THE
Halcyon
Bird

THE *Demon Catchers* OF *Milan*

BOOK 2

THE Halcyon Bird

KAT BEYER

EGMONT

USA

NEW YORK

For Gay and Michele—
may we journey to yet more lands

EGMONT

We bring stories to life

First published by Egmont USA, 2014
443 Park Avenue South, Suite 806
New York, NY 10016

Copyright © Kat Beyer, 2014
All rights reserved

1 3 5 7 9 8 6 4 2

www.egmontusa.com
www.katspaw.com

Library of Congress Cataloging-in-Publication Data

Beyer, Kat.
The halcyon bird / Kat Beyer.
pages cm. — (The demon catchers of Milan ; book 2)
Summary: Mia Della Torre is happy to be settled in Milan, learning her family's
ancient trade of demon hunting, and able to put her fear of her own, personal
demon aside—until she falls in love and realizes how much more than her own
happiness is at stake.
ISBN 978-1-60684-316-1 (hardcover) — ISBN 978-1-60684-317-8 (eBook)
[1. Demonology—Fiction. 2. Demoniac possession—Fiction. 3. Americans—
Italy—Fiction. 4. Family life—Italy—Fiction. 5. Love—Fiction. 6. Milan
(Italy)—Fiction. 7. Italy—Fiction.] I. Title.
PZ7.B46893Hal 2014
[Fic]—dc23
2014001937

Printed in the United States of America

Nascondiamo le nostre armi in bella vista.

We hide our weapons in plain sight.

—*G. Della Torre*

Table of Contents

1200s Pagano DELLA TORRE
Martino DELLA TORRE, *capitano del popolo*

1300s Alcione DELLA TORRE
3 children, one who survived the Black Death

1700s G. DELLA TORRE
founded candle shop at age 21, 1733

Francesco DELLA TORRE

1900s

Gianna DELLA TORRE
1911

Roberto
1933

Matteo ⋯⋯ Calandra
1968 *1971*

Mia Gianna   Gina Laura
1996   *1998*

Della Torre Family Tree

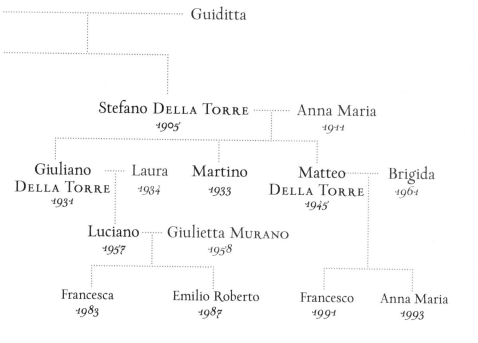

Guiditta

Stefano DELLA TORRE · · · · · · Anna Maria
1905 · 1911

Giuliano · · · · Laura · · · · Martino · · · · Matteo · · · · · · Brigida
DELLA TORRE · · 1934 · · · · · · 1933 · · · DELLA TORRE · · 1961
1931 · 1945

Luciano · · · · · · Giulietta MURANO
1957 · · · · · · · · · · · 1958

Francesca · · · · · · Emilio Roberto · · · · · · Francesco · · · · Anna Maria
1983 · · · · · · · · · · · · 1987 · · · · · · · · · · · · 1991 · · · · · · · · 1993

THE
Halcyon
Bird

ONE

Il Giorno di San Valentino

It was only a small candle. The first match went out, but the second took, and Nonno Giuliano nodded at the tiny flame like an old friend.

The man on the floor lay perfectly still, his eyes on the ceiling, in the middle of a rug full of shattered glass, his head twisted at a frightening angle. My cousin Emilio watched the candle take fire, then opened a palm-size notebook and began to read.

The man on the floor chuckled as the thing inside him stirred.

Beside Nonno, my cousin Anna Maria held a hand mirror. She waited like a guard, her eyes on the man on the floor.

The man turned his head, slowly, from one awkward angle to another. I could hear the bones in his neck grinding. He seemed to be listening to Emilio, but it was hard to tell. In the dim light, we could see his face, being molded like putty from the inside.

Emilio paused at the end of the page and looked at Giuliano. His grandfather lifted his hand. "Bell," he said.

My cousin Francesco was holding the bell. It was his own, a miniature beaten brass bell from Guatemala that hung from a bright strip of fabric. He swung it in a careful circle, and it rang sweetly.

The man on the floor shuddered.

All our ordinary weapons, hidden in plain sight.

I didn't have a weapon. Instead, I got to stand next to the man's wife. "Keep a hand on her arm and an eye on her heart," Nonno had told me when we arrived. With my free hand, I touched my demon-catching case where it sat in my breast pocket, wondering why I had bothered to bring it.

I kept my hand on the woman's arm, rigid under my fingers. She stared at her husband. I had heard her voice when she called Giuliano, steady and even on the phone, not panicked like an ordinary client's.

"Yes, we handle such things," he had said. He never said the word *esorcisti*.

Francesco kept ringing the bell, and the man began to roll back and forth. A red rash like a burn began to spread up his arms. I glanced at my cousins, my heart pounding, and I could see that Emilio, Anna Maria, and Francesco were frowning, their expressions almost identical. I knew those frowns; I knew they were afraid, and so was I. But Nonno's breath rose and fell at the same even pace. The flame in front of him fluttered patiently with each breath.

The man began to scream in pain, batting at his arms. His cries were his own, not the voice of a demon. I tried to stay focused, tried not to get caught up in his suffering.

Giuliano gazed steadily at the man, one hand resting lightly on the table. At length, he raised his other hand, and Francesco silenced the clapper of his bell between two fingers. Nonno gestured for Emilio to begin reading again, but when Emilio tried to raise his voice above the man's cries, Giuliano shook his head. Emilio nodded and lowered his voice.

I waited for the woman beside me to ask why we weren't trying to do something to ease the man's pain, but she didn't. She wasn't even shaking as much as I was.

The screams changed to roars, and we heard the demon's voice clearly at last, raging and laughing, forcing its way past the man's whistling vocal cords. The roars had a distant quality, as if the demon were speaking from far away, from beyond the corners of the room. Francesco rang the bell again.

Again, the demon bellowed. Again, Nonno nodded, again, the bell, again, the laughter, while all the while Emilio droned on. . . .

"TACE!" thundered Giuliano.

I jumped. My ears rang in the silence that followed.

The man froze, and so did everyone else. I felt the woman's arm tighten with shock under my hand.

"Lei mi sentirà," said Nonno, his voice calm again. *"Lei mi sentirà. Mi dirà il suo nome.* You will hear me. You will tell me your name."

Another burn began to appear on the man's arm, spreading slowly this time. He—or the demon—did not seem to notice it. Giuliano held his gaze.

"Il mio nome è Vendetta," whispered the demon, cold, guttural.

Oh, please, I thought. *For real?* "I call myself Vengeance." *This one should be easy, at least.* The melodrama of demons!

The woman groaned, and I glanced sideways at her. Nonno said to Francesco, "Three counts and pauses, until I say to stop." Francesco nodded and rang the bell three times.

"Why have you come?" Giuliano asked.

"Il mio nome è Vendetta," repeated the demon, rolling the man's head away, but at the ringing of the bell, he dragged his eyes back to Nonno and Francesco.

"Why?"

"Il mio nome è Vendetta!" screamed the demon, until the bell yanked his attention back again.

"Very well. And have you had your revenge?" Giuliano asked softly.

"I am taking it now," the demon told him.

"How does it feel, then?"

"Like a relief."

"Truly?" asked Nonno.

The demon ignored him, twisting the man's body, raising more burns, his hands an angry red. I felt nausea overcome me like a wave at the sight. *If you're serious about this, you have to learn to face these things,* I told myself sternly. The burns on the man's arms began to darken. Giuliano nodded, and Francesco rang the bell again, pulling the demon's attention back once more.

"You cannot know what it's like to have your heart broken by the one you trusted the most," snarled the demon.

"But I do," Nonno replied.

I flicked my eyes toward him, and I saw that my cousins had done the same. Giuliano had been married to Nonna Laura since they were practically kids. What did he mean?

"Not like this . . . or you would be like me," the demon said.

"Would I?" asked Nonno, sounding curious.

The demon said nothing. His form crawled underneath the man's skin, as if by shaping his borrowed flesh he could shape his own thoughts.

"Were you invited?" Giuliano asked gently.

"Yes!" came the snarling answer.

"You are lying," Nonno said.

I knew he was right. How did we both know?

"I was called! I was told to come!" snapped the demon.

"Who would do that?" asked Nonno.

"I came because her heart commanded it!" the demon cried, and thrust one of the man's hands awkwardly in the direction of his wife.

Only Emilio, Francesco, and I turned to look at her; Anna Maria kept her eyes on the demon, her mirror in her hand, fierce and ready, and Giuliano did, too. This was just as well because at that instant the demon snaked the other hand toward Nonno's ankle. Nonno jumped back, nimbly for an eighty-year-old man, and laughed.

"Nearly got me, then," he said.

Bizarrely, the demon laughed, too.

"I did, didn't I?" he said.

For a moment, I imagined a world where we were not all enemies. But there was something in the man's twisted face, the way the demon forced his lips to smile, that broke my heart with its cruelty.

The woman didn't speak, even now. She only looked down at the man. I felt her arm soften under my hand, for a brief moment; then it tightened again.

"You see?" the demon said. "He broke her heart. I torment him as he has tormented her."

The demon began to laugh again; but now, beside me, I could see that as the woman looked down at him, the lower lids of her eyes seemed to swell slightly. It took me a split second to realize that this is what tears look like close up, before they spill out. Giuliano gazed at her for some time, keeping his feet out of the way of the man. Then he turned back to the demon.

"I do not think you were invited," he said. "But will you leave when you are asked?"

"Never! Not until my work is finished!"

Nonno turned to Emilio, who nodded and opened his notebook to a different page. When Emilio began to read again, he didn't consult the page, but glanced down at it occasionally, like a singer who knows the music in front of him by heart.

"We will not wait, we will come, we will reach for you, we will bind you with chains of oaths and exhortations. Render up the body you have infested, the spirit you afflict, release them unharmed, and we will not confine your spirit in the close places, the dusty dark of the ancient underworld, but rather return you to your home in the Left-Hand Land."

I'd heard this ritual before, at the exorcism of Lisetta Maria Umberti. That time, it had not really worked, at least not right away.

This time, the man's mouth opened wider, until I thought his jaws might crack, releasing a roar that hurt my ears and seemed too big for his body. The man arched his back, and I could hear his own screams joining with those of the demon. Giuliano whipped the candle into his hands, shielding the flame, and knelt close to the suffering body. A knot of wind seemed to fall from the man's mouth, tumbling across the room to the flame.

The man collapsed back onto the floor, his eyes fluttering, his body slack.

"Did you catch him?" Emilio asked doubtfully.

"No," said Nonno, sounding uncertain for the first time.

"But he's gone, isn't he?" asked Anna Maria. "I'm not getting anything in the mirror, either."

Giuliano got to his feet slowly as I waited for the woman beside me to sag with relief. In fact, I waited for her to do something, anything; she'd been so still the whole time.

Nonno looked at her.

"You may come to your husband now," he said.

There was a terrible pause, which gave me time to realize how much I'd missed while watching the man on the floor. I still had my hand on his wife's arm. She turned and gripped my wrist, so swiftly I had no time to move. She grinned, and I saw, too late, who looked out of her eyes.

"He should have come to her long ago," said the demon, this time from the woman's mouth. "He should not have betrayed her. He went to that other woman, over near the Stazione Centrale. A waitress in a café! After all his wife had done for him."

I met the demon's eyes in shock, trying to get hold of myself as the woman's fingers squeezed my arm. I could feel the pulse in her fingers: her own heartbeat and the pulse of the demon, an irregular, frantic rhythm. I had felt this once before, at Lisetta

8

Maria Umberti's exorcism, when my demon's pulse began to tap at me, pushing toward me, reaching out. Another wave of nausea swept over me. Would this demon's pulse reach for me, too?

"I'll take better care of her," whispered the demon. "She'll never know a moment's sorrow with me. It won't be like the last time."

"What happened last time? Did she die?" Giuliano asked.

"I didn't do it," whispered the demon. "She wanted to die."

"You keep coming back, don't you?" Nonno said softly. "You keep hoping that the human spirits will survive in the bodies you take. You want to care for them, don't you? You want a love returned."

"Yes," said the demon, so faintly that I could barely hear him.

"But the bodies, the spirits, they can only bear your presence for so long," Giuliano said. "I am not pleased that I must tell you this, but it is so." He smiled gently. "Your name isn't really Revenge, is it?" he asked.

"No," the demon hissed.

"Do you wish that was all you needed?"

"Yes."

"What do you long for? Might we give it to you?"

"You might," conceded the demon. The woman's fingers tightened their grip on my arm, and I whimpered at the pain. "You might, but I do not trust you. You will return me to the Left-Hand Land if you can. You are not here for *me*. You are not

9

here for *her*. You are here for that wreck on the floor."

The man had begun to groan in pain. The burns on his arms were starting to fade.

Nonno nodded. "Sometimes we arrive to help one person and leave having helped another," he said. "We assume nothing. We do the work that must be done. If you are the one we must help, then we will help you."

I wasn't sure I believed this, and I could tell the demon wasn't sure, either. True, I had been there before when we had helped a spirit, one that had returned from Majdanek concentration camp, but that had been a ghost, not a demon.

"I suspect a trick," the demon said.

Giuliano laughed.

"It is a fine trick," he said. "It rescues everyone: you and those you occupy at the same time. Who loses? Not you. Not anyone."

"Not even you?" asked the demon.

"I look after myself," Nonno replied with a wide, open smile.

I could see the demon considering this.

"What is your real name?" asked Giuliano.

"I cannot remember it," said the demon, and I could hear just how far his voice had traveled to reach us.

"Anger abrades memory," said Nonno.

"Grief abrades it!" snarled the demon. "You cannot know how I grieve!"

Giuliano shrugged his shoulders. I noticed my hand was going numb; every time the demon spoke, he made my arm shake.

"What would you like your name to be?" Nonno asked. "If you could be done with the name Vendetta?"

"*Pace. Speranza.* Peace. Hope."

"Not joy?"

"I have lost too much for that."

"You are sure?"

"Sure," snapped the demon.

"You want peace; you want hope."

"Yes."

"You find them by caring for women who have had their hearts broken?"

"Yes. I make them happy!"

"By taking revenge on the men who have hurt them, or by occupying them?"

I could see the woman's face being pushed and pulled from within, just as her husband's had been. I remembered my own possession with a sudden vividness—the way it felt to have no control over my body, to be jerked about like a puppet and punished with pain when I fought back. But I could recall the power, too—the way I could see through walls, hear people's thoughts. I shivered, and the demon Vendetta turned the woman's eyes toward me, his secret, terrible smile pulling her lips thin.

"You know, don't you?" he hissed. "You know."

I had to swallow hard to speak.

"I do. But I never wanted to," I said.

I held his eyes with my own, trying hard not to watch the way the woman's irises writhed under the demon's control.

"Let her go," I whispered, my jaw tight from the pain of his grip. "You think you help, but you don't. Let. Her. Go."

Out of the corner of my eye, I saw Giuliano start toward me. I looked back into the demon's eyes and saw them beginning to withdraw, saw the skin of the woman's face begin to deflate, felt a movement in her hand, as if the tide were going out of her body. . . .

"NOW," roared Nonno, and Emilio leaped forward and ripped the woman's hand from my wrist. The demon threw her head back and roared. Giuliano cried words I could not hear and held up his candle. This time, the roaring narrowed to a distant point, and a miniature whirlwind spiraled down into the candle flame. In a moment, the flame flickered and died. The room stood silent. The woman slid slowly to the floor, caught at the last minute by Francesco, who sank to his knees, gently bringing her to rest. I realized Emilio was holding me up.

"Happy Valentine's Day," I muttered, looking down at them, husband and wife, both unconscious on the floor. I wondered what their story was, what had drawn the demon to them.

Emilio shifted his weight behind me and I remembered where I was.

"Steady, wait," he counseled in my ear as my legs buckled under me. I forced myself up and took a step out of his arms.

"I'm fine," I said, gritting my teeth. I couldn't see his face.

Nonno was kneeling on the floor, his fingers on the man's wrist; Anna Maria was checking the woman's pulse.

"Fine," she said, looking up at Giuliano.

"Yes," he agreed.

The woman stirred first; she sat up abruptly, snarling, "Get out!" Then she looked up at us. "Oh," she said, sounding hoarse. "What . . . ?" She rubbed her eyes. "I can't remember a thing," she complained.

"Good for you," said Nonno.

"Rufo!" she said, catching sight of her unconscious husband. "Rufo!" She looked up at us with an expression I had not seen before—genuine fear. "Will he be all right?"

"We must wait and see. He stirs," Giuliano pointed out. The man was rocking his head side to side just as he had earlier, but this time I could see that he was using his own muscles.

"Mother of God," he said at last. He looked up at his wife, not rising from the ground, and she stared back.

After what seemed like hours, he said, "I have broken your heart, my dear."

"Yes," she whispered.

"What now?" he asked.

She waited a long time to answer. "I do not know," she said softly.

43

Nonno stood and began to put his tools in their case. Anna Maria followed suit. Emilio turned and opened his notebook again, this time with pen in hand, and began making notes. I kept staring stupidly at the couple on the floor. They seemed to have forgotten us. Then I collected myself and turned to see what Emilio was writing. Out of the corner of my eye, I saw Francesco slide a tiny leather cover over the clapper of his bell and tuck it away in his case. *That's all?* I thought. I wanted to know the answer to the man's question. But instead, we helped them rise, and Giuliano fetched them each a glass of wine. When he had satisfied himself that they would do for now, he counseled them to sleep and to skip work the next day, if possible.

"I will come by in the morning to check on you," he said. "You should not be troubled again tonight. I see no need to leave a sentinel."

"You are confident," said the man.

"I know the signs," Giuliano replied. "You'll do, for tonight. Sleep. You've both gotten off lightly. Rejoice in it. People die of this, yet you live. Now go . . . sleep."

They obeyed him in a daze, but I still wanted to know, *What now?* I took comfort from the fear in the woman's voice when she'd woken up, and from the look in the man's eye. Maybe there would be a happy ending, after all.

I reached into my coat pocket and drew out my case, the case I'd longed to open when everyone else opened theirs. I turned it over in my hands, looking at the list of names stamped in gold on the leather, beginning with *G. Della Torre,* the founder of our candle shop.

We stepped outside into the freezing February night. The Via Mario Pagano stood empty, but the smell of diesel fumes lingered.

"What time is it?" asked Anna Maria.

Francesco pulled out his phone and smirked at his sister. "Not *San Valentino* anymore," he said. Anna Maria rolled her eyes, but it was Emilio who swore, and then promptly apologized to his grandfather. Nonno shrugged and asked, "You think she won't forgive you?"

Emilio frowned. We all knew his girlfriend Alba wasn't the forgiving type.

Italians, famously in love with love, have imported Valentine's Day, and Emilio and Anna Maria had both had dates. Francesco had been disappointed, too; he'd had plans to go out with a bunch of his university friends.

Not me; I was the only one who'd been glad when Giuliano had gotten the call about this case.

Nonno walked behind us, his hands clasped behind his back. Francesco slowed down to walk beside him. As we crossed the Piazza Niccolò Tommaseo, Anna Maria asked Emilio in a low voice, "Have you thought about telling Alba what we do?"

He looked straight ahead and didn't answer at first.

"What about the rule?" he asked at last.

"What about it?" replied Anna Maria. "Don't you think it's maybe a bit antiquated? Anyway, so many of our neighbors know, perhaps one of them told her already?"

I blinked, but Emilio only laughed. I love the way his face changes when he laughs; he is as handsome as Apollo, with curly blond hair and high cheekbones—but the sun really shines out of him when he laughs. Anna Maria, walking beside him, made quite a contrast to her cousin, pale and dark-haired. In her brother, Francesco, the same features are overemphasized—huge nose instead of an elegant one, gawky instead of slender, hair sticking out in every direction instead of a sweeping mass of curls. Anna Maria is beautiful enough to model, which is what she does. Francesco's main talent seems to be the ability to bump into things.

Nonno Giuliano had passed some of his features on to Emilio, his grandson, and his niece and nephew shared the family traits: the high cheekbones, the far-seeing eyes, the generous mouth. Emilio had his sturdy frame and straight back.

"Can you see Alba talking to any of our neighbors . . . or listening to them? Seriously?" asked Emilio.

Anna Maria shrugged and grinned. Francesco laughed.

"You're right," she conceded.

"Anyway, it's not like . . . like we're superheroes or something," Emilio went on, looking at me. I thought maybe he was saying this for my benefit. "No. I will follow the rule."

What the heck is the rule?! I wanted to scream. Then I

reminded myself that the tool case in my breast pocket was nearly three centuries old, made by the same man who had made Emilio's case. Even though there was a demon following me, I had a right to ask questions, didn't I? They could choose whether it was safe to answer them. "What rule?" I asked.

Anna Maria looked at me. "Sometimes I completely forget that there's all this stuff you don't know, because you didn't grow up with it." She clouted me on the shoulder. "You're really changing, you know that?" She looked down at my ankles and added, "And growing, too, still. Remind Francesca: new pants, immediately."

"Yes, ma'am," I said, rolling my eyes. Anna Maria is three years older than I am, which should not be old enough to act like my mom, but that doesn't stop her. Emilio looked over at us, smiling wryly.

"And the rule . . . ?" I prompted. Emilio opened his mouth, but Anna Maria broke in.

"The rule we're talking about is that you don't tell your lovers what we do. You don't even tell your wife or your husband, until you've been married a year and a day. It's an old, old rule, and I don't know who decided it."

"The first references are from notes from 1322 and 1343," said Emilio. "Baldassare Della Torre was practicing at the time, with his cousin Martino and their families. But many of our customs are from much further back, before we began writing things down."

Anna Maria waved her perfectly manicured hand. "I think it's outdated. Nowadays, people live together for years without getting married. You're sleeping under the same roof, you're in the same bed every night. How would you not figure it all out, for heaven's sake?"

"How would you know that you had anything to figure out?" asked Emilio.

We turned into the Via Giovanni Boccaccio, and Anna Maria glanced back to make sure Nonno and Francesco were far enough behind us before she said, "So you're going to let Alba think you're cheating on her, all this time?"

Emilio smiled.

"How is this any of your business, Anna Maria?" he replied.

"Fair enough." She shrugged.

He nodded. "But just so you know, no, I don't like having her think that—except sometimes—when it's not such a bad thing, maybe, that she jumps to that conclusion."

"It's not like you come home smelling of some demon's perfume," I pointed out.

They stared at me for a moment. Then they both burst out laughing.

Emilio wiped his eyes. "Thank you, dear Mia. I wasn't looking forward to Alba's anger, and now you have lightened my heart."

I tried not to feel smug, and failed. Why did he bother with Alba? I wondered. She seemed so high-maintenance.

"And what will What's-His-Name say when you see him next?" Emilio asked Anna Maria.

"I don't know if I will see him," she said thoughtfully. "This might have been it, for him. It was the third date I'd canceled. Anyway, he wasn't who I wanted to go out with for the *festa*, but my other guy already had a date."

"I can't keep track of them," said Emilio.

"Yes, you can't even remember Mario's name," she pointed out.

"I didn't, either," I admitted, realizing she probably didn't care whether I remembered this guy's name or not.

"Well, *somebody's* got to!" she said, laughing. "I keep forgetting how to tell them apart, myself. Mario is the snowboarder, and Fabio's the lawyer who has almost certainly neglected to tell me that he's married, and Gerhardt is the visiting professor of aeronautics, who may have forgotten whether he is or not."

"No models?" I asked.

She shook her head.

"*Stai sputando nel piatto dove mangi*—don't spit on the plate you're eating from," she said. "Anyway, the ones that aren't gay are either high all the time or unfathomably narcissistic. Or just too stupid to do anything but . . ."

She caught Emilio's eye and stopped.

"I know what you were going to say," I said grumpily. "No need to hold back on my account."

"Not that that's a bad thing . . . being good at only one

thing, I mean," Emilio said lightly. "In moderation."

"Moderation's a bad thing, too, sometimes," said Anna Maria, looking as if she was trying not to smile.

"Yes. Well," Emilio said.

"So," I mused, "we have to wait until we're married, and then a year and a day, huh?"

"That's the rule we're supposed to follow, yes. I'm not sure my father did, to tell you the truth," said Anna Maria. Emilio flicked his eyes at her in surprise. I tried to imagine gruff Uncle Matteo and proper, glamorous Aunt Brigida—who was a number of years younger than her husband—breaking a rule.

"Oh, Papa and Mamma were together for ages," she added. "If they tell you when their first date was, and then the date of the wedding, and you add that to Francesco's birth date, you know they were a couple for a long time before they were married. Or he was a miracle birth. Now, I love my brother," she finished. "But he's no miracle."

"Someone will think he is," said Emilio. "Just wait."

"He has to get near enough to talk to her, first," retorted Anna Maria, as Francesco and Giuliano caught up to us.

A minute later, we saw Anna Maria to the door to her parents' apartment in the Via Melone, then made our way to the shop in the Via Fiori Oscuri. Francesco and Emilio kissed us good-bye and headed back to their flat a couple of blocks away in the Via dei Giardini. I tried not to wonder if Alba was waiting there. I rubbed at my cheek where Emilio had pecked it, leaving behind his pinesap scent; just a cousinly, Milanese good-bye kiss.

"I always forget that Francesco's older than Anna Maria," I said to Nonno as we stepped inside the shop, shutting out the cold winter air. "He's like me and my sister, Gina. She's a year and a half younger, and people always think she's the older one. She's got it more together."

He was moving around the little shop with paneled walls and wooden shelves full of candles. Sometimes he would stop to sniff one or touch another. I watched him, knowing he probably wouldn't explain what he was looking for. Sometimes he explains everything, like he's talking to a child, and other times, he seems to think the knowledge will stick better if I have to claw it out of the woodwork myself.

Before we'd left to go to the exorcism, he'd asked me to put out each flame with the old silver snuffer. I'd noticed their oddities a while ago—how one always left behind a whiff of swamp gas, and another expired with a faint giggle. Long ago, Emilio had made me promise I would never blow out any of the candles with my breath, but would always use the snuffer. Now I thought I knew why: nearly all of them were inhabited, either by imprisoned demons, or helpful spirits, or both. On those rare occasions when someone came into the candle shop to buy a candle, we had to get a new—and empty—one from the back. It scares me, when some tourist leans in close to a flame, and I wonder if they are about to accidentally swallow a demon.

But my family has been doing things this way for centuries; I'm pretty sure there are more protections than I know about.

I love the candle shop. I love the smell of the wood and the beeswax, the ghosts of sulfur matches, and the way that, when the door to the street closes, I feel like I am in another century. For me, the shop really has been a sanctuary, and still is.

More than anyone else at the exorcism we had just left, I knew what that man and woman had gone through. I knew what it meant to have another mind invade my body.

I hadn't really allowed myself to remember, not all the way. Not yet. Sometimes a part of it would come back to me, and I would remember floating through the air, making the books on the shelves ripple like dominoes. I tried not to remember what it was like to fling my sister against the wall.

I was pretty sure she knew that I wasn't the one who had done it.

I remembered drifting down the stairs, the photos on the wall beside me falling and shattering, the sight of broken glass below my feet. I blinked and came back to myself, standing in the candle shop, Nonno Giuliano's eyes on me.

"You don't need to be older than your sister," he said. "You are old enough, as you are. Sit down! We need to write up our case notes before we go to bed."

He pointed at the chair across from him, and we both sat down at the desk, worn and oiled smooth by twelve generations of hands. He pushed a notebook in front of me. I saw it was already labeled: *Mia Gianna Della Torre, Taccuino numero 1.* He told me, "Write precisely what you remember. Each detail, even the ones that do not seem significant. Tell what you smelled and tasted. What you heard and saw and touched. And the impressions that came into your mind. See if you can remember the order of events. Practice! We will keep these notes for your great-grandchildren to read."

No pressure. I hadn't realized until then that every family member who was present for an exorcism kept notes.

I began to write and wrote until the words blurred in front of me. "Bed," Nonno said, and steered me toward the stairs. He did not follow me, but stayed at the old oak desk, writing about lost souls in the lamplight.

TWO

The Demon's Sonnet

Every morning, the smell of Nonna Laura's coffee tugs me back from my dreams. After the *San Valentino* exorcism, I woke up remembering what it was like to be able to see through walls and listen through skulls—memories of terrible helplessness and secondhand power, of being able to see and hear what others couldn't.

But I could smell the espresso Nonna was making in the kitchen, so I got up and got dressed.

"Buon giorno," she muttered as I came in and kissed her on the cheek. She clashed dishes into the drying rack above the sink. I did a quick mental check to see if I was the reason she was crabby and decided I probably wasn't.

"It's my leg," she said, answering my unspoken question. "It's sore again. Makes me cross as a bear. Did you sleep well? Coffee?"

"Yes, please," I said. She always offers, as if I might have changed my mind overnight, and I always accept. "Can I do anything? Run errands for you this morning?"

"No, because you need to study."

Plan foiled. I would much rather have stepped out into the chill February air, smelling of diesel and rosemary and baking bread, than stayed inside with my books, even though they meant survival.

She set a *caffè latte* in front of me. I swirled it around in the bowl, gazing down, and then took a sip.

The Italians take their coffee seriously, and Milan is full of excellent cafés. I don't know what Nonna does differently, but her *caffè latte* is always perfect. I took my time with it. The books could wait.

While I sat, my cousin Francesca and her fiancé Égide emerged from their room down the hall and came into the kitchen, kissing Nonna on the cheek and saying yes to coffee. Égide helped himself to a pastry from the breadbox, and held one up to Francesca, who nodded. He set them on the same plate and sat down beside her. Nonna put her espresso maker back into action. It looks like a double showerhead for dolls, with a miniature platform for two espresso cups. The first time I saw it, I'd been fresh off the plane from Center Plains, New

York, still rubbing the jet lag out of my eyes, still in shock. Five months later, I felt like I had always sat at this kitchen table, had always heard Francesca ask Égide, "What time is the hearing?"

"Ten. But they'll postpone it."

"Again?"

He shrugged. Égide can shrug more elegantly than any Italian. He's a tall, slender man with the darkest, smoothest skin I have ever seen, the gift of his Rwandan parents. Here, in this casually racist country, I've seen him walk up to a stranger to ask if the metro train has left, and heard them snap, "I don't want to buy anything!" They don't notice his expensive, beautifully tailored lawyer suit. It's not like the Milanese to miss a detail like excellent tailoring, but with Égide, they do.

Most of the time, he ignores it magnificently, as does Francesca. She is as pale as he is dark, with long dark-brown hair that she wears in an elegant knot. Both Francesca and Égide always seem so calm, which, since they are lawyers, kind of surprises me.

The doorbell to the apartment rang.

"Mia," said Nonna, concentrating on the coffee. I jumped up from the table and pressed the intercom button.

"Who is it?"

"Brigida and Matteo. Just for a minute."

Aunt Brigida swept in, tall, perfectly made-up, with magenta nails like claws, and opinions about everything. She kissed me on the cheek and asked, "Everyone's still having coffee?" as if we were all running late for something.

Uncle Matteo followed her, smelling of cigarettes, and kissed me, too. "Keeping well?" he asked. "How do you like getting around on your own, now you don't have to stay inside all the time?"

"I love it," I replied fervently.

His eyes crinkled. "The freedom or the city?"

"Both," I said.

He nodded.

Aunt Brigida was setting a bag on the kitchen table. "Two bottles of the red from Lucia and Mario, that sponge I was telling you about, and your shampoo," she told Nonna.

"Thank you," Nonna said. "Coffee?"

"We're just stopping by," said Aunt Brigida, just as Uncle Matteo said, "Yes, please!" They looked at each other. "Yours is the best in town," Aunt Brigida conceded, and took a seat at the table while Nonna set the coffee shower in motion again. Uncle Matteo pulled out a chair for me, then sat himself.

"What's on the docket for today?" he asked Égide.

"Political asylum for three Sudanese women fleeing"—he paused and rolled an eye toward me—"their enforced traditions."

"Ah," said Uncle Matteo, who clearly knew what Égide was talking about, even if I didn't. I made a mental note to Google Sudan's traditions.

"But they'll postpone the hearing," Égide said.

"Our government specializes in postponement," said Uncle Matteo. "We've taken many years to perfect our skills in that direction."

Even though Uncle Matteo was speaking Italian, I heard my father's voice for a moment. My father's name is Matt, too, and though his voice is pure American, he looks like Uncle Matteo, and Dad would totally be complaining about the government.

Like Dad, Uncle Matteo gathered thunderclouds on his brow more easily than his older brother Giuliano. Nonno either had a lighter heart or a milder temper, which had always suprised me, since he was the hardworking head of a family of demon catchers. What we'd witnessed the night before was nothing compared to some of the cases I knew he'd worked on, including my own.

Last October, when the same demon that had killed both Nonno's middle brother, Martino, and Nonno's son, Luciano, had crossed the ocean and taken over my body and my mind, Giuliano and Emilio had arrived to rescue me. That was the first time we'd met them, since my own grandfather Roberto had never even mentioned their existence. Grandfather Roberto, cousin to Nonno, had left Italy in 1958 for reasons he never told any of us. He had certainly left out the part about coming from a family of exorcists.

It had come as a shock to Dad when the priest, calling Rome for help as I thrashed around in the air, had been refused:

"Under no circumstances was an exorcism to be performed on a Della Torre," Dad had repeated later, dropping his deep voice even deeper. "Their exact words, Father Amadoro told me later. Can you believe it?"

I could now.

After Nonno and Emilio had come to Center Plains and performed the exorcism, they had brought me to Milan, to a strange and unexpected homecoming. I hoped, if his spirit was still out there, my grandfather would one day forgive me.

My demon had come back to Milan, too. And for the first few months after I arrived, I had had to stay inside our apartment or in the candle shop, going outside only with the family to protect me. Finally, Signora Negroponte, a witch from Lucca who is a family friend, had helped me find a talisman that would protect me outside. She and I had spent quite a bit of time testing different objects, a harrowing process since it involved me stepping out into the street to see if the demon would come while I was holding a sacred acorn or wearing a smear of evil-smelling paste or clutching a splinter of wood pulled from our stairs. In the end, I found my talisman myself: a bell that had hung on the door of the shop. It was smaller even than Francesco's Guatemalan bell and had a miniature bird engraved on its side, the same one that was carved in stone above the shop door. Now I wore it on a leather string around my neck.

"In Italia i treni arrivano tanto in ritardo che bisogna fargli

il test di gravidanza," Uncle Matteo was saying. "In Italy, the trains are so late they need a pregnancy test." Égide threw back his head and laughed at the ceiling. I knew that the family hadn't been all that excited the first time Francesco had brought home a six-foot black man (in some ways, sadly, they aren't that different from other Milanese), but they seemed to have gotten over it. Aunt Brigida scolded her husband halfheartedly, but Nonna was laughing, too, finally taking a seat at the table with her own coffee.

Uncle Matteo took a long, appreciative sip of his. "Ah! So good," and Égide nodded.

I asked myself for the first time why we had never met any of Égide's family. I knew his father had brought him over from Rwanda, and that was all. I also noticed that Uncle Matteo didn't ask Francesca about her work.

"We have to get going if I am to walk you to the office," Égide said to her, and she nodded.

"We'll get out of here, too," said Aunt Brigida. "Any errands, Laura?" she asked, looking at Nonna.

"Nothing, thanks."

The kitchen emptied; I picked up the cups and took them to the sink, looking out the window at our lavender plants and the courtyard next door while I ran the hot water.

"Thank you," said Nonna, still sitting at the table. The winter sun picked out dust motes in the air. After a while, she asked, "How did last night go?"

It seemed to me that there was another question she really wanted to ask instead, and I wished I could work out what it was.

"Pretty well," I said. "The demon jumped from the husband to the wife, but we got him in the end, and I think they will be okay. I hope they will stay together."

"You think that would be the best thing?" she asked.

"Yes. Or . . . I don't know," I said. "But it was the *Festa di San Valentino*, after all. I guess they could work it out. They seem to love each other."

"It can take more than that," she said, turning her cup slowly.

"But isn't there always a way? Can't people work it out? Isn't true love that important?"

Nonna looked at me. "Are you sure they are true lovers?" she asked.

I frowned at the ceiling. "No. But . . . how can you tell?"

At that, she laughed.

"Are we the ones who can tell?" she shot back. Then she glanced at the clock. "Go read your books," she said. "I'll need you in the afternoon, to help with dinner."

I gave her a kiss and headed down the wooden stairs to the shop. Nonno was already sitting at the desk, reading the paper.

"Doing all right after last night?" he asked, glancing up.

"Yes, thank you."

"Read for a while, then go for a good walk, to the Parco Sempione. Take the air, walk among some trees. You'll be remembering things, under the surface. Any dreams?"

"Yes . . . of . . . of that time," I said.

"So. Walk. But start your books first. And then, after lunch."

"Okay."

The pile of books on the table had not shrunk since yesterday. I pulled it to me. I really was getting interested in all the history I had to read, but still, I think a part of me will always be a B student, looking for a way out of homework. I opened my study notebook and sighed. Nonno looked up from his newspaper and grinned.

"Try this," he said, handing me the front page. "Glance at the headlines and tell me what you think relates to the history you've been reading. Which headlines have their roots in the past?"

I took the front page, greasy with ink, and glanced down, still thrilled that I could read it so easily. There was a trial featuring a couple of bankers. One of the people interviewed was a Piero Leone Strozzi, and I knew there was a famous Florentine family of bankers named Strozzi. Had a branch moved to Milan at one point? One of the guys on trial was named Lorenzo Benedetto Rota. "A relative of that famous composer guy, the one who wrote *The Godfather* soundtrack, is being charged with corruption," I ventured. "Does that count?"

He nodded. "Do you think that family has made a habit of corruption?"

"I don't know," I said. "I guess I'd have to look it up."

I read another piece about the Sanremo Music Festival. Nonno nodded again. "It's new, they only started it in 1951, as part of the effort to revitalize their city after the war." I thought about how 1958, when my grandfather had left Italy, seemed like a long time ago to me. "Its founders have interesting roots, too," Nonno went on. "Perhaps it's related to the *famiglia* Rota? I can't remember, myself."

There was an article about the upcoming election, another about Italian politics in general, and one about the financial crises across Europe. I felt suddenly overwhelmed. Did Italy's political problems begin during the *Risorgimento*, the nineteeth-century movement toward Italian reunification—or during the first time Italy had been united, under the ancient Romans? Did the financial crises have their roots in the banking systems of the Middle Ages or in the invention of numbers, or of money? Or with the development of carbon-based life-forms on Earth?

An old man had entered the shop. I saw him out of the corner of my eye and looked up.

I hadn't heard the shop bells jingle to announce him, and that was the first clue. The second clue was that the light didn't fall on him the same way it fell on Nonno; this old man's face seemed to remember another sun. I waited for the third clue, for him to speak words that I could hear only in my thoughts, but it never came; the old man said nothing. He turned and raised his eyebrows at me.

Nonno said, without opening his mouth, "Allow me to

present you with the newest one. Cousin Roberto's grand-daughter, from America, Mia Della Torre. Mia, this is Respicio Della Torre, a relation of ours from the eighteenth century." I looked more closely at him, annoyed at myself for not having noticed the family resemblance. The three of us shared the same high, square cheekbones, the same pale eyes, the same generous, sad mouth; yet at least twelve generations lay between him and Nonno. Signore Respicio bowed to me, and I saw that his clothes were old-fashioned; he wore a closely fitted, drab jacket, and tight pants that ended just below the knee, and white stockings smeared with dirt. His elegant shoes had buckles on them, and he wore his curly gray hair in a ponytail. I glanced at Nonno, not sure what to do, but he didn't offer any advice, so I bowed, and said in my mind, *"Cugino, è un piacere di fare la sua conoscenza,"* as formally as I could. He smiled faintly, bowed again, and turned toward Nonno, holding out his hand. Giuliano opened his palm and Respicio put something in it. I blinked. When I opened my eyes, he had departed.

I knew what I'd seen: a messenger, a suicide, one of the spirits who has to keep to this world even though he or she tried so hard to leave it. These spirits could earn release by doing tasks, however, and some of those who remained trapped in Milan helped our family. I had never seen one before that did not have anything to say; usually the opposite: they were often crabby, or angry, or sad, or didn't want to do what we asked of them.

Giuliano opened his hand. In his palm was a signet ring. It faded away as we both looked at it.

"He never speaks," said Nonno. "As you see, he's been with us longer than most; I think he has a great deal to work off. Our family did not record his death as a suicide. We might have been too ashamed, or too determined to have him buried inside the churchyard. He left a widow behind, and more than one child. I can't tell how he provided for them, and I think he did not. Our family had hit hard times, and I do not think anyone else could take them in. Do you understand what that would have meant? They would have starved, or died of overwork or abuse, or the widow would have had to become a prostitute, and might have died in childbirth or of disease. It was a terrible thing, what he did, you understand."

"I can't imagine it," I said. "Or maybe I can. It makes my stomach turn."

He nodded. We sat in silence for a moment. Then I said, "The way he spoke by handing you an object, that was interesting. What does it mean, that ring? I didn't get a good look at it."

Giuliano laughed. "I didn't, either. That's the trouble with Respicio. Every time he brings me an object in order to give me a message, he knows precisely what he means, and I usually have no idea! And then it's too late."

I laughed, too. Then I said, "Maybe . . . maybe that's why it's taking him so long to do his service to the world?"

He frowned. "Even with rings, and old wine corks, and a

book of calculations for the stresses on bridges and arches, and once, a dead rat . . . a messenger can get a lot done in half a century, and he has been here more than two."

He looked out the window. "A signet ring," he mused. He turned to his open notebook and began to sketch what he could remember of it, asking me to look over his shoulder. He thought he had seen a compass on the face; I couldn't recall anything like that, but I might not have been close enough.

"Could be a Masonic symbol," he said.

I thought of all the puzzles I was trying to solve, about my own demon, and about the family and my grandfather. I thought about how each exorcism so far had seemed like a puzzle, where we had to figure out what made the demon do what it did. If we were successful, we could save lives.

I looked around the room, at the flickering candles on the shelves, and I smiled. I had fallen in love with history and the riddles of demons. What had begun as a desperate road to survival had started to bring me joy, too.

I tried not to think too much about how my demon would almost certainly kill me when (not if) he succeeded in possessing me again. Even so, I'd felt a thrill when we had worked out the nature of the spirit from a concentration camp that had plagued Signora Galeazzo, or when my demon had recited ancient Greek the third time I had encountered him. Or when he'd spouted poetry.

Because I knew now that my demon was a poet. Or at least

he recited poems. I have memorized the lines he spoke to me in Italian:

> *No, brothers, when I die I will not feel*
> *cool coins on my eyes, nor the Trojan bronze*
> *that pulled my breath with it when it withdrew—*
> *but brothers, by Hera I beg of you:*
> *no soldier's songs when the gluttonous fires*
> *lick at my corpse on our sandy pyre,*
> *no "he died for our cause," no show of spears—*
> *for I will feel those lies, those words that praise*
> *this waste of men and boys and harvest days.*

> *Better for me if this vast field of spears*
> *had been spears of wheat in my Sparta's fields,*
> *and far better for us to outlive our fame,*
> *for mouths are not fed by a hero's name—*
> *better my firm sword arm should only wield*
> *my cup—let it shake as I gray and die,*
> *at peace with men—with gods—with soil and sky.*

I have only ever heard this sonnet once, recited to me by a startled boy my demon had borrowed for a mouthpiece. But I remember every word of it, and I made sure to write it down afterward.

"Poetry!" I said aloud, breaking out of my thoughts.

"What?" asked Nonno, who had been gazing thoughtfully at his sketch of the ring.

"I've got to start trying to find that poem by my demon."

Giuliano knit his brows. "You haven't found it yet?"

"No, of course not. I haven't started looking," I grumbled.

"Well," he said, "I should scold you. But your freedom is so new to you, and as far as I can tell, that bell around your neck is giving you some time."

He paused, then looked at me. "No. I will scold you. Find the poem, Mia!"

He cuffed my shoulder. Then he stood up, putting his notebook away in a desk drawer and tidying the books with swift hands.

"In fact, come!" he said, grabbing his coat off the back of his chair. He paused at the door and asked, "Do you have the poem in your notebook?"

I stared at him, even more annoyed by this question than by his pompousness or his peremptory command. "Yes, it's in my purse."

"Good. We'll take that walk now," he added as I scrambled into my coat and followed him out the door into the freezing industrial fog of February. I pulled my scarf from my pocket and twisted it around my neck; I'd found it at the Thursday market in the Via San Marco, one of the first Italian things I'd ever bought for myself, edged with dangling circles of lace. I matched Nonno's quick step as he turned down the Via Brera toward the center of the city. We threaded our way through the art students in front of the Pinacoteca, dodging their giant portfolios, and headed out of the pocket-size piazza into the narrow part of the Via Brera, before it crosses Via Monte di Pietà and Via dell'Orso, and the people stop being students and start being NATO and EU employees.

"We are going," said Nonno, "to a place where you can look for the poem. I know I said you should go to the Parco Sempione, but we are out in the fresh air, now—or fresh fog anyway—so let us go to the library first."

We turned right at La Scala, and I wondered if Emilio was going to get us tickets to the opera, like he'd said he would. All I knew of opera involved scratchy dresses and long songs that made no sense, so I hoped he wouldn't. We headed down the Via Santa Margherita and crossed the Piazza dei Mercanti, past the ancient, covered marketplace that gave the square its name. I asked Nonno to slow down so I could look at the great iron horse rings in the walls, the high arches over the empty, raised platform where the market had once stood.

"One of the oldest buildings in the city, covered with the young," Nonno said, laughing. There were people my age all over the steps and leaning against the columns, holding hands, hanging out. Maybe they were older than I was, but they didn't look it.

At home in Center Plains, they would be in trouble. Some-body from the shops around the piazza would have called the school. I thought of my high school, of the ice in the parking lot on February mornings like this. I suddenly wished all the girls back home could see me now, walking through the heart of Europe's fashion capital, looking like I belonged there. I wanted to casually answer my cell phone, *"Pronto,"* and have an animated conversation in Italian, preferably with some gorgeous guy.

I sighed, looking over at all the teenagers, and Nonno smiled at me.

"Not enough people your own age in your life, I think," he said as we went on. I didn't say anything. I wasn't sure I truly minded; I didn't hang out with people my own age at home, except for my sister, and she's one and a half years younger, even if everyone always thought of her as older than me. But to have a crowd of friends like the ones sitting on the steps; to have something to do on Friday nights besides help Nonna Laura cook fish; to have a boyfriend to post pictures of on Facebook—well, I did wish for that.

What did it matter, anyway? I was probably going to die, killed by the demon that had taken two of my cousins in the last century, and killed another young woman practically under my eyes. She had come back to herself before she died, that was true. But, like many others, she had died because she'd been possessed. Sometimes all we could do, I had learned, was make sure they died free of whatever creature had attacked them. It seemed a pretty miserable victory.

"Anna Maria can't really introduce you to anyone," Nonno was saying. "She left school at fifteen to become a model, and she never seemed all that interested in making friends her own age. I don't want you meeting the kinds of people she works with, or the men in her life," he added. "Your father would not be happy with me. He's angry enough that we had to take you away, isn't he?"

"I think he's getting over it," I said. "But I don't think it matters: I don't live the life that other girls my age live, do I?"

He nodded. "It's a lonely matter, being a member of this family," he said. "When you can get away from all the other family members," he added, grinning.

I grinned, too, in spite of myself. "But that's not what I meant," I said. "I mean, with . . . with someone chasing me."

"I was thinking of that, too. Yet so many people have a demon after them, you know," he told me.

"You mean, like a metaphor?" I asked, feeling impatient. "Because mine isn't a metaphor."

He could only shrug in agreement. We had been waiting to cross the busy Via Orefici, streetcars rumbling along while cars and *motorini* zipped past. Now we stepped hastily into the street, taking advantage of a window in the traffic and getting sworn at by a biker, the dog in her basket yapping as if it were swearing, too.

"Have patience with an old man!" Giuliano called after her, and then we were across the street, heading for an old building far up the Via Cesare Cantù. "It first opened to the public in 1609," he told me as we got closer and climbed the dimpled stone steps. "The Biblioteca Ambrosiana," he said.

There was no sign over the door, just a poster for an exhibit. Inside, the hallway smelled like the Church of Santa Maria del Carmine, where my family occasionally attended services. It occurred to me as we pushed through the glass doors that it smelled kind of like our shop, too.

"Here," said Nonno, opening another door, and we entered the great library.

"Libraries always take me by surprise," Nonno reflected in a whisper. "I always expect them to be bigger than they are." The Biblioteca Ambrosiana's main room was carpeted in red, and its walls of books rose to the arched ceiling. There was a walkway that ran around the walls, one tall story up, so that patrons could easily reach the higher tiers of shelves, and there were ladders, too. Otherwise, I supposed, only really tall people could be hired as librarians there.

People spoke in soft, echoing voices in what seemed like a hundred languages. If I had shut my eyes, I would have thought the books themselves were speaking, in all the tongues they were written in. At the center of the room, pages from Leonardo da Vinci's *Codex Atlanticus* were displayed in special cases. Giuliano agreed that we might go and look at these for a moment, so I got to see Da Vinci's famous, elegant mirror writing up close. I studied his sketches and notes, including a prophecy, of all things: "Men shall speak with and touch and embrace each other while standing each in different hemispheres." *The 'men shall speak' came true,* I thought. Nonno laid a hand on my shoulder. I turned and followed him off to the side.

A cheerful, youngish man in impeccable clothes sat behind a desk. He stood up immediately and held out his hand. When he smiled, dimples appeared in his cheeks, and his eyes seemed to be full of light. I tried to stop myself from thinking cute-guy thoughts—he had to be at least as old as Emilio, who is nine years older than I am—but I couldn't help myself.

"Giuliano Della Torre," he said. "It has been much too long."

Nonno smiled at him and shook his hand, nodding agreement. "Fernando Vesuvio, allow me to introduce my cousin in the third degree, Mia Della Torre."

My American last name is Dellatorri. But I heard Nonno say the Italian name clearly. I stood up straighter.

"Piacere," said the young man, shaking my hand also. "Welcome to our library."

"Thank you," I said. "It's beautiful."

"It is, isn't it?" He turned and gestured around him. "I love it."

Remembering my own, spontaneous love for our shop, I asked impulsively, "What's your favorite thing about it?"

Nonno turned his head sharply, and I knew this was too personal a question for a stranger in Milan. Fernando widened his eyes and laughed.

"I don't know if I can answer that," he replied. "But it is a good question. Let me offer a question of my own: What are you here to find? Because you know your cousin here never comes without some unbelievably hard historical question."

"Most of the time you can answer them," Giuliano pointed out.

Fernando laughed again. He had a wide-open laugh that was still not too loud for the library he worked in.

"It is not so much a historical question as a literary one this time. We need to find a poet," Nonno told him.

"We have some," Fernando informed him gravely, his eyes dancing.

Giuliano turned toward me. Now that the moment had come, I wasn't sure I wanted to show the poem to anyone outside my family. My hands felt heavy and stiff as I fumbled with the zipper to my purse. As I passed the poem over to Fernando, it seemed to jump out of my hand; he feinted to catch it, not looking in the least surprised. He leaned back against his desk and began to read, and I realized he was the first librarian I had ever seen who did not wear glasses.

When he finished, he looked up at me with an alert expression in his eyes. "Is it a translation? What do we know?"

"We don't know anything—" began Nonno, and then waved a hand at me.

"It's true," I said. "It was recited to me in modern Italian. The person who recited it didn't tell me who the author was," I added, feeling embarrassed. Although I suppose it wasn't completely a lie.

"Ah," said Fernando. He looked out across the room, down the walls of books, over the heads of whispering tourists gazing at Da Vinci's notes. "I'm having trouble even placing the era. Sometimes it doesn't matter, you think you have it and it turns out that the writer was far ahead of his time, or far behind it. Or her time," he amended, looking at me. "But I am no reader of poets, really. I know the masters but not their students. I think we need a poet for this, an educated poet, one who isn't afraid to know all those who came before him. Or her," he repeated, again looking at me.

Giuliano asked, "Aren't all poets educated?"

Fernando laughed again, and said, "You'd be surprised. You grew up in an age when they were, they had to be. But . . ."

As he went on talking, I glanced over at the display cases and froze: there was a man, looking at the page that contained the prophecy with a famished look in his eyes—a dark-haired, handsome man, with a red scarf around his throat. It was Lucifero, the Satanist who had tried to harvest my demon from me on our one, utterly disastrous date, when we had had hot chocolate in the Galleria. He was alive.

THREE

The Odd Matter of Signore Strozzi

Don't look up, don't look this way, I thought. I tugged Nonno Giuliano's sleeve.

"Yes?" he asked, turning away from Fernando.

"Lucifero," I whispered.

"Hmm? Ah," he replied, following my eyes. "Fernando, perhaps we could continue our debate in the Sala della Rosa? Someone we wish to avoid."

"He's seen us," I whispered, despairing, even though I wasn't perfectly sure. I couldn't see how he could miss us, standing over by the librarian's desk. I didn't understand how Nonno could stay so calm; he and Fernando kept their voices even as the librarian directed us to follow him through the door beside his desk.

"I can't be away long; Marco is at the other end of the room, but it takes two of us," Fernando said. "In any case, I don't believe I can help you. We must find a poet for that. But I will take you to look at some that had an interest in Greek history and pacifism."

"You don't think it was written by a Greek?" I asked.

At Lisetta's exorcism, my demon had smugly spoken ancient Greek to Uncle Matteo. (Uncle Matteo had answered him in ancient Greek, too, which I hadn't expected at all.) I had begun to wonder if we were dealing with a human spirit, one that had walked the earth a very long time ago.

"It certainly seems intended to sound that way, but somehow I do not think a Spartan wrote it," Fernando murmured as we passed into the Sala della Rosa. A couple of patrons at the reading tables raised their heads at his voice. "I believe they would have considered such a sentiment unworthy of their warlike traditions."

"Oh," I said, disappointed. If I had to have a demon chasing me, an ancient Greek one would have been cool, especially one who might have been at the Battle of Thermopylae. And knowing that about him, I might have had a way in to his mind.

Fernando shrugged, going to a shelf of poets and pulling down volume after volume.

"I am not an expert on Spartan culture, so I only guess," he added. "Remember that I could be wrong." He set a pile of books on the nearest reading table. "I cannot send these home with you, but if you haven't time to look at them now, please note down the titles of any that seem promising and come back. Here are some neoclassicists, among others; and you might try, just for a lark, a bit of Leopardi."

I nodded.

"Today we will simply make a list of titles," said Nonno. "I have no wish for a meeting with Lucifero, do you, Cousin?"

"No," I said.

I still felt cold and afraid, but I was annoyed, too. I vividly remembered what it had been like when I couldn't go outside because of my demon. I didn't want Lucifero to keep me from staying here in this palace of books, and talking to Fernando. And I certainly didn't want him finding out about the poem.

"It was a pleasure to see you again, Signore Della Torre," Fernando said, giving me back my notebook. "And a pleasure to meet you, Signorina Della Torre."

"Likewise," I said, accepting the hand he offered me.

"I should get back," he said. "Awkward if someone steals a page of the *Codex*."

Nonno and I matched his wry grin, and he left us with a pile of books on a table. I sat down and pulled out a pen, beginning a quick list of titles and authors.

"Note place and date of publication, too," said Nonno, who seemed to be idly scanning the shelves.

I couldn't help myself. "Why?"

He raised his eyebrows.

"We are dealing with a demon of place . . . or so we think. And if we can get a date, a time, a place to search, anything, that would be good, don't you think?"

I bowed my head, embarrassed.

"The more information you can find, the better; you will save yourself time and trouble later, when you find a clue and want to place it in context."

I went as fast as I could, and thankfully Lucifero did not come in. Finished, we slipped out through a courtyard.

"I feel cheated," I said.

Nonno looked surprised. "How so?"

"It's like so many things I want to do . . . spoiled by someone evil," I said.

He nodded. "Yes; it can be difficult to enjoy what we are given when the shadows crowd around," he said.

I remembered once seeing a glimpse, over his shoulder, of soldiers marching down the street. We had been standing in the candle shop at the time, and I had never been sure afterward if I'd seen what I thought I'd seen.

"Someday," I asked, "would you and Nonna ever tell me about when you were young . . . about the war, maybe? I mean if you could talk about it."

"Someday, perhaps. Not today, not now. It's time for lunch, and there is a place on the Largo Cairoli I want to take you. Then you can have your walk in the park; then come home and study."

He stopped in the middle of the street and frowned at me. "You already checked online, didn't you?"

I frowned back. "Of course! But there wasn't a thing. You'd think there would be."

He smiled. "It shows how old I am, that I didn't think to ask that until now. And how young you are, if you think that everything can be found on the Internet."

His grin took the sting out of his words. I had to admit I'd been pretty surprised not to find a single line about the poem.

"The Internet feels so vast, doesn't it?" Nonno went on. "It feels as if it ought to encompass all things, when really it touches on only a small part. This poem, I expect, is hidden in a letter or in a book nobody's bothered to translate. Or there is no written copy of it, at all."

"Don't say that," I said. "I'm already feeling hopeless."

He snorted. "Despair is for the weak-minded. We haven't even started yet," he said.

We were in the Via Orefici now, weaving in and out of the shoppers, the tourists, the businesspeople in a hurry. I could see the Largo Cairoli up ahead. Beyond it was the Castello Sforzeco and the Parco Sempione.

We walked up the Via Dante, and got a table in a restaurant on the left-hand side of the Largo Cairoli right before the Foro Buonaparte.

"You don't think Lucifero might be following us?" I asked as we sat down.

"Oh, I think it very likely," he replied, looking a lot less disturbed than I felt. "We can watch the entrance to the restaurant from here, and keep an eye on the promenade, too."

If I hadn't been so worried I would have enjoyed watching all the people going by on the sidewalk outside our window. Beyond the sidewalk, cars and *motorini* circled the Largo as if they were in a race with no finish.

"Should we go home instead?"

"No. Laura's out, and I want to eat here," he stated.

The waiters knew Nonno, and one of them came over to shake his hand and thank him, profusely and loudly, for making his sister well again. I shifted uncomfortably in my seat, looking around us; Nonno stopped him.

"*Basta, basta,* gently, my son," Giuliano told him. "You are very welcome, and I will thank you to speak in a lower voice."

The guy looked crestfallen.

"I am so sorry, Signore."

"No. I can understand your joy! It's only that we do not speak of these things too loudly in public, you know," Nonno said kindly. "And I am delighted to hear your sister is better. I must pay her a visit soon."

Lunch was delicious. I had the mushroom risotto, which looked like it had been poured into a mold: a perfect, round, flat-topped mound with crisp edges. I felt a bit bad when I put my fork into it, but ruining a work of art never tasted so good.

We didn't see Lucifero again. When I said I was worried

about walking alone in the park, Nonno overruled me.

"You have your cell phone. And you must not let fear of him interfere with your daily life. What can he do to you? Scream like a madwoman if he gets near you; there will be plenty of people in the park at this time of day."

I still didn't want to go. Even without the possibility of running into Lucifero, wandering around among the leafless trees and half-dead winter grass didn't seem like all that much fun. I went anyway, sulking at Nonno as he waved airily at me before heading back toward the Via Brera.

After half an hour exploring, however, I had to admit I felt better. I had a good meal inside of me, and I liked watching the scattering of cold-season tourists staring up at the castle battlements and buying postcards and models of the Duomo at the stand across the moat. The Milanese were out with their vast assortment of dogs, sometimes several at a time. One sour-faced woman had five dogs: a solemn German shepherd, a brace of greyhounds, a busy-looking terrier, and a Chihuahua in a sweater and booties. They all got along, but their legs had different plans. I watched until she noticed me, and then pretended I hadn't been looking.

The Parco Sempione is beautiful, and it stands in the heart of the city. Emilio told me once that the city used to be full of orchards, long ago; I thought I could imagine spring in a city like that, with blossoms everywhere. In Center Plains, spring brought a snow of white apple blossoms in April or May. I thought of Gina walking through slush to get to school, then I remembered that Luke probably drove her these days. I thought of the kids on the steps in the Piazza dei Mercanti again and turned toward home.

"You didn't tell me about Lucifero," Gina said that night over Skype. She looked seriously alarmed.

"I know," I said. "I was too embarrassed."

She glanced over her shoulder, then asked, "Did you tell Mom and Dad?"

"Of course not. They would only worry even more."

"Well, I'm worrying now!"

My sister doesn't freak out about things. She can see the funny side of the biggest, blackest argument between our parents. She even teased me the day I left for Milan, still exhausted and shell-shocked after my possession. Seeing her like this, I started to worry again myself.

Behind her on the screen, I could see our living room: a faded poster from some 1980s band and family portraits on the walls, including Grandfather Roberto, my father's father. Mom passed through the living room, carrying a plate and a glass, a romance novel under her arm; her end-of day ritual. I heard Dad's voice call out, asking where something was. Mom answered back, and I knew she was saying, "You left it in the something-something, don't you remember?"

I wanted to be there, to be close enough to touch the picture frames. I wanted to go into the kitchen and microwave some milk for hot chocolate, and bring out two mugs, one for me and one for Gina, and sag down onto the couch in front of the TV. I wanted Mom to lean around the door and say, "It's a school night. Just this show, okay?"—and then disappear again, only to reappear and say, "Hey! Wait a minute. Did you guys finish your homework?"

Gina and I looked at each other and I felt dizzy, thinking about the cold ocean between us.

"Is it spring there yet?" I asked suddenly. "Any sign of a thaw?"

She raised her eyebrows.

"We've had a couple of really warm days . . . odd weather. Then freezing again. Don't try to distract me."

"I'm being careful, Gina. We can't exactly have him arrested. And I'm not the only one keeping an eye out."

"Okay," she said, but I could see she wasn't convinced.

"Let me tell you about the cute librarian," I said, and she relented, listening patiently to a description of Fernando.

Unfortunately, as the cold, foggy weather continued, I didn't get another chance to see Fernando. He and Nonno talked on the phone a bunch, so I did hear his laugh. I didn't see Lucifero, either, so I felt like I was coming out even. Fernando put us in touch with a very crabby poet who ignored Nonno's messages.

The sun came out, briefly, for Nonna's birthday in March. Francesco stopped by after lunch, it being a half day for lectures at the university. We shared the desk in the shop, our books spread out before us, while Giuliano worked on accounts and case notes in the back office.

I love studying in the shop. I love doing anything at all in the shop, even sweeping the floor. Actually, I really do like sweeping; it's a simple job, and I know, more or less, when it's finished. I also know that with the dust of centuries hiding in the floorboards, I could sweep it over and over and never stop pulling dirt out of the cracks. I love how, when I come in from the street, the city disappears, and around me there is only the silence of centuries, the flickering candles, the measured, calm greetings of my cousins. Time moves more slowly in the candle shop, I'm sure of it.

Francesco looked from his pile of books to mine.

"What are you working on today?" he asked.

"I got interested in Da Vinci after we saw the *Codex Atlanticus*," I told him. "I'm reading about his involvement with the duchy, and his inventions and stuff."

"I've always wondered if one of us met him," he said. "I wonder what they would have talked about."

"Do you think he believed in the existence of demons?"

"I don't know," said Francesco. "I think he mainly believed in what he could see. He was so intensely interested in the material world, you know. Yet I think if he had seen a demon in action, he would have believed in it, and not everybody does that."

I thought of the sketches, the prophecy, the imaginative world I'd seen in Da Vinci's pages, and wasn't sure I agreed with him.

The bells on the shop door jingled, announcing a man about Emilio's age, who said gruffly, "Signore Della Torre?" No *buona sera*, or any other kind of greeting for us. He looked around as if Nonno might be sitting on a shelf or hiding behind a candle. I glanced at Francesco. He seemed annoyed, and neither of us moved for a minute. Then I got up and gently tapped on the door of the back office.

"Coming," said Nonno, who had probably heard the guy anyway. He carefully put away his notes, then followed me back.

"Ah! Tommaso Strozzi. Good evening," said Giuliano. "Come sit. May my assistants stay?"

The young man grimaced, as if to say he didn't much care either way.

Francesco and I cleared the table, and I was sent to get wine and glasses. I hurried, not wanting to miss anything, and got back in time to hear Nonno finish his polite inquiries about Tommaso Strozzi's mother, and aunts and uncles, and so forth. As he invited Tommaso to tell his story, I remembered how hard I would have had to work, even a month before, to understand their swift Italian. Now it was as if I flowed along with the stream of words, and rarely hit one I didn't understand. I noticed every detail about Tommaso; his expensively cut dark hair, his fingers, thick with rings, the heavy smell of his cologne, rising over the scent of melting wax from the shop, the sturdy swell of his neck, his silk scarf. I realized I found him disturbingly attractive, though I had no idea why. I blushed and looked out the window.

Tommaso Strozzi was telling Giuliano that his father had recently begun to believe that his hands were rotting off. He spoke hesitantly, though nothing about him suggested that he would normally hesitate about anything, like punching a man, or kissing a woman, for example. When he detailed his father's behavior, he glowered as if he were furious. I had a sudden flash of memory, seeing the same expression on my father's face on the day he found out his own father was dying. I looked at Tommaso again, and this time, I could see the pain behind the stiff pauses. He finished his story at last, and then added, "Forgive me for saying this, but I would never have come to you, except that my mother said this wasn't for the doctors at the mental hospital. She seemed to think something like this had happened before."

"In your family?"

"Oh, no! At least, I don't think that's what she meant. She said something about another family."

"This is certainly not unheard of. And she's right, the psychiatrists, they don't always understand the causes."

"Perhaps," said the young man, lifting his eyebrows ever so slightly.

Watching Francesco, I saw that he betrayed no more

concern about the young man's skepticism than Nonno. When Giuliano began to ask Tommaso Strozzi specific questions on the details of his father's condition, I looked away again, annoyed that I found him so attractive. That was when I first noticed the candle.

As I turned to look at it more closely, Tommaso's and Nonno's voices slid away from me; the room, full of minute fires, shrank down to that single failing light. Then it went out, briefly flickering blue, which was not how a candle flame died when it had enough wick. There was no orange coal gleaming in the wick, no smoke. I stood up and put one finger close to the wick, taking great care not to touch it. I couldn't feel any heat; the candle was as cold as if it had not been lit.

It's an old family problem, I thought. *It comes in families of bankers. The key that opens the door is*—and then not a word but a sensation came to me, a taste, stagnant and musty, like a pond with no way for the water to flow in or out. Still gazing at the candle, I asked myself where all this had come from.

As the room snapped back into focus, I noticed Francesco watching me, but I didn't meet his eyes. Giuliano stood up and bowed slightly toward the man at the table.

"We will call on your father as soon as is convenient for him," said Nonno.

"Of course. Thank you for being so understanding."

"There's nothing wrong with skepticism. That is not where the trouble lies. *Buona sera.*"

They met each other's eyes for a moment. Then Tommaso nodded. Still ignoring us, he said *buona sera* to Nonno and stepped out the door.

I could tell Giuliano was about to ask us what we thought of all of this, when the church bells started to ring, and he said, "*Santa Maria*, is that the time? We have to get ready for Nonna's birthday dinner."

I stole the first shower, because I still had to buy a present; then I went to the bike stand in the Via Brera.

Milan has these wonderful bikes. They're cream and yellow, like a lemon meringue pie, and they have the city coat of arms printed on them. If you have a membership in the bike-sharing program, you can go to a *stazione* anywhere in the city, swipe your BikeMi card, and take out a bike for thirty minutes, which is always way more time than you need to get to the next stand.

The bikes are stout and come with a lock and a basket, which is perfect for carrying a history book, a panino, a can of *aranciata amara*, and a spare sweater. I flew all the way to the Libreria Rizzoli in the Galleria, and bought Nonna one of her cheesy romances. The covers look the same as the ones my mom reads, but the words are in Italian instead of English. I had the store lady wrap it in their fancy wrapping paper, found a bike at the Duomo *stazione,* and took off again, this time for the Navigli neighborhood on the south side of the city, a place I'd never been. I had to use my tourist map to get there.

I parked my bike at one of the *stazioni* on the Viale Gorizia and went to wait near Nonna's favorite restaurant. Emilio had asked me to come early, and I was glad it hadn't been too hard to find this place. I leaned against the wall, gazing at the shops on the other side of the canal, holding Laura's present.

It was a pretty part of the city, and the evening was unusually warm. Everyone seemed to be taking advantage of the balmy air and the stillness. Voices echoed up the street from the far side. Couples held hands as they walked along the canal, or stood close together, looking down into the water.

I wanted to pretend, just for a moment, that I was alone only because I was waiting for someone to come hold my hand. In the last few months, I hadn't had time or energy to be sad about the fact that I was going to be alone forever, because only a crazy Satanist like Lucifero would ever want to date me.

A nearby couple was kissing. He was handsome, with dark hair that could take a bit of ruffling. He held on to his girlfriend like she might fly off the bridge. I knew I probably shouldn't watch them, but I couldn't look away.

Then I reminded myself that I *was* waiting for someone. In fact, I was waiting for the most beautiful man in Milan, even if he wasn't mine. I touched my hair and straightened the hem of my dress, just as Emilio turned the corner, walking up the street toward me. Every woman paused to look at him— probably trying to figure out who he was smiling at. Even the girl on the bridge stared over her boyfriend's shoulder at him.

He was close to six feet tall and wore an open-necked white shirt and a cream blazer with a line so perfect it might have been tailored for a god. He had high cheekbones and golden skin, and his blond hair caught the evening sun. His eyes were the same color as the storm that had passed over us in the afternoon, leaving rain in the gutters, washing the city clean for this clear almost-spring night.

I heard a thudding in my ears, and for a moment thought I heard the hearts of all the women on the street, not just my own, pounding away.

But, of course, it all was completely pointless: my pounding heart, the pristine evening, my pretty dress, the looks the women gave him. It was just Emilio. I sighed.

He came up to me and said, "*Buona sera,* Mia. Not waiting inside?"

"No, it's too nice an evening," I replied.

He nodded in agreement, kissed my cheeks, and held out his hand for my parcel.

"I've asked them for a table by the window. They don't have outdoor seating, but the food's worth staying inside for, even on an evening like this. Ah!" He looked up at the sky and took a deep breath. "Nights like this I want to flee our lovely, smoggy home. I want to go out to the country, or to the sea. Or just fly up into the sky," he added, and smiled at me.

Sometimes I think that all I want in this world is for Emilio to go on smiling at me until we both grow old and die. But, aside from the fact that he's my third cousin, he's utterly out of my league *and* he's taken. We crossed the street and went into the restaurant.

They had already set up a long table for us, with bowls of gardenias all along the center, and a view of the canal. Emilio thanked them.

"I love the light on the canal," I said as we sat down.

"Dock," Emilio corrected me. I rolled my eyes. A waiter lit candles, one by one. When he left, Emilio picked up one of the candles in its holder, tipping it this way and that, staring into the flame.

"Thanks for meeting me," he said at last. "I think we've got at least a half an hour before the others arrive."

"You never did say why you wanted me to come early," I prompted.

He shrugged.

"I have a hunch," he said.

"What kind of a hunch?" I asked.

"You look nice in that dress," he said.

I rolled my eyes again.

"Wait and see," he said. "And tell me what Tommaso Strozzi told my grandfather."

I blinked. It still surprises me, the way such a big city can be so like a small town—at least if your family has lived there for centuries.

"How did you know he'd come by?" I asked. Emilio smiled.

"Bernardo Tedesco stopped in at the bank to deposit last week's checks. He said he'd seen Tommaso with you and Nonno this afternoon."

"Nobody else dropped in. I don't know Bernardo."

"He was just passing by. You'll meet him sometime. His grandfather was friends with Nonno, his father was friends with my father, and so on."

"And you guys are friends?"

"I'm friends with his older brother. Bernardo just followed us around and bugged us when he was little."

"Like Anna Maria?"

He smiled.

"Like her and Francesco, both," he agreed, but he seemed distracted, looking over my shoulder. I tried to catch his eye.

"What's going on?" I asked.

"Don't turn around," he said.

"Okay."

Now he looked directly at me, and I felt afraid. He leaned across the table and gently took my hand.

"They're actually a bit late. I thought they'd be here sooner," he said. "Lucifero and his friends."

My hand convulsed under his; he tightened his grip.

"Don't turn around! It's all right, Mia. They've been following us on and off for some weeks. Mostly you or me, as far as we can tell. They think I don't recognize them. Somebody generally knows where you are, so I felt no need to tell you. You keep on the alert anyway, which is good."

"I do," I agreed, but it was hard to speak.

He should have told me, I thought. *He should have told me!* And worse, I hadn't noticed on my own, except that once at the Biblioteca Ambrosiana.

I thought back to that peculiar first date with Lucifero: how I'd snuck out to meet him, walking part of the way with Francesca and Francesco, how looking at him had made my stomach quiver. Not anymore, not in a good way, anyway. Why would anyone ask for possession? Yet Lucifero had. "Power, quick power," Nonno would say.

"Where is he sitting?" I asked, when I was sure I could control my voice.

"Over your right shoulder, two tables down."

I knew I shouldn't, but I had to look. I caught one short glimpse of him. At first, I couldn't figure out exactly why he looked abnormal. He seemed brighter—not like Emilio, who seems to shine in the dark, but bright and flat like an advertisement that grabs the eye without filling the heart. It was bizarre. I felt sick.

"What do you think they're planning?" I asked Emilio.

"I don't know," he said. "But I thought if we could give them a few moments where we seemed vulnerable, that might bring matters to a head. Nonno and Uncle Matteo will be here soon, and Anna Maria and Francesco, too, so we'll have plenty of backup. Let's just continue talking, and I'll keep an eye on them."

I couldn't decide who I wanted to murder more, the serenely self-confident man in front of me, or the handsome Satanist at my back.

FOUR

A Weapon Hidden in Plain Sight

T ake out your case, slowly," Emilio advised. "Set it open in your lap. I'll do the same if something distracts them."

I reached in my jacket pocket and clasped the heavy, leatherbound case in my fingers. I slid it onto my lap and opened it, touching the mirror, the candle stub, the tiny brass bell, the fountain pen I'd wedged next to the new leather notebook.

"You have no idea what they're going to do?" I repeated.

"None."

I glared at him, and he laughed.

"Life's not interesting if you always play it safe," he counseled.

"Just how unsafe do you think this will be?" I grumbled, and then, still glaring at him, I recognized the ice-cold feeling between my shoulders, a telltale sign of a demon.

Emilio saw me flinch.

"Pick up the bell and mirror and set them on the table," he went on in the same calm voice, never releasing my shaking hand. "Now."

I could feel some power seeking a way in. The bell I wore around my neck, nesting in the hollow between my collarbones, began to shiver but did not ring. I had never even considered whether it would protect me against any demon aside from my own enemy.

The bell from my case tinkled, too, as I set it on the table. I nearly dropped the mirror. With his other hand, Emilio slid them across in front of him, around the place mats and silverware, the glasses and napkins. He held up the mirror, low, hidden more or less from the view of the tables around us, and aimed it over my shoulder.

"Look at yourself," Emilio whispered, and I thought he was talking to me until I heard a low, guttural growl beside my ear. I was pretty sure that even if the demon roared, Emilio and I would be the only ones that could hear it.

"Know yourself," Emilio whispered, and the demon growled again. I knew now it wasn't my demon—it didn't sound like him, more like some angry animal.

"Now," he went on, looking into the space over my shoulder, "come to me."

Something pounced at the table, blowing over glasses and flinging cutlery into the air. Emilio dropped my hand and leaped up at the same time—as if he'd been expecting this—then, grabbing the restaurant candle between us, he cupped it in both hands and murmured a singsong chant. I couldn't quite understand the words; they sounded Italian, yet thicker and rougher.

He interrupted himself to say, "Ring the bell."

I felt slow as I reached out and grasped the bell. I rang it, once, twice, three times, pausing carefully in between, even while something whirled above the table. On the third ring, I heard a sigh from among the spilled glasses, and the candle in Emilio's hands flared wildly.

"Got it," he said. I looked down at the ordinary restaurant candle between his fingers. All our weapons, hidden in plain sight . . .

One of the waiters arrived at the table now, and Emilio apologized to him for the mess. "I'm clumsy." He shrugged.

The waiter laughed and tipped his head at me. "Don't try so hard to impress her," he advised, and we all laughed. For about the millionth time, I speculated what it would be like to be on a date with Emilio. I supposed I'd be the one spilling water everywhere, because I'd be so nervous. Or maybe I'd just be overjoyed and wouldn't notice I was tipping glasses over.

"What are they doing now?" I asked in a low voice, once the waiter had left.

"They're gone," said Emilio. "That must have been their best shot, so far. Interesting . . . they must have learned quite a bit, to be able to call up a being and direct it at us like that. I wonder who has the talent, and who has the skill, and if they are the same person . . . our Lucifero, perhaps?"

I glared at him and said nothing.

"What?" he said, looking genuinely surprised. "Upset about something?"

"You should have told me. I should have known they were following me and what we were getting into."

He furrowed his brow. "What would you have done differently?" he asked finally.

I didn't have an answer.

"Three months ago, we had to spend all our time protecting you. Now things are different. You can run risks you never could before. Isn't that a good thing?"

"I'd still like to know I'm running them," I countered, surprised that I could actually find the right words when I needed them. This kind of discussion isn't my strong point.

He shrugged again. "Fair enough," he said. But I wanted an apology, and I knew I wasn't going to get one. Does being that good-looking mean never having to say you are sorry? I decided to ask Anna Maria, although I thought I knew what she would say.

I turned to look at the empty table where they had sat. "I hope they paid their bill, is all," I said. Emilio laughed.

"Early!" cried Nonno, spotting us across the restaurant and leading Nonna Laura to us. We stood up to wish Nonna a *buon compleanno* and receive her kisses. Then cousin after cousin arrived: Anna Maria, texting her way between the tables; Uncle Matteo, earnestly bickering with Aunt Brigida about which way to the restaurant was quickest, even though they had already arrived; Francesca, carrying a bright parcel wrapped in hand-printed paper; Égide and Francesco talking and moving in hilarious contrast—the one all grace and dignity, the other knocking over some poor woman's wineglass, and having to stop and apologize. The last to arrive was a stranger, a tall man with a triangular face, black hair shot with gray, and a goatee that made him look like the devil.

Everyone knew him but me, apparently, because they all called out, *"Dottore! Dottore!"* cheerfully across the restaurant, and Nonna smiled with genuine pleasure: "You came!"

"Of course, I came, Nonna Laura," the man rebuked her, smiling, too. He handed her a box smaller than the palm of her hand, all done up in silver paper with a wide silver ribbon and the label of some fancy store.

"Dottore Komnenos, allow me to introduce our young American cousin, Mia Della Torre. Mia, this is our Venetian cousin, Dottore Augusto Komnenos."

"Piacere," said Dottore Komnenos, holding out his hand. I took it, and my own shy *piacere* felt awkward on my tongue again, as if I hadn't said it to every new person I was introduced to in Milan.

Nonno took charge of the menu, conferring with his wife.

Apparently, this wasn't a meal we would get to choose.

"Venice?" I asked Dottore Komnenos while Nonno and Laura discussed antipasti as seriously as the coming election (more seriously, in fact).

"*Sì.*" He smiled. "Is that so strange?"

I ducked my head.

"All the family I've met come from Milan."

He laughed.

"We're all over the world, under a number of different surnames. My mother was a Torriani, for example, another derivative of Della Torre. I like your own Dellatorri."

He'd seen my name written? He seemed to guess the question.

"Yes, in e-mail. Of course your family talks of you."

Of course. But not like an ordinary relative who has come to visit, I felt sure. Was he in the family business?

"I hope they said good things," I said.

"Oh, yes," he answered with a wry smile.

"But Venice," I went on, hoping I wasn't being rude. "I've never been there. Are all the streets really canals?"

"Almost all of them. You can't go everywhere by water. You need sidewalks."

"It sounds amazing, though."

"I suppose it is," he said. "I grew up there, and so for me the remarkable thing was cities with stone streets; I'd never been in a dry city until I was seven, so I remember my first one quite well: Sienna, with her Piazza del Campo paved in waves of stone. My father never really liked Venice, but then he was Greek, as you might guess by the name; he liked dry countries, and the damp was hard for him. He knew my mother would never leave her city, though, so he didn't try to make her," he added, smiling.

I thought about the things people do for love, and how everybody here seemed so wise about love. Everybody but me.

My eyes must have wandered, because Dottore Komnenos asked me politely what I was thinking.

"I was thinking about what people do when they love someone very much," I said, feeling shy about confessing this to a stranger, even if we were related. Would my dad do what Dottore Komnenos's father had done—stay in a place he didn't like for the woman he loved? Dottore Komnenos turned his eyes on me, and I saw the family resemblance in them very clearly.

"Yes," he said. "All kinds of strange things. Like writing bad poetry, or naming stars after them."

"Or inventing a dessert," I put in, "like that nobleman who supposedly created panettone for his baker girlfriend."

At that moment, we realized that the others were listening. They gave their own suggestions.

"Sending a girl thirty pounds of foul-smelling German sausage that everyone has to think of ways to cook for weeks, months," said Francesco, with a mischievous glance at his sister.

Anna Maria blinked her perfectly made-up eyes at him and shot back, "Or learning how to snowboard so you can follow her to Livigno and break your leg on an Alp."

Her brother stuck out his tongue. Emilio and Dottore Komnenos laughed.

"Touché," said Emilio.

"Oh, yeah?" retorted Francesco. "What about you, Emilio?"

"Oh, the antics of his women," said Anna Maria, rolling her eyes. "You should see them."

Dottore Komnenos seemed interested. "Really?"

"They all try to get him to chase *them*, and try to look like they're not really chasing *him*. That girl who used to run into you at the baker's by accident every single day."

"The one who took a job at the bank," said Francesco. "What did she say in that elevator, to put you in such a bad mood?"

"This isn't nearly as funny as you think it is," Emilio said, and I was surprised to see he seemed really annoyed. "They have hearts, you know."

Anna Maria snorted. "So serious! They have more heart than head, from what I can see." She turned to Dottore Komnenos. "They walk into lampposts looking at him. No dignity, that's what I don't like."

"Is love such a dignified thing?" asked the doctor, looking her in the eye.

Now Emilio smiled, because for once Anna Maria seemed

to be at a loss for words. But after a minute, she said, "No, not really. But that's all the more reason to keep your dignity as long as you can. Those girls should have some self-respect." She turned to Emilio and went on in a kinder voice, "That's the thing I notice about the ones who catch you; they have self-respect. You don't go for the other kind."

"Thank you for the compliment," he replied with only a touch of sarcasm in his voice. He turned when his grandmother tapped his shoulder, and Francesco murmured in an undertone, "The current one has maybe too much self-respect," which got a choking laugh out of both me and Anna Maria.

Dottore Komnenos raised his eyebrows. "The famous Alba," he said. "Will I meet her tonight?"

"No," Anna Maria shook her head. "She and Nonna don't get along too well."

"There's someone who doesn't get along with Nonna Laura?" He sounded as if he didn't believe it.

Anna Maria shrugged.

"It is pretty unheard of," reflected Francesco.

We went on to something else, and the antipasti arrived, accompanied by the owner of the restaurant, who wished Nonna a *buon compleanno* and then explained where each kind of sausage and cheese had been produced; some of them by a farmer my family knew. For a fierce moment, I wished I'd been born here, among my cousins, so that everything and everyone they were talking about would be ordinary and familiar to me, and I'd know the names of all the dogs at that farm, and the way the hills looked behind it.

I was starting to share the national obsession with food, so the conversation kept my attention; on the other hand, my stomach didn't care where the food was from. I watched the progress of the giant platter down the table with all the attention of a wolf, wondering when I had gotten so hungry.

"I could eat an ox," I said. Emilio, looking up, smiled and said, "Catching always makes me hungry, too."

"Catching?" Nonno asked softly, his eyes alert. He glanced at his wife.

"Tell me later," he said. I widened my eyes at Emilio. Were we in trouble? He shook his head very slightly.

The dinner was delicious: *risotto alla Milanese* infused with saffron, its bright yellow color belying its subtle flavor; fried pork cutlets with a truffle sauce; a salad with radicchio and endive; and a custard dappled with cinnamon and scented with orange blossom water. I couldn't get enough of the custard. Aunt Brigida gave me and Francesco the rest of hers to fight over.

After dinner, Dottore Komnenos walked with us. Apparently, he had a small apartment near the Porta Nuova he stayed in sometimes.

"You don't mind the stone streets after all?" I asked, feeling brave enough to tease him.

He smiled. "Sometimes during the night, I wake up and

look down into the street, and wonder why it does not sparkle under the lamps."

I wanted to visit Venice.

We walked along the canal for a little while, enjoying the evening. Later, heading back to the metro with everyone, I thought about Lucifero.

"He doesn't seem to have reacted to possession the way I did," I said to Anna Maria, who stopped texting to look at me. We'd wound up ahead of the others, who were arguing about the best way to cook the meal we'd just had.

"I mean," I went on, "I really . . . it took so much out of me. I don't think I really started to feel like myself until Christmas."

She shrugged. "You were also learning a new language and living in a new place," she pointed out.

"Still, I don't think I'd have gone around setting demons on people," I said. "Not after what I'd been through."

"You weren't dumb enough to invite a demon in," said Anna Maria. "Maybe that's the difference."

I had been wondering about that, though. Why had my demon gone after me in the first place? He had crossed an ocean to find me, something he had not—as far as anybody seemed to know—done before. Before me, he had chosen and killed strong people, like Emilio's father, Luciano. I wasn't some practiced demon catcher, I wasn't a Luciano, not by a long shot. So, if I wasn't his usual kind of victim, why had he gone to the trouble to target me? Had I inadvertently invited him in? Was there something about me that called to him?

I feared the answer to that question, but I had to find it. I set these thoughts aside, looking at Anna Maria. "What does Lucifero want?" I asked. "Nonno says quick power. But why? What happened to him?"

Anna Maria snorted.

"Don't make excuses for him! He may be good-looking, he may be charming, he may have asked you out on your first date, but those aren't reasons enough. I've been on several photo shoots with him, and he's a diva, a pain in the butt . . . messing with the photographers or stressing out the makeup artists. What does it matter if he had a horrible childhood? People live through terrible things all the time, and still go on to live good, happy lives. They even use their experiences to help others. It's no excuse, ever."

I thought that was pretty harsh. But then she said, "Like you, Mia. The same demon possessed you, and instead of going crazy, or looking at how evil the world can be, you've already helped Signora Galeazzo and Signorina Umberti."

"Signorina Umberti died," I retorted, holding up a finger.

"Yes," she said simply. "But then, even Nonno couldn't save her. And you helped her get free. She didn't die possessed, she died herself, her own self."

We walked on in silence for a moment.

"And that is very, very important. We can't lose ourselves," she went on fiercely.

I stopped thinking about Lucifero and started wondering about Anna Maria. Had she always been like this? Emilio said that as a kid she'd badgered the family to let her learn to be a demon catcher, finally sneaking into an exorcism when she was eight. They gave up after that. Why did she want this so badly? She wasn't born until a year after her uncle Luciano died, so she didn't have Emilio's motivation to become a demon catcher; but then again, Emilio had always wanted to be one, even before his father was killed. Since Emilio was a man, nobody had argued—no, his mother had, after she had lost her husband to the profession.

This family was complicated.

As we boarded the metro, Anna Maria and I melted back into the puddle of Della Torres. Nonna pinched my arm.

"Thank you for the book," she said. "I'll start it tonight."

I leaned down to kiss her cheek, saying, "Happy birthday, Nonna." I felt a pang of guilt that I'd hardly talked to her during the meal, but she'd been surrounded by us, by family, so maybe it was just fine.

When we reached Lanza Brera–Piccolo Teatro metro stop, we kissed Dottore Komnenos good-bye as we stepped off. I watched him wave at us through the window as the train pulled away. Emilio fell in beside me on the stairs and asked again to be told about Tommaso Strozzi's visit to our candle shop. I'd already heard him talking to Nonno and Francesco about it, but he seemed to want my point of view, which pleased me a lot.

Emilio nodded thoughtfully as I told him what had happened; he raised his eyebrows when I told him about the candle, the stink of pond water, and my idea that this was a special trouble in banking families.

"Is that the first time you've noticed something like that, while a case is being discussed?"

"Yes, I think so."

He pressed his lips together.

"What's wrong?" I asked.

"Nothing. It's just further proof that we need to keep training you, regardless of the risk that the demon may learn what he does not already know," Emilio said.

"I've been meaning to ask about that, actually," I said. "Why is everybody so worried about what he can learn through me, when he's already learned whatever he can from—from your great-uncle and your . . ."

"From my father," he finished for me. I gave him an awkward, sad grin.

"Sorry," I said.

"Don't be," he replied tersely. After a moment, he went on. "Great-uncle Martino was Nonno Giuliano's middle brother. The demon killed him in 1957, when he was twenty-four," Emilio said after a moment. Neither of us pointed out that this was only a year younger than Emilio was now. "Martino was young, but when the demon possessed my father, he was attacking a far more seasoned exorcist. Now, if the demon had gained all of my father's knowledge, that would have been a problem. Indeed, we run that risk over and over when we face different spirits. So we have to sequester parts of our minds, and even our souls. You are already learning the foundation for that. My father, they tell me, was quite good at it. Though there's no telling whether he broke down at the end."

I could imagine breaking down. If I hadn't been rescued by Nonno and Emilio, I would have. Emilio's voice sounded awfully cold, especially considering what he was talking about. I had been looking up the street, paying attention to his words, but now I turned to see his face, his expression hard and tight, like he wasn't letting anything out.

"Do you think he did?" I asked, keeping my voice soft, so that he could pretend not to have heard me if he needed to. He shot me a quick glance and one corner of his mouth turned up.

"No, I don't," he said, his voice full of pride. "The man I remember . . . no."

Luciano: the root of his name was *lux*, light. I could see the light in Emilio's face while he remembered his father.

We had reached the door to the candle shop. Even though only Nonno, Nonna, Francesca, Égide, and I lived in the apartment, the whole family had ended up walking together, because nobody had wanted the conversation to end. Now Emilio seemed surprised to find himself at the shop door.

"I was going to go home," he said, laughing. "Never mind.

. . . No, wait." He turned to Nonna. "My beautiful grandmother, I have a bottle of *sciacchetrà* back at the apartment. Should I run and get it, so that we can have another birthday toast upstairs?"

Nonna waved her hand airily, queen for a night: "Do as you will, my peaceful subjects!" Emilio turned and dashed away; I watched his bright head flicker in the streetlight from the Via Borgonuovo. The rest of us went through the shop and upstairs, me floating along in the middle, letting myself get lost in the rapid rise and fall of my family's voices. When we were all settled in the living room, I asked Francesca, "What's he getting?"

"The *sciacchetrà*."

"The what?"

"*Sciacchetrà*," she repeated, pronouncing it like "shah-keh-TRA." It had a beautiful sound. "It's a dessert wine from the Cinque Terre."

I had no idea what or where the Cinque Terre was, but sometimes I get tired of asking for explanations, so I let it go. Emilio returned, breathless, looking like a little boy as he held up a long, slender bottle of amber liquid. Nonno had already gotten out glasses for everyone. I watched as he poured, because I'd never seen wine that color. Emilio raised his glass and we all followed.

"To the best grandmother in the world," he said, still looking like a kid. "A very happy birthday."

Nonna shook her head. We all clinked glasses and drank. It wasn't like any wine I'd ever had before. It was sweeter, and thicker, and I could taste the grapes, and a sun like honey, and something else, a raisiny taste, if raisins came from the heavens.

"It's made from grapes grown on the original rootstock brought from Greece a couple of thousand years ago," said Uncle Matteo. "These were among the few vines in Europe that escaped the vine blight in the last century. You know about that? You Americans saved us. We grafted our ancient grape varieties on to your rootstock, since our own were dying. Nearly every wine in Europe owes its survival to you."

I wanted to say, "Not to me, specifically," but instead I accepted his thanks solemnly, feeling a sharp pain in my heart when I heard him say "you Americans." It wasn't because of all the lame things my country was doing at the moment, but because I had finally started to feel like part of the family. On the other hand, it was nice to hear that we had done a few things right over the years. Grape rootstock, the Marshall Plan, stuff like that.

We ended the evening by singing some song that Nonna was trying to remember the words to, and some pop songs that everybody knew because you couldn't avoid hearing them on the radio.

"Ma gelido sarai," I sang to myself as I struggled with the zipper on my dress, thinking what it would be like to kiss various people.

"You don't quite have it yet," Signora Gianna told me, speaking out of the air above my head. I jumped, having forgotten for a moment that I shared my room with a couple of nosy and opinionated spirits. I reminded myself to try to find out which member of the family Signora Gianna had been, and to try to work out who her gravel-voiced friend was (I still just called him Gravel). I wondered why I kept forgetting to look her up, once I was out of the room. It was still hard to even talk about her to Nonno and the rest of the family.

"Try again," she prompted. "Listen, first." And she sang:

Gelido come
Mi guardo allo specchio
E non mi vedo più
Qual è il mio nome,
Qual è la mia città
Dov'è che abito

Which I would translate sort of like this:

Freezing like when
I look in the mirror
And I cannot see
What my name is
What is the city
In which I live

Signora Gianna has a beautiful voice, and I got lost,

listening to her sing, so I was surprised when she said, "Now your turn." I thought about asking who had appointed her my singing teacher, but I didn't. Instead, I tried again, and this time I sounded much better. We ended up singing the whole thing together before I fell asleep.

In the morning, Giuliano informed me that I would be going with him to visit Piero Strozzi, Tommaso's father, because the only time the banker would see us was over his lunch break, and none of the others could get off work or school to go with us. Giuliano had insisted on seeing him in his home, a point that Signore Strozzi had made some difficulty over, since they were very busy people. Why couldn't Nonno come to Signore Strozzi's bank, or meet him for lunch? There were several very private tables at his favorite restaurant. But Giuliano was firm, and we were to see him today at noon at his home.

The Strozzis lived on the other side of the Castello Sforzesco.

We headed down the Via Madonnina toward the Foro Buonaparte. Nonno stopped to talk with another old man, their voices echoing across the cobblestones. As we continued on our way, he said, "He used to live down the street from us during the war. We would drive the Germans crazy, throwing rocks from windows and dodging away before they could see us. Nobody wanted them here, never mind that we were allies."

Just at that moment, a herd of German tourists emerged from the Via Madonnina, following their leader, who held a fake daisy on a long stick. I thought Nonno would lower his voice, in case one of them understood Italian, but he didn't.

"They were pompous and loud. They really thought they were the master race, building a better world. But you and I have glimpsed what they built—a monumental sorrow."

I knew he was talking about the spirit that had possessed Signora Galeazzo, a spirit that had taken many years to return from Majdanek concentration camp to her home here in Milan. Giuliano followed my gaze to that pack of earnest, sensibly dressed older people. For a moment, I thought I could see what he saw, but then I thought, *They're just people.* I remembered Emilio's warning, before we entered the house of Signora Galleazzo five months ago. *Trust your own senses. . . . Don't just believe what you are told. You're not a child.*

One of the Germans turned toward us, and I saw his eyes flicker and change before I realized what I was seeing: another soul looking directly at me—one that gave me a cold shudder as I recognized it. *You again?* I thought, and my stomach turned over. Then the man's eyes flickered once more, and he was only a slightly bewildered-looking tourist with his wife's shopping bags in his hands. A young, black-haired Italian going the other way stopped and took a step toward me, and I saw the same soul looking out of his eyes, before it flickered away yet again, into the eyes of a young woman standing nearby, her gilded blonde hair floating around her face, and then, fluttering like a candle flame, it blew into an old man just beyond her, his own tired eyes vanishing for a moment. He was holding the hand of a small boy, who looked up at me and spoke in my demon's voice. I stopped still.

"I will come for you," the child said simply, his voice deep, gravelly, horribly familiar. The grandfather frowned down at his grandson; the air opened and parted; the boy blinked in confusion, himself again. I smelled cinnamon in the air.

FIVE

The Banker's Hands

Giuliano touched my arm.

"About time," he said when the old man and his grandson had walked on, both already forgetting what had happened. The Germans swirled sensibly around us and vanished down the Via Mercato.

I shivered.

"Really?" I managed.

"Yes," he replied firmly.

"Did you smell it?" I asked. "This time?"

"Smell what?"

"The cinnamon," I said, still wondering why the demon had sounded so cold, but so full of longing. "He always leaves behind the scent of cinnamon."

"I remember," he said. "From Lisetta Maria Umberti's exorcism."

I shuddered. That exorcism had taken place about a block away, inside the Church of Santa Maria delle Carmine. My demon had taken over an art student and had been able to enter the church because the sign for Christmas Eve Mass had said ALL ARE WELCOME. I had held Lisetta's wrist, feeling the double pulse of her heart and the demon's presence beating against my fingers. I remembered visiting her in the hospital afterward, seeing her gray face as she slipped away from us, weakened beyond recovery by the ordeal of possession. Suddenly, I felt deeply grateful that the couple we had rescued on *San Valentino* had survived.

"Cinnamon," I repeated. "Why, though?"

I thought of the stagnant smell that had entered my mind when Tommaso Strozzi had come to see us. I thought of the smell of the roses outside Signora Galeazzo's house, the smell of bitter almonds—of Zyklon B gas.

"Do they all leave behind different scents?" I asked Giuliano.

"I don't know if every single one does," he replied, "but many I have encountered do."

We kept walking but my legs felt weak. By the time we crossed the Foro Buonaparte, I found myself shrinking against the tall, dark buildings, my stomach heaving.

Nonno took my elbow in a tight grip and hurried me forward. His fingers drove into my arm, and I yelped.

"Ow! You're hurting me," I said.

He loosened his grip but said, "You can't get lost in your fear. You need to snap out of it."

I thought this was pretty unfair. Nothing more frightening had ever happened to me—or to anyone I'd ever known.

Giuliano went on, "He can't come in while you wear that bell, and it was about time he turned up: we want him where we can see him, not off making trouble with someone else, do you see?"

I muttered something that probably sounded like I was agreeing with him. I didn't want to admit that when he'd pinched my arm, I'd stopped feeling sick.

We contined walking on the Foro Buonaparte after navigating through the Largo Cairoli, with its traffic and swirl of foreign languages—Russian, Portuguese, Greek, French, and, startling me, English, which for a moment I didn't understand. I hadn't spoken it since my recent Skype with my parents and Gina. As we entered the Via Vincenzo Monti, where the Strozzis lived, I asked Giuliano about the man and woman from the night of *San Valentino.* Had he stopped in on the couple since then?

"Two phone calls, one with the husband and one with the wife," he replied. "Would you like to come with me when I visit them?"

"Yes, please," I said, wanting to know what had happened to them.

"Good," he said. We crossed the street in silence.

Nonno said, "This is one of the big avenues, as you can

see, that the city planners created, working on the same principle as Baron Haussmann did in Paris—you need to be able to get soldiers to the center of the city if there's a revolt. But it backfired in Paris, and here, too. They didn't think about *whose* soldiers."

I didn't say anything, watching him stare into the distance. Once, I had thought I had seen the soldiers from his memories marching past; now, I saw only the street we were on.

The Via Vincenzo Monti was full of traffic, and some of the shops looked pretty fancy. The tall door to the Strozzis' apartment building was made of well-polished wood, and the brass intercom plate shone like a gilded mirror. No flowers grew beside the door, like the rose outside Signora Galeazzo's that had smelled of bitter almonds and snow, giving us a clue what lay inside. I thought again of the stagnant-water smell on the day Tommaso Strozzi had come to see us, as Giuliano stepped up and pressed the button for their apartment.

"I believe they own the entire building," he told me.

The intercom gave a burst of static. "Who is it?" asked a woman's voice.

"Signore Della Torre and his assistant."

"Come up, then."

Nonno looked down the wide entryway into the courtyard of the building, then pressed the button again.

"What?" snapped the voice.

"I don't know where your apartment is," he said simply.

89

"Straight through the courtyard, staircase on the right, number seven," she said impatiently, as if he were at fault.

The courtyard's garden was as carefully manicured as the door, a wreath of clipped bushes waiting for spring. Yet the soil smelled dank, as if there was nowhere for the water to drain. Around the garden smooth stones were set in patterns, white and red and black. The walls were faced with cream-colored marble, a fine pattern in different colors of stone running in a band around the whole court. We climbed a marble staircase and came to the Strozzis' front door, with its polished brass fittings.

Signora Strozzi didn't look like her voice at all. I had expected someone narrow-faced and tight-lipped, angry even. But she had a wide mouth and high cheekbones, arched eyebrows, and what novels called "the remains of great beauty." I could hardly tell she was wearing makeup, and she had a chic haircut and huge diamond earrings.

She looked at Giuliano, then at me, and gave me a twenty-four-karat frown. I looked around, taking in the silk-lined walls, the antique benches, and the dark portraits.

"My young cousin, Mia," Giuliano explained, introducing me. "She is studying with me."

Signora Strozzi grudgingly greeted me and let us into the house. Even though we were arriving precisely at noon, we had already eaten lunch, for Giuliano had told me beforehand that we wouldn't be offered a meal. "You'll see," he said. I didn't, yet.

Signora Strozzi allowed us to take seats in the hall, on a bench with clawfoot legs, upholstered in red silk. Across from us hung the dark portrait of a man in antique clothes who had Tommaso Strozzi's eyes. Once she'd seen us seated she disappeared down the hall.

"So they're bankers?" I asked softly.

"Yes," replied Nonno.

"And Signore Strozzi thinks his hands are rotting off," I mused aloud.

Giuliano didn't show that he'd heard me. I saw his hands twitch. One moved absently to his breast pocket, touching the bulge of his case. I took the hint and sat quietly, staring up at the man in the painting, with his measuring eyes, and his square, thick-fingered hands covered in ornate rings. One had a tiny mason's compass and square on it, like I'd seen on buildings and on some costumes in the parade for Sant'Ambrogio. And, I remembered with a start, in Respicio's hand. I nudged Nonno and pointed. He nodded, frowning.

The man also wore a single enormous pearl earring in one ear and a big gold chain draped over his shoulders. He himself had nothing of the elegance of his clothes, however. His hands looked like wrestler's hands, like he could throttle anybody who made him mad; and the set of his jaw and the look in his eyes seemed to bear out this promise. It was the look of someone who wouldn't let anyone stand in the way of what he wanted.

I'd seen that look in Lucifero's eyes, I realized now.

I'd seen it in Giuliano's, too.

When we were finally ushered into Signore Strozzi's study, I began to understand what Giuliano meant about not being offered lunch, and also why he had wanted to see Strozzi in his own home.

"Go ahead and sit," Signore Strozzi said, and we did. "I'm only seeing you to placate my wife," he told us bluntly, as he took a seat behind his broad desk. He could have been the son of the man in the portrait. He was certainly Tommaso's father. He tapped one thick finger on the desk, and sure enough, there was a heavy ring, set with a black stone inlaid with a gold compass.

"I understand," Giuliano said calmly.

"And this is your apprentice?" Signore Strozzi asked abruptly, gesturing at me.

"Yes, one of them," replied Giuliano.

"We can speak freely?"

"Of course," said Giuliano, frowning. Signore Strozzi went on looking hard at me.

"If you have doubts about her discretion . . ." said Giuliano, and made as if to rise from his chair.

"Of course not," Signore Strozzi shrugged, and I knew he was lying. I also realized that he thought of us as servants, which was why we were not offered lunch. I hadn't run into this before. Most of those my family helped treated them as respected doctors, or neighbors, or friends—at least as equals. This man had an air that made me want to apologize for not wearing nicer clothes. I snuck a glance at Giuliano, who sat straight and silent in his chair, looking at our client with his far-seeing Della Torre eyes. At last, he asked, "Why did your wife ask you to see us?"

Signore Strozzi snorted and looked down at his hands. He gazed at them for some time, spreading his thick fingers wide on the polished oak of his desk, letting each separate ring tap the hard surface.

I remembered the night we exorcised Lisetta Maria Umberti, how Nonno had come to each of us, looked us in the face, and let the silence grow until it became a space of its own within the room, a protected place, where the unseen might be seen, where secrets might be spoken aloud. Was that what he was doing now? I found myself attending to my breathing, for a moment thinking of the wooden folds of the robe on the Madonna statue in my room, the one I meditated on, with the blue tinting and the gilded stars peeking out of the drapes; I could picture the edges of the robe where the paint had worn away, leaving half stars, and shades of blue paint and wood grain blending with each other.

The silence, the protected place grew around us, but still Signore Strozzi sat without speaking, and I tried to see how we could get him to trust us enough to unburden himself, for it seemed clear that he did carry a burden.

"My wife," he said at last, "believes . . ."

We watched him decide not to tell us the whole truth.

" . . . believes I'm crazy."

He paused.

"She called you and not the doctors because she relies on your discretion. The man who referred you said you are known to be 'as secretive as the Vatican.' "

He looked up.

Giuliano smiled briefly. "More secretive than that, I hope," he replied. He waited, then added, "We have to be, you see. Our lives depend on it."

Is that how you do it? I thought. *Show them that you are vulnerable, too?*

Signore Strozzi looked him in the eye. "My wife believes that I imagine that my hands are rotting off. I don't know where she gets this idea."

"She had mentioned this to me," Nonno said. "Your son, Tommaso, also."

"Ah! She poisons his mind!" Signore Strozzi growled. I saw the thick fingers tighten into fists. "My own son! And he believes it."

"And they are quite wrong?" Giuliano suggested. "Their fears are baseless?"

"Yes. I think I know why they do it, though."

His eyes took on a manic gleam.

"They want to control me. My wife has never been content with everything I buy her, and my son waits and waits to see me in my grave."

I hadn't liked Tommaso, but, to be fair, I hadn't gotten that feeling from him. He had seemed deeply worried about his father.

I could see Nonno watching Signore Strozzi's clenching hands, as if he were working something out. I looked at them, too, then up at the banker's angry eyes.

"Such family matters are beyond our help, I fear," said Giuliano. "I can always listen, and offer the advice of an old man with a family of his own. The family is always complicated; it's one of the first things we learn in our profession."

"I fear this family is beyond any help," replied Signore Strozzi angrily. "What did I do to deserve such a wife? Nobody warned me against her, not even my uncle, who was always very hard to please. Ah!"

I thought about what lengths Signora Strozzi and her son had already gone to to help him, tracking us down by word of mouth, for there was no other way—asking around discreetly until they found us, checking to make sure they could trust us. In spite of this, Signore Strozzi sounded so ungrateful. Were all rich people this untrusting? I wasn't sure if my family here counted as rich, even though they owned a couple of apartments in the center of the city. In fact, I hadn't thought about it until that moment.

Nonno rose.

"I understand," he said gently. "Perhaps the best I can do is give you my card, and tell you that we will be happy to aid you should you ever need us. And we are, as you have already learned, more secretive than the Vatican." He smiled faintly as he said this.

He stood up. I started to rise as he took his card from his case and handed it across to Signore Strozzi.

"Please just place it on the desk," Signore Strozzi said. "As you see, in my condition . . ."

He held out his hands, and looked down at them, frowning. "You should not have to see them this way. I cannot think for the life of me why Fiamma didn't wrap them this morning! She's a good wife," he went on, smiling apologetically, "but she doesn't always remember everything."

The smile transformed his face; he looked warmer and kinder, which made the whole moment even more unreal. Giuliano changed gears faster than I did; I was still staring at Signore Strozzi's healthy, heavy hands, full of rings, and wondering at his kind words for his wife when Nonno sat back down, dropping the card on the desk in front of Signore Strozzi. I sat down again, too.

"She wraps them in the morning?" Giuliano prompted.

"And the evening. It helps, though I fear it can't quite take away the smell, for which I apologize. You are very good to come to me, *dottore.* I know house calls aren't common any more, but I would prefer not to come to the clinic for this. My situation, my station in life, you see."

"Of course, naturally," said Nonno. "Perhaps you could answer a few questions for me?"

"Certainly, *dottore*. But first let me remedy this; it must disgust you and your assistant."

"We are used to such things; please do not trouble yourself."

I nodded, too, trying to keep my incredulity from showing in my face.

"Very well, if it is not too much for you, *dottore*."

"I assure you, it is not. It will help us, too, if you leave them unwrapped, for then we can examine them more closely in a moment," Giuliano told him. "So, please, tell me, signore. When exactly did you first notice there was something wrong with your hands?"

Signore Strozzi's brow furrowed; he looked at the ceiling. Again, I felt sure he was calculating how much to tell us. "At least since October. I cannot remember the exact day, for my head was full of particular business at work. We bankers have had some hard years recently, you know. So much scandal, so many troubles in the market."

I couldn't shake the feeling that he was keeping an awful lot from us. I remembered the trial I'd seen mentioned, the composer's relation—and then thought of my father, swearing at the news, calling men like Signore Strozzi the biggest thieves ever born, liars and cheats, the curse of the ordinary man. I remembered the marches back home, the calls to have bankers jailed. I knew kids who had cut school for weeks to Occupy Wall Street. Gina and I hadn't gone, partly because we knew we wouldn't have whole skins if we'd ever dared to come home, and partly because the idea of camping on the streets of New York scared us even more than the thought of our parents' anger. I looked back at Signore Strozzi, wondering if he had committed some of the same crimes that the American bankers had been accused of. Giuliano seemed sympathetic, tipping his head in agreement with Signore Strozzi. "So about the time of the difficulties with the banks, perhaps? Didn't all that start in October?"

Signore Strozzi replied, "It started long before that, but yes, I suppose all that scandal was just breaking out in the press in October. What a mess. Well, we've nearly cleared it up."

"So your hands began to trouble you in October."

"Yes, I believe so."

"Did you first notice the trouble at home or at work? At a particular time of day, perhaps?"

"Not that I can remember," said Signore Strozzi thoughtfully. "Let me see . . . I suppose I was at home when I first noticed. Yes, at dinner; it became difficult to hold a fork and knife."

"Ah," Nonno said, as if he'd just learned something very significant. "And was there pain then?"

"Not so much pain as numbness, and the smell of course. My wife and son did not notice it right away. But then, sometimes they don't notice anything!"

Giuliano leaned forward, gazing more intently at Signore Strozzi's hands.

"And the state of your hands now . . . ? Is this what they looked like at first? Or have they grown worse, or improved?"

Signore Strozzi looked up at him blankly.

"I'm sorry?" he asked. "What about my hands?"

"Their condition," Nonno prompted.

Signore Strozzi held them out in front of him, flexing those powerful, grasping fingers. He laughed.

"Ah, you've been talking to my wife. Well, look at them! Perfectly healthy. I think perhaps I should send you to examine *her,* don't you think?"

Again, I watched Giuliano switch gears while I struggled to hide my surprise. "I will certainly have a chat with her, if it's what you desire," he said.

Signore Strozzi considered this, and replied, "Yes, I think you should. She's probably gone out shopping by now. Perhaps you might stop by another time."

"We would be glad to," said Nonno, rising and collecting the large black case that Signore Strozzi must have mistaken for a doctor's bag. I had noticed that it had names embossed in gold on it, just like our small cases. I stood, and Signore Strozzi acknowledged me vaguely, but only shook hands with Giuliano.

Once Nonno and I were in the street, we walked in silence for a block or so. As we passed a shopwindow full of fluttering spring dresses, he said, "Tell me what you observed."

"You mean besides the way he switched back and forth, with no warning, not even a change of expression?"

"That, and all else you saw."

I told him, and as I talked, I began to see even more, like how his attitude to his wife shifted with his beliefs about his hands. Giuliano raised his eyebrows approvingly at this observation.

"You are doing well," he said, smiling. I smiled back. "You are helping me organize my thoughts, too," he added. "It's a tricky case."

"Is it?" I asked. "Is it one of the harder ones you've had?"

Nonno grinned wryly. "It's far too early to tell. It depends, too, what you mean by 'hard,'" he said, his face darkening, and I thought of the things he had been through, the terrible decisions he had had to make. I knew he had had to choose to let his middle brother, Martino, die, in order to prevent my demon from gaining power in this world. The choice had also cost him his beloved cousin, my grandfather Roberto, who had left Milan because of what had happened. All this, and he had lost his son to the same demon, too.

"But as you see, we must spend time with a client," he went on finally. "It is nearly always best to listen, to wait, to humor them.

"And this can be treacherous, Mia, especially with a very cunning demon, like the one I believe we are confronting. You must find a way to remain an observer, while at the same time doing your best to climb into their shoes, to understand them."

I blinked. "How can we do that? It sounds impossible."

He raised one eyebrow, the corner of his mouth lifting in a smile like his grandson's, and nodded.

"Oh, yes, it's probably impossible. But we must do it just the same."

He looked at me, tipping his head like a bird.

"I have noticed that the young are so impatient."

Adults are always saying stuff like this. I usually just switch it off, unless it's Mom or Dad, in which case I argue, but I had already found that even when I was annoyed with Giuliano, he was still worth listening to.

"You think you can learn it all in a minute," he went on. "But the truth is, *cara*, the most important things take an age just to understand, let alone master. My Laura did not learn to cook in a day, you know, and we did not learn to be married in a month, I can tell you. Remember the conversation you had with your cousins on Nonna's birthday? About love?"

I nodded.

"Anna Maria doesn't know everything about love just yet," he said.

"Even I know that," I replied, laughing.

"Yes," he agreed, smiling at me. "That will take time, too. Patience, and time, just like you will need for learning our work. Speaking of Anna Maria," he added, "I want you to ask her for some help finding an account of a case concerning the ruler of Milan during the 1740s. She has been going through some notes and needs to refresh her memory as well. So when we get home, I wish you to call her and ask her. Yes?"

I texted her instead. She answered right away. "I'll be over for dinner, will bring them. Of course he didn't say when, exactly, in the 1740s."

I texted, "Of course not," and she wrote back, "Ha, ha, ha. See you then."

Nonna roped me in to make ravioli for dinner, stuffed with wild mushrooms a friend had brought from the south.

"You've been having a busy week," she said. "Did you like the Biblioteca Ambrosiana?"

"I did," I said. "I wish we could have stayed longer."

"You'll get more chances," she said lightly, passing me a ball of dough to knead. "It's beautiful, isn't it? . . . More flour on your hands."

I dusted my hands thoroughly and worked the dough, thinking over Signore Strozzi's behavior, and then the moment when I had heard my demon's cold, gravelly voice in the piazza, and smelled cinnamon in the air.

"Be kind to the dough!" Nonna said with a laugh. "Don't take your thoughts out on it."

"Sorry," I said. "It was not the most—comfortable—day."

I realized immediately this was a ridiculous thing to say to a woman who had been married to a demon catcher for sixty years. She waited for me to go on.

"The interview went okay. Signore Strozzi is kind of a jerk."

She grunted agreement and took the ball of dough from me.

"Peel and mince," she commanded, passing me a head of garlic and some shallots.

"But on our way there, we saw my demon."

Nonna lifted her head like a deer, listening.

"Corporeally?" she asked.

"If you mean did he take over one body after another, just for a second, yes," I said.

She asked, "Did he say anything?"

"He said he would come for me," I told her, forcing out the words.

"Let him try," she said, almost growling.

I blinked and felt my spirits rise, seeing her fierce expression. She put a hand on my shoulder.

"You are not alone, Mia," she said. The doorbell rang and she dropped her hand. "Go get that." She placed the dough on a floured board, still looking dangerous. I could picture her braining a demon with the rolling pin.

Anna Maria was waiting on the doorstep with a bottle of wine and a loaf of bread. She bustled in, uncorked the wine, washed her hands, and picked up a knife.

"You want this parsley chopped?" she asked her great-aunt.

"Yes, very fine."

She sat down at the kitchen table with the cutting board and went to work. I finished the garlic and shallots. Anna

Maria and I put together the rest of the mushroom filling—the chopped parsley, garlic, and shallots—before Nonna Laura took it from me and sautéed it in a pan. Then she added the grated Grana Padano.

I was still thinking about Nonna's fierceness when I started spooning the mixture onto the sheets of pasta.

"You're overfilling those," Nonna pointed out. "They'll explode in the broth. Your head's in the clouds."

I laughed.

"Sorry, Nonna. Should I start over?"

"Yes, please."

I began the process again.

"Is it a guy?" asked Anna Maria.

I blushed, even though I had nothing to blush about.

"No," I said. "It never is, with me."

"Lesbian?" she asked coolly. Nonna stiffened beside me.

"No!" I said quickly. Then I felt bad, acting so narrow-minded. Anna Maria laughed.

"It's just," I struggled. "Guys. I never have any luck. Come on, you know about my first date, right?"

Nonna patted my arm. "Give it time," she said.

Anna Maria nodded, though I guessed that she had more advice than that. She gave it to me after dinner, when we headed down to the shop office to go over the notes she'd brought.

"Guys are pretty simple," she told me. "You just need practice. You're too shy, for one thing. You need to get over that.

You're quite pretty, in a mousy kind of way, and you're dressing better now, thanks to Francesca's shopping expeditions. But you've got to get out more, too. I think Nonna would skin me if I took you to clubs, though.

"And if you do decide you are a lesbian," she added as she took some notebooks down from a shelf, "I know some great gay bars." She opened a drawer and took out a slim satin-covered box.

My face felt hot, even though I knew for sure I liked guys. "Thanks, but I think I'll be okay," I said.

Most of the time I can't believe that Anna Maria is only three years older than I am. She seems to have lived an entire lifetime.

"You'll have your chance," she said, smiling, as if reading my mind. "Don't worry about it so much; that's the first thing. You've got to relax."

It's always so unhelpful when people say that. I sighed and reached for one of the notebooks she'd set on the table.

"No, wait," she said, opening the satin box. "Put these on. Don't handle the books with bare hands. They're too old."

She handed me a pair of white cotton gloves, the fingertips smudged faintly brown with leather dust, and the backs stitched with neat rows.

"I feel like Mickey Mouse," I said.

She shrugged, pulling on her own gloves. "I bet Mickey Mouse has perfectly kept hands," she said. "I'd hate to let him loose in our archives, though."

I laughed.

We each cleared a space in the piles of notes and accounts that always covered the office table.

"We are looking for an account relating to the Austrians who ruled Milan in the 1740s," Anna Maria said. "We served on a few cases in their court. There's something about altering a building at the palace. There may be more than one case. If a client likes what we do for them, we often get called in again, of course. There are families we've served and aided for centuries."

"Like the Strozzis? Have we helped them before?"

She looked up and creased her elegant brows, thinking.

"I don't think so. But we've helped a lot of people over many centuries, so I could be wrong."

She pulled a book from the shelves, one of the thicker history books that I hadn't yet found my way through. She flipped quickly through as if seeking a page by feel, then laid it open on the table and ran one gloved finger down a list of names and dates.

"In the 1740s, the ruler of Milan was the Archduchess Maria Theresa of Hapsburg. She had briefly visited the city in 1739 on her way home from Tuscany," she said thoughtfully. "She had a whole pile of other places to rule, so we were just another dot on the map. But she did have a governor in Milan to rule for her, who used the Palazzo Reale as his residence."

She looked up, lifting an eyebrow, then went on, "Otto Ferdinand, count von Abensberg und Traun, was the governor from 1736 to 1743, and Prince Georg Christian von Lobkowitz governed from 1743 to 1745. Before the Austrians, the Spanish and French fought to control Milan."

"Never a dull moment," I joked. "Why does everybody always war over this city?"

Anna Maria replied in an offended voice, "Why not? It's the greatest city in the world."

"Oh, I didn't mean to . . ." I began, and she laughed.

"No," she said, and I realized she'd been teasing me. "It's money, trade, location. It's a gateway between the Alps and all of Italy to the south, and between Venice in the East and Genoa in the West. Plus, we have always had the most skilled artisans, the best armorers . . . and the best clothiers. We led fashion long, long before today."

She opened her notebook, writing down the names she'd mentioned. I watched her, with her perfect hair and clothes, her pristine skin and elegant features. I'd seen her photograph in magazines, and on a billboard, too. I always wanted to point her out, and say, "That's my cousin."

Who would guess that that face hid a mind full of history, or that she sometimes came to her photo shoots straight from an exorcism?

"Okay," she said, pushing a pile of leather-bound notebooks toward me. "We need to look for these two names, or a variation on them. I know Nonno thinks I've got all this in my head now but I don't. I've always been interested in the nineteenth century, not the eighteenth. Although I've often speculated about G. Della Torre, the one who founded our shop. These cases would have happened during his time, you know.

"Of course," she added, "with some clients we had to use code names, particularly if they were nobles. So if you see some unusual name repeated, something that doesn't look normal, note the page."

She passed me a pad of what looked like very slender, cream-colored Post-its. "Use these," she said. "Always. They are acid-free and won't harm these old manuscripts."

I nodded, opening the notebook on the top of the pile. The spidery, gorgeous cursive handwriting of our ancestors was hard to read. There were records of visits, like the one Nonno Giuliano and I had paid Signore Strozzi; detailed notes of exorcisms, with commentary on what had worked and what hadn't. We wound up with a list of page references, with short notes beside them. The notebooks began to bristle with acid-free markers.

It may not sound all that interesting, but we had a good time. We each had a notebook in G. Della Torre's handwriting, as well as the notebooks of three other ancestors working at the same time. I liked reading G.'s notes the best, because they were the cleverest, and the funniest. He said things like, "Giovanni does not remember a thing about last night, which must count as a blessing; what a shame that everyone else will."

Sometimes he gave me a more direct idea of who he was: "I felt as excited by this discovery as I did the day I snuck my father's copy of *Scienza Nuova* out from under his nose and read the whole thing in a night."

Around ten o'clock, Anna Maria slapped the table and said, "Ah!"

"You found it?"

"I think so. Prince Georg. 'A strong presence, easily detected by my assistants . . .' "

She paged forward, white gloves fluttering in the lamplight.

"Here. 'I have elected to build a Second Door on the side of the palace; it took some time to convince the prince, for he did not easily understand the idea of a demon of place, Austrians lacking subtlety—or this one at least. Like every other client, he commanded us to make as little fuss as possible; this suits my instinct as a demon catcher, since I would avoid the fate of my great-grandfather.'"

She paused and looked up at me.

"I can't remember who his great-grandfather was. We did get tried as witches, sometimes, you know."

"What, like, burned at the stake?"

I think I must have sounded facetious, because Anna Maria replied, "Well, yes. That was if you survived the trial; they had some pretty harsh methods for testing people for witchcraft, you know."

She frowned and went on with the notes. "'The demon has certainly disturbed the palace with his antics, all of which show a ghoulish sense of humor: meals uncovered before

Prince Georg appear to be maggot-ridden, though they left the kitchen in perfect order; wine turns to foxglove on the palate, then to wine again, terrifying guests (many of whom already have reason to fear poison); sleepers wake to find corpses in bed with them, only to watch them fade into nothing.'" Neither Anna Maria nor I could figure out what about this demon made it a demon of place, except that it haunted the palace.

We learned that G. built a false balcony and door on the side of the Palazzo Reale over one of the tall windows; then used a ritual called the *Canto della porta d'Orchoë* to enter what he referred to as the Second House. Unfortunately, he and his assistants arrived at an awkward moment, interrupting an assignation between the prince and a married Italian noblewoman.

"'The prince was vastly displeased,' he wrote, 'having forgotten that I had named that night for our entrance, but the lady became quite intrigued once our presence was explained, as I fear it had to be; she was too intelligent a woman not to have guessed the significance of bell, book, and candle, and begged to be permitted to observe our experiments, though warned of the danger.'"

Anna Maria rubbed her eyes. "Well, we found it. Now we can stop for tonight," she said.

I blinked. "Why? It's just getting good."

She laughed.

"I don't know about you, but I'm exhausted, and I have to work early tomorrow. Let's go to bed."

Up in my room at last, I didn't go to sleep right away. I thought about the demon's voice, and the smell of cinnamon. About Lisetta Maria Umberti, gray-faced from her struggles with my demon. Her body had looked so empty after she was gone.

I wanted answers. I wanted to get this bastard, this demon. I wanted to understand who or what he was. I felt my stomach turn with anger, and with fear.

I sat on my bed, my case open beside me. I fingered my tools absently, turning a silver nail over and over. It had a square head and four flat sides that tapered to a point. It looked like it had been made by hand. I could tell from the feel of it that it wouldn't hold a house together nearly as well as one of my father's steel nails. It had a beautiful roughness to it, though.

"Don't try to tell me about humans," Signora Gianna snapped, and I wondered how long she and Gravel had been arguing while I'd been lost in thought. "I am one! Or was one, anyway," she amended thoughtfully.

"And I've watched you for ages! I know something . . . me."

I'd figured out by now that Gravel wasn't human, that his gravelly voice reminded me of my demon's. Yet it didn't make sense, a demon here in this room, in this house so carefully warded against them. I remembered the first time I had heard these two voices, the night after I had arrived in Milan; they had been discussing my wardrobe. In the end, I'd worn the outfit they had chosen. But it had been months before they'd spoken directly to me, and even now I knew only Signora Gianna's name. Gravel was simply a name I'd made up, like Pompous, which was the name I'd given Signora Gianna before I knew her real one.

"Watching is not the same as being," replied Signora Gianna. "Me, I know."

"Being is not the same as watching, either," Gravel snarled. "Maybe I see what you don't."

"Maybe, but I know I see what you don't, because you never had a heart like mine."

"How do you know what I began as?" answered Gravel.

I was used to their bickering, but this sounded like real anger, the kind of fight where, if these were living people, they'd start throwing dishes in a minute. Or books.

"I don't know why we're talking about this," snapped Signora Gianna. "We've talked it over hundreds of times, and it makes no difference. By now, he's been dead—oh!—five years? A thousand? I can't tell anymore. . . ."

Her voice began on a raging note and ended on a lost one.

"I don't want to stay, my dear," she said. "I see them make the same mistakes we did, over and over. I'm losing track of myself, of you, of time and place. Part of me floats free, part of me is tethered; all of me is divided."

When Gravel spoke again, his voice was gentle, soft even, despite its gritty accents.

"I know, my dear," he said. "This part, I do understand, believe me."

They were both silent for some time, and then he added, "Besides, neither of us knows where I came from anymore. I've forgotten. It's been so long. Before you came, I was only anger, nothing more. I was on my way to being one of those who leaps out from the gargoyles on the sides of buildings, tipping the scales of human decision, so that a man who might have left his wife decides to murder her instead. But for you, I would have been . . ."

He trailed off.

"That, my dear," he growled, "is why we must stay. They need us now, especially. The girl, she needs us. They all do. You felt how he tested the wards at the beginning, and he does so now, again and again. They need our help, so that they can help one another, instead of giving in to jealousy or fear."

This was one of those times when I'd felt like they hardly remembered I was in the room unless I spoke to them. Signora Gianna mentioned losing track of things. Perhaps she also lost track of human presences? And who or what was Gravel? Why had he forgotten where he came from? How old was he?

I couldn't ask them directly. I'd tried, a week or two earlier, and they had just vanished into thin air, leaving behind a familiar feeling of emptiness.

Now, the air above me held a feeling of silent communion. The fight was over. They'd agreed on this matter—a matter of love.

I went to sleep wishing, once again, that I knew more about love, and about my family.

SIX

The Most Beautiful Man in Milan

Nonno Giuliano was very pleased that Anna Maria and I had found the entries for the Second Door. We read on, learning about the kinds of wood G. Della Torre had used, the number of silver nails, and the real iron nails that had been used to keep the thing from falling off the wall of the palace. It seemed half a practical structure, half a balcony made of dreams.

I mentioned this to Giuliano one morning about two weeks after our visit to Signore Strozzi. He was too distracted to hear me. Without raising his eyes from the notes he was writing, he said, "Go and see if Nonna needs your help with lunch." I nodded and went up the stairs, wondering why I didn't complain, like I would have if my mom or dad was telling me what to do.

Nonna Laura did need help with lunch, which was going to be a mushroom risotto to start, then a veal cutlet with a *contorno* of winter greens, and an orange salad to finish.

"The last of the oranges from our tree, this year," she told me sadly, handing me a bowl of them to peel.

"We have an orange tree?" I asked, looking around. She laughed.

"Not here," she said. "We have a place by the sea. We'll take you there in the summer. These," she added, pointing to the oranges, "Francesco brought back. Peel them and slice them to make circles, so." She gestured with her hands. I started peeling.

"Everything all right?" asked Nonna, sitting down opposite me with a bunch of asparagus and beginning to snap the ends.

"Yes," I lied. She nodded. For a while, the only sound in the kitchen was the snapping of asparagus and the whisper of orange peel. I watched the misty spray of orange zest burst from between my fingers.

Nonna did what she always does, snapping asparagus, waiting.

"I miss home," I said, giving up. She looked up and pressed her lips together in sympathy.

"Skype isn't enough," she agreed.

"They are saving money to come over," I said. "I know I shouldn't try to go home yet."

At that moment, I asked myself, really for the first time,

whether I could go home. There was more than a fair chance that when the demon and I met again, I would die. I knew that.

"I miss home, yet at the same time I don't know if I'll ever really want to go home, or if I'll ever have the choice," I said, surprised by my own words.

She nodded, snapping away.

"Of course, I don't know if you could stand to have me live here forever," I added.

"We'd manage," she said, her eyes sparkling. "You are very helpful around the shop," she added. "And your cooking is really improving."

Francesca came home for lunch, bringing a loaf of freshly baked bread. Nonno glowered at her, his expression reminding me of my dad. "What are you doing home so early?" he asked.

"I'm tired," she said with a shrug. "I don't have court this afternoon, so Marcello said I should just take my work home." She sat down, rubbing her eyes. "Oh, and Égide will be home late, he's got a hearing for the Sudan case. He may have to go to Rome next week."

I remembered that Rome was where Francesca and Emilio's mother, Giulietta, lived. After their father, Luciano, died, she'd eventually moved back with her family in the capital. Maybe Égide would visit her while he was there. I saw Nonno look down at his plate.

Hating to see everyone look so sad, I said quickly, "Is this the same Sudan case he's been working on?"

Francesca smiled faintly and said, "Yes. It's three women with their daughters, seeking asylum from the Sudan. There's so much pressure right now, so many people wanting to get into the European Union. Once you have a passport, you know, all Europe is your job market. It's a big deal."

One of the immigration offices was a few blocks from our apartment, in the Via Montebello. I had seen the line going down the street, heard twenty languages being spoken at once. Francesca and I had gone over there a couple of times to walk Égide home after a case, stopping for gelato if the day hadn't gone well for him, or shopping for dinner, if it had.

After lunch, Nonno went back down to the shop while Francesca took a nap. That left me with Nonna and the dishes, and I found myself telling Nonna about summer in Center Plains: the humidity, the summer jobs, the smell of cut grass, the nights when we went to the movies just to get into an air-conditioned building. I had to explain what air-conditioning was. She said, "Mostly, we just go to the sea when it gets that hot. It sounds like our way is better."

I didn't mention that I was fairly sure Aunt Brigida had air-conditioning. Nonna was always pleased whenever the Milanese way was proven, yet again, to be better than that of the rest of the world.

"I guess so," I said.

I ended up taking a nap, too. Later, Nonna stopped me on my way downstairs and said, "Can you catch up with Nonno and give him this list for the shops?"

I took the list and barreled down the stairs and through the back office. Emilio, who must have come in when I was asleep, raised his eyes and said, "Watch it!"

"Sorry!" I called, looking back at him from the doorway, before turning and running into someone, hard.

He grunted.

"Uh—oh—sorry," I said again, and found myself face-to-face with the top button of a man's blue shirtfront. I looked up. What I saw made me jump back, even more embarrassed.

Up until then, I'd thought Emilio the most beautiful man in Milan. Over the centuries, Etruscans, Romans, Vikings, and Arabs had passed through the city and left more than money and architecture behind. The man in front of me had classic Milanese looks—dark hair with deep reddish tones; pale blue eyes; high cheekbones; translucent skin.

He looked down at me and grinned.

"In a hurry," he stated, in a level tenor that sounded younger than he looked but was as beautiful as the rest of him.

"Sorry," I began. "I thought—"

Nonno laughed behind him.

"Mia, meet Bernardo Tedesco, grandson of an old friend of mine," he said. "Bernardo, this is Mia Della Torre, our young American cousin."

"Ah! Emilio was telling me about you," said the most beautiful man in Milan.

Crap, I thought. *What did Emilio tell you? Lame, clumsy . . .*

Bernardo just smiled and looked at me like an Italian

man looks at, well, a woman, I guess. *"Piacere,"* he said, and I remembered my manners, finally.

"Piacere," I replied, and put out my hand.

"You are enjoying Milan?" he asked.

I thought of Anna Maria, and replied, "Who wouldn't?"

He laughed. "Well, this time of year, just about anybody," he said. "The city is full of freezing fog, most of the time."

"The other night was perfect," I blurted out, remembering Nonna's birthday dinner.

"True," he agreed, his eyes twinkling.

"We should go," said Giuliano, touching Bernardo's arm. "We can talk on the way."

"Oh, right. Though you'll have to ask my father about most of the details, like scheduling," said the most beautiful man in Milan. "Good-bye," he told me. "It was a pleasure to meet you."

"Yes," I said. "I mean, it was a pleasure to meet you, too."

He laughed again and buttoned up his coat before following Nonno out the door.

I completely forgot to give Nonno the shopping list, and ended up having to track him down; I was glad of the excuse to catch up with him, hoping he was still with Bernardo. He wasn't.

I knew Emilio had mentioned Bernardo on the night of Nonna's birthday party, but I didn't know anything else about him, or why he had been visiting Nonno. It took two long days to find out.

Studying wasn't enough to distract me, even though I was searching for the demon's poem. The next afternoon, I skimmed volumes of minor poets and struggled, more slowly, through collections of letters, looking for one line, one reference. I felt the old, familiar urgency—I had to solve the riddle before the demon found a way around my bell. My quest tugged at me, but now I felt another pull. I couldn't stop thinking about Bernardo, about the way it had felt to slam into him and hear his voice.

You met the guy for five minutes, I told myself. It didn't matter. My eyes drifted away from the pages as I tried to figure out how old he must be, and whether he had a girlfriend. I kept thinking about how blue his eyes were, and how before I had come to Milan I had never seen such a combination: the pale, pale skin, the dark red-brown hair, and the eyes like borrowed sky.

The shop bells jingled, and I came out of my reverie to see Signora Strozzi closing the door behind her, and looking around as if she were surprised to find herself in such a place. Maybe she had all her candles delivered.

"Buon giorno," she said in a bright voice, and actually smiled at me.

I stood up.

"Buon giorno, Signora Strozzi," I replied, more warmly than I meant to. "What can I do for you today?"

"I have come to speak to Signore Della Torre. Is he in, please?"

"I am," said Giuliano, emerging from the office. He came forward and clasped her hand, glancing at me. "*Buon giorno,* Signora Strozzi; it is good to see you again. Please sit. May I get you anything to eat or drink?"

She shook her head, taking the chair he offered her.

"You know my assistant," he told her. "May she remain?"

Please say yes! I thought. I didn't want to miss this.

"It would be helpful to the case if she did," Nonno added gently. "Young eyes see many things old ones do not. And young ears hear better," he finished with a deprecating laugh.

"That's fine," she said without a smile this time.

She was wearing the same enormous diamond earrings I had seen last time. As she turned her head, they caught the light, and flashed like a warning.

"He's getting worse," she said abruptly. "He was up in the night, screaming."

She glared at me as if this were my fault. Giuliano caught her eyes and held them with a kind look.

"I am very sorry to hear that," he said. "It is indeed the kind of thing that gets worse before it gets better. Fortunately, we have discovered a possible solution."

"Oh?"

The relief and eagerness in her voice gave her away. I realized she hadn't been glaring at me at all; she had been glaring because of how helpless she felt.

"Yes," said Nonno. "It is a complex but ancient practice.

Have you ever heard of the Second Door?"

"No."

"It is a magical door, one that we build in this world in order to enter another." In answer to her frown, he added, "I know you are still having a hard time believing this."

He waited. She said nothing.

"But," he went on, "you had the sense to send for me in the first place, which suggests this is not the first time you have run across the supernatural in your life."

"It is not," she said, sounding slightly proud.

"So . . ." said Giuliano, "it is possible for you to believe that a door made of ordinary wood can serve such a purpose. And we have built such doors before. My ancestor indeed built one for the rulers of Milan, more than two centuries ago."

"Really?"

He smiled at her.

"Yes, indeed. A door on the side of the Palazzo Reale. It was for one of the governors, you know, during the Austrian occupation," he added with a wave of his hand. "Not a Milanese. But we have done them for other Milanese, too."

In spite of herself she seemed interested. She smiled, and I saw the worry lines, the shadows of sleeplessness on her face.

"The Palazzo Reale," she repeated. "My husband's ancestors funded the renovation. And you built a door on the side of the palace, a permanent door? Did your ancestor cut a hole in the wall? Is it still there?"

"No, no. A Second Door is a kind of false door," Giuliano answered. "We generally build it over a large window, or better yet, a set of French doors on a balcony. I think I saw a balcony at your house?"

"We have more than one."

"Excellent."

"But you can't permanently damage our home."

"Of course not. We would remove the Second Door afterward as if it had never been there."

"My husband will not approve."

Nonno nodded and spread his hands out on his trouser legs. He met her eye.

"Can you convince him?" he asked.

She raised her eyebrows.

"I see I need not ask," he said dryly.

"But why this . . . carpentry project? Why not the bell, book, and candle, all that?"

I was curious to hear how Nonno would answer this one.

"Are you familiar with the instruments of your husband's trade?" he asked.

"Some of them," she answered guardedly.

"The different kinds of loans, the ways he and his ancestors made money from loans to princes, funding their military campaigns, and so forth?"

"Yes," she said.

"Our work is much the same: different situations require different instruments. I would not use only the rituals of expulsion in this matter, just as your husband would not use a home loan to fund a war."

Signora Strozzi did not look impressed. She pressed her lips together, holding his eyes.

"And the cost?"

"Well, it is not cheap," Giuliano said bluntly.

"Price is no object," Signora Strozzi said firmly. I saw her chin lift. Nonno had said the right thing.

Then why ask about it in the first place? I thought. *Because she's proud, and she wants to show that they are rich*, I answered myself.

"I will think about it," she said, and stood, clasping her expensive purse in both hands. The shop bells jangled as she left.

"So, how do you think that went?" I asked Giuliano. The air seemed lighter now that she had gone.

"She will agree to it," he said. "And she will convince her husband."

He was right. She called the next day. Even though I couldn't hear her words, I could tell from the tone of her voice over the phone that she was back to her grumpy self, now that she had gotten what she wanted.

That night, Nonno turned to me and said, "I want you to help build the Second Door, Mia. You and Anna Maria both need the practice."

At the time, I had my mouth full of *budino al cioccolato*, which I think was deliberate. I could only nod.

Emilio was over for dinner, he and Alba having fought again.

"Bernardo can't start until the week after this," Giuliano grumbled to his grandson. "Even though I told him it's urgent."

I put my fork down and asked cautiously, "Are Bernardo and his family . . . Do they do what we do?"

"No, they are building contractors only. They know a bit about our work, as much as any of the neighbors. They send us clients once in a while."

He went back to his thoughts, looking crabby.

"He and his father have some project they are finishing up for one of the universities, and when I suggested to Rinaldo that he hire someone else so we could get Bernardo sooner, he just shook his head."

"He has always said Bernardo is the best apprentice he's ever had, even so young," said Nonna.

"He's not so young anymore," said Anna Maria, sounding irritated. "He's my age, after all."

I looked up. Bernardo was only nineteen? My heart seemed to bump up into my throat and come to rest on my tonsils. I hadn't been able to tell how old he was. I mean, he was definitely older, but not too old, really. I took a deep breath, feeling relieved—then quickly checked around the table, to see if anyone had noticed my expression. I was pretty sure they hadn't.

"Yes, and you are positively elderly," Emilio teased Anna Maria.

"Oh, no, not as ancient as you," Anna Maria replied generously, and everyone at the table laughed.

"Like you," Nonno said to Anna Maria in a reproving tone, "he has come far for one so young."

If he was trying to put her in her place, he hadn't succeeded. She had her mind on another question. "Why do we need a contractor anyway? Haven't you guys done this before?"

Emilio laughed.

Giuliano answered, "Oh, yes, but always with help. If we were just building a simple frame on the ground floor, I wouldn't worry. But we need something on a second floor that will actually hold us all long enough to enter, and get out again, maybe several times. I'm not interested in doing this myself and ending up with a family of demon catchers with broken bones. I know what I'm good at, and what I'm not."

"Nonno, you know you won't be working on it much anyway. It will be the rest of us," Emilio said.

"This is true, Giuliano," Nonna said to her husband.

Nonno shrugged, and said, with the corner of his mouth turning up ever so slightly, "A heap of demon catchers with broken bones."

Anna Maria laughed, and Emilio said to her, "Now you know why. And who."

"But there is the danger that Signora Strozzi might change her mind," Emilio went on, serious again, looking at Nonno.

"The demon might change *his* mind beyond repair," agreed his grandfather.

"Yet the *famiglia* Tedesco has a living to make," Emilio

said, gently. "We can't pay Bernardo what others can, especially when we can bet Signora Strozzi will argue about the price for the job."

Nonno snorted. "Too true," he growled. "It's the poor who give more than they can, out of gratitude."

"That always breaks my heart," Emilio said. "Like that family from Sardinia, with the Etruscan seven-repeater."

Everybody else at the table was listening. An Etruscan seven-repeater is a demon of Etruscan origin that attacks the same family line, once every seven generations. According to Emilio, Etruscans had powerful magic, and these demons originate from curses they laid on their enemies. The tricky thing about a demon that attacks so rarely is that often the folks who suffer from it don't remember the last time their family had some kind of occult trouble by the time it shows up again.

"Are we looking at a family repeater here?" I asked.

"We don't have any record of it, but I am wondering," said Nonno, lifting his eyebrows at me. Then he smiled. "You and I will be hiding behind piles of books tomorrow," he said. "But for now," he added, raising his eyes around the table, "let's change the subject. Thinking about rich people is bad for the digestion."

Emilio laughed, and helped him turn the conversation, leaving me free to think about Bernardo.

Of course, I hadn't the faintest idea what I would do when I saw him again. Giuliano had said it would be a week before

Bernardo could help us. That meant the following Thursday, so I kept track and waited.

On Wednesday night, I sat up in my room, laying out different outfits for the next day.

"What are you doing, dear?" asked Signora Gianna.

"Uh," I answered, searching for a better explanation than the truth.

"It won't do to keep a young man so much in mind," she said gently.

How did she know?

"The Tedeschi are a good family. He's a good choice. But don't keep him in your thoughts so much; it's better to wait and see, you understand? You do not know him yet, and you must decide if he's worth your time."

I almost laughed. It's not like I was planning to marry the guy.

"Oh, Signora Gianna," I said, "He won't think I'm worth his time, anyhow."

"Really?" she asked. "How do you know?"

"He's older. And he's gorgeous."

"And gorgeous older men never look at you?" she asked.

"Well . . ." I began. She had a point. Even though looking at women was a favorite sport for the men of Milan (and all of Italy, from what I'd heard), I had to admit some pretty handsome men had turned my way lately.

"You see!" Signora Gianna said, accepting my unfinished

thought as an answer. "I wonder about young women today. You don't seem able to put a value on yourself. In my day, we knew we were treasures to be sought after. We would have made this fellow work to get to know us. The art of fascination."

"Isn't that kind of devious?"

"Devious?" She laughed. "This is love we're talking about!" She paused, then added in a more reflective tone, "I don't know about devious. Why should we just throw ourselves at some man like a parcel of rags? We always thought we were worth more trouble than that. And you know, they don't like what they can get easily. They like the chase."

I'd heard this before. "It doesn't seem very . . . feminist."

"Is it feminist to think that you are not worthy of him, instead of waiting to see if it's the other way round?"

She had me there. What had men been like in her day and age? Had it been easier to get a date?

"If I sit around all day, waiting for guys to chase me, I will die old and alone," I pointed out.

Signora Gianna guffawed, startling me. "Unlikely," she said. "After all, you are a Della Torre, my dear. But you don't sit around at home, silly girl. You go about your days. And then they begin to call on your elders. Or at least that's what they did when I was young."

"Things have changed a lot," I informed her.

"Some things do not ever change, my dear," she said firmly.

"What did you mean, I'm a Della Torre?" I asked.

"Oh." I could hear the smile in her voice. "For those in the know, we make *excellent* wives."

I noticed that Gravel hadn't chimed in. "Where's your . . . ?" I asked, not sure what to call him.

"My familiar? He's out patrolling."

"Oh," I said. I started to formulate a question, but she got in ahead of me.

"Think about what I've said," she finished, and then I felt the change in the air that meant she had gone. I turned over the new ideas she'd given me. It seemed kind of unfair to the guys to expect them to do all the work, but then, it was pretty unfair to expect us to do all the work, too.

Just the same, I spent another hour deciding which outfit I wanted Bernardo to see me in the next day.

It didn't matter. Thursday came and went; I knew I hadn't missed his visit while out getting groceries for Nonna because nobody mentioned him that night at dinner, nor did he turn up over the weekend.

On Monday, Emilio texted me to change into the work clothes he'd left out for me and be ready when he came home. I found them on my bed: a worn canvas shirt and heavy canvas pants, a lot like the kind my father wears, and nearly as big. I rolled up the sleeves and the pant legs and looked at myself in the mirror. I looked like a little girl playing dress-up in her father's closet. I laughed at myself. Who would want to chase me after they'd seen me in a pair of canvas pants, anyway? Oh, well.

Francesco stopped by in the late afternoon to receive an order of lumber from a squat, scowling old man who came in a truck that was probably as old as he was. We parked the wood in the courtyard below our apartment, and two young kids, a boy and a girl who had just moved in across the way, crept out and started climbing on it almost before we'd gone back to the shop.

About half an hour later, after Francesco had left for his next lecture, Emilio pulled up in a white van that I'd never seen before. If anything, he looked handsomer in an old canvas work shirt and paint-spattered jeans than he did in his usual crisp, clean clothes. It was deeply unfair. He looked me over, taking in the dress-up clothes.

"Good," he said. "Come help me with these," he added, pointing at the boards.

When Emilio and I finished loading the van, he sat down on the back bumper to wait, and I followed his lead. He seemed antsy about something, at least as antsy as he ever got about anything, and when his phone rang he jumped, looked at it accusingly, and put it back in his pocket. I thought he and Alba had made up, but maybe they hadn't. I heard the chime of voice mail and decided not to ask him whom he had ignored.

Sitting next to Emilio, I liked breathing in his pinesap smell, feeling the warmth of him. We watched our breath frost the air.

I looked up just as Bernardo turned down into our street.

He had the most beautiful walk, sure and graceful, a long loping stride that brought him to us before I had a chance to catch my breath—only to have it taken away again, by his pale blue eyes, the clean angle of his chin, his white skin, and his dark, reddish hair.

Emilio stood up and clasped his hand, giving him a kiss on both cheeks. I didn't expect to get the same treatment, but I did; I guess I rated as a member of the family. Bernardo's aftershave smelled delicious.

"Thanks for picking up the van," he told Emilio. "I couldn't get away. Ready?" he asked us. We climbed in, me wedged in the rickety backseat next to all the lumber, and Bernardo drove us off back down the way he'd come, swerving around a well-tailored old woman on a bike with a dog in her wicker basket. Then he jerked hard left into the Via Borgonuovo, and again into Via Fatebenefratelli. He drove calmly, his hands loose and relaxed on the wheel, but the van moved like a Milanese, hopping up the narrow streets, yanking us from lane to lane on the wider Foro Buonaparte, revving at the stoplight. Bernardo and Emilio exchanged heated views on the soccer game that would be on TV later—Emilio was coming over to watch it at our place—and then they talked more quietly about some business trouble Bernardo's uncle was having.

"It was a bad idea to begin with," Emilio said. "I love the guy, but he should have gotten advice."

"He should have gotten *good* advice," corrected Bernardo, laughing ruefully.

I liked his laugh. He didn't sound mean, or even particularly mad at his uncle.

Since they were both pretty much ignoring me, I watched him, thinking about what Signora Gianna had said. But how could I tell if he was worthy? All I could do was stare at him. He laughed and swore as a blonde woman in a dinky Smart car cut him off.

"Gorgeous," he said to Emilio.

"Maybe," Emilio shrugged. "Not gorgeous enough to drive like that," he added.

They both laughed then. I envied her.

Bernardo wore a canvas work shirt, too, a dark navy, with *Tedeschi Imprenditori Edili* embroidered on the pocket and over the shoulder yoke. The navy fabric set off his pale skin. To me, he didn't look like a building contractor; he wasn't sunburned enough. His toolbox, rattling beside me, looked real enough, with *Bernardo* carefully spelled out in square letters on the dented lid.

It reminded me of my father's toolbox, even though it was smaller and steel-gray, not a huge black Craftsman like Dad's. I looked up at him again, and this time I looked at his hands, which looked older than the rest of him; they were strong, and long-fingered, with big joints and surprisingly well-kept nails. They were hands that could do this kind of work, I thought. I thought other things about them, too, which made it hard for me to look at him in the way Signora Gianna had suggested.

He turned, suddenly, and asked me a question. I was so embarrassed that he'd caught me looking that I didn't hear what he was saying.

"I'm sorry?" I asked.

"The van's too loud?" he asked. "I was just asking if you needed anything to eat before we get there."

"Oh, no, thank you," I said, and felt my face get hot. Immediately, my stomach growled and I wanted to change my answer.

Emilio glanced back at me and said, "There's a wine bar around the corner from the apartment that does really nice *aperitivi.*"

"Oh, yeah!" Bernardo said. "Let's go there after we get everything roughed out. Is anyone else coming today?"

"No, just the three of us."

"It will be enough." Bernardo shrugged and turned to me again. "You know which way to hold a *cacciavite*?" He asked.

"A . . . ?"

Emilio thought for a minute and then supplied, "A screwdriver," in English.

"Oh, yeah. My father's a carpenter," I said.

Bernardo's eyes lit up. "Really? In America? Does he do this kind of work, too, for your family?"

"No, not the same," I replied, embarrassed. Maybe he didn't know the story—but his family had been friends with ours for so long, surely he knew my grandfather had left for America after his cousin's death, and had cut ties with those who had remained behind? Maybe Bernardo had never heard. "He has a toolbox like yours, though," I volunteered.

Bernardo was looking for a place to park, but I saw him give a slight smile as he said, "He does, does he?"

Then we were out of the van, scoping the area. Emilio had obviously been here since my visit with Nonno, because he led the way, not into the courtyard of the Strozzi apartment building, but into a nearby courtyard, where five BMWs were parked in a row, facing the doors of a bank. Bernardo teased, "How come you don't drive a BMW, Emilio?"

"Because I don't work for the Intesa Sanpaolo," Emilio replied, a hint of scorn in his voice. Bernardo chuckled.

We walked to the bottom of the parking lot, looking up until we found the tall window we were going to use, and then went back to start unloading lumber and scaffolding. We got the scaffolding assembled and stowed the lumber beneath it. By the time we stopped for the night, we were covered in sweat, even though the air was still crisply cold. As we were sliding the last planks into place, Signora Strozzi came walking down the lot, her diamond earrings flashing their warning. She stood looking at our afternoon's work with her hands on her hips, eyeing the scaffolding.

"*Buona sera,* Signora Strozzi," I said when I realized that I was the only one she recognized. I was used to Emilio handling this stuff. "May I introduce you to my cousin Emilio Della Torre, and to our friend Bernardo Tedesco?"

"*Piacere,*" she said, shaking hands with both of them. I had thought she wouldn't; none of us were remotely clean. But she smiled much more warmly at each of them than she did at me.

"Where is Signore Della Torre?" she asked Emilio, sounding polite but concerned.

"Probably at the candle shop," he told her cheerfully. "He's getting too old to do anything but order us around."

She smiled the same grim way her son had.

"Well, I told him that the building was not to be harmed, and no mark to be left on it," she said.

"Oh, he made sure we knew," Emilio said, nodding. I wanted to add, "I know! I was there, Signora Strozzi!" But I didn't.

Signora Strozzi went on examining the scaffolding.

"How long will it take?" she asked abruptly.

"That depends," said Emilio. Bernardo had walked off to the side, looking up at our handiwork. I drifted over to him as Emilio went on, "You know how it is. If I give you a time, the bottom will drop out of the lumber market the next day, and I'll have to tell you something else."

She shrugged, running her eyes over Bernardo in a way that creeped me out. I shook my head, trying to clear it.

"A month?" she persisted.

"Could be a month," Emilio conceded. He met her eyes,

and held them. "We will be in time, Signora Strozzi," he said in a low voice.

"You had better be," she replied, matching his tone.

He did not blink. And in the end, she was the one who looked away. After a moment, he said, "This stage is always an anxious one. Your concerns are normal," so much like a doctor I wanted to laugh. *Concerns?* I thought. *This woman is terrified . . . and furious.*

She didn't answer him, but looked up at the side of the building, as if scanning it for new scratches and dents. Then she said, "*Buona sera.* Pleased to meet you," and walked to the front entrance of the apartment building. Bernardo came back, raised his eyebrows, and said mildly, "That went well, I thought."

Emilio caught his eye and they both chuckled.

"We are workmen to her," Emilio said.

I turned to Bernardo and said, "Her husband didn't even offer me and Nonno anything to drink, the day we came to interview him."

"Servants," agreed Emilio. "Sometimes it's like that. Depends on the family."

"Same thing in my business," said Bernardo. "Our society, with all of its class restrictions. In America, it's more equal, isn't it, Mia?"

I started to say yes, and then thought of all the housewives talking down to my dad and the other carpenters when they left sawdust on the carpet.

"Sometimes," I hedged. "Some people treat you like servants and other people treat you like equals."

He looked disappointed but not surprised.

"That's too bad. I had heard it was different, and it's hard to tell from TV," he said.

"Oh, it's different." I smiled suddenly.

"Tell us on the way to the wine bar," suggested Emilio. "Because, I don't know about the rest of you, but I must eat immediately."

I had been too excited to work with these guys to remember how hungry I was. Signora Gianna would have had a word or two to say about that, I thought. But I felt proud, proud of what I had learned, proud of my dirty work clothes, as we headed off to the wine bar. As we turned down the street I wondered what my father would think of me. Would he be proud, too?

SEVEN

In Which I Prove (Again) That I Am Not Cool

The bar was a normal Milanese one, smelling of fried food and wine and smoke, with a marble countertop covered with dishes. When we walked in in our sweaty, dirty work clothes, a couple of patrons gave us a look, but the barista eyed Emilio and Bernardo the way any normal, breathing woman would, and said, "What would you like, *ragazzi*?" They both ordered prosecco. Then she said, "And for the boy?"

I looked over my shoulder, not sure who she meant, before realizing, my face hot, that she meant me. For a moment I saw myself in the mirror and thought, *I'd make a cute boy.* I blinked.

Bernardo and Emilio thought this was hilarious and didn't

correct her. I didn't, either, deciding instead to fill a plate with appetizers from the bar: hand-sliced salami, *mozzarella di buffala,* pickled asparagus, olives, and a small piece of foccaccia. Emilio lumped a couple of slender fish in oil onto my plate, saying, "You should try these," even though I made a face at him. "Be a good boy." He grinned.

I stuck out my tongue. When we sat, I felt even more depressed by her mistake. Did I really look like a boy?

Bernardo smiled at me kindly.

"You don't see a lot of women in my trade," he said. "And people look at the clothes. Do you feel bad about it?"

"I did, but now I'm not sure," I admitted.

"You make a cute boy," Emilio said, echoing my own thoughts in a thoroughly irritating manner.

"It's true," Bernardo agreed helpfully.

I stuck out my tongue at both of them this time, and they laughed again. Bernardo sampled a slice of salami and shut his eyes, chewing carefully. I was glad that Nonna Laura, Nonno Giuliano, Francesca, and just about everyone else had patiently scolded me for the last five months to get me to stop "eating like a wolf." In the States, people who eat too much eat like a horse, but in Italy, they use wolf, instead. Maybe that's where we got the expression "wolf down your food"?

Watching these two hungry guys eat slowly, I could really see the difference between them and the young guys on my dad's jobs. I thought maybe there might be other differences as well, and had to keep my eyes on my plate for a while, until my face (and the rest of me) stopped burning again.

"This is really good," Bernardo said, pointing at the salami on his own plate. "Where's it from, do you think?"

"It reminds me of the salami from the market near the Stazione Centrale," said Emilio. "I think he gets most of his stuff from a farm on the way to Vigevano. But I don't know. Alba and I found his stall by accident, and now I have a hard time going anywhere else."

I had gotten more used to hearing her name, now, and it was easier with Bernardo sitting there, too. Then a pit opened up in my stomach: What if Bernardo had a girlfriend? What if there was an Alba in his world, too?

"Everything better now?" asked Bernardo.

"Oh, yeah," said Emilio.

"You're lucky," Bernardo told him. I pretended I wasn't listening.

"Women are a pain," Emilio said, just as if I really wasn't listening.

"Hey!" I said, looking up.

Bernardo's eye sparkled. "Yeah, Emilio! Hey!"

"Oh, but you're a boy," Emilio explained.

I smacked him with a piece of bread.

"Stale joke," said Bernardo.

I wanted to hear more about why Bernardo thought Emilio was lucky. Instead, Bernardo said, "The farm we always go to, up near Como, has the best salami I've ever tasted. And the cheese, oh, the cheese. You have to taste it to believe it."

"Didn't we go up there one year?" asked Emilio. "My mother brought us. And Rodolfo tried to kiss my sister. They did have incredible soft cheese. Incredible."

"I remember that," said Bernardo.

These men were so confusing; was Bernardo referring to the cheese or the kiss?

"Francesca hit him with a huge squash, didn't she?" Bernardo recalled. Emilio laughed again, and so did I.

"No, really? A squash?" I asked.

"A big one, a Chioggia."

"Those are really good," Emilio put in. "I like ravioli with a squash filling."

"She just whacked him over the head with it? Did it break?" I asked, ignoring my cousin.

Bernardo grinned. "I wasn't there. But you're not supposed to do that with the farm's produce. Rodolfo behaved like a gentleman, though, and took the blame."

"Must have been the only time," put in Emilio, tearing his thoughts away from food for a moment.

"That he treated a squash like a gentleman?" I asked.

They both burst out laughing, and Bernardo gave me an appreciative look.

"A squash *or* a woman," Emilio said.

"Oh, I don't know. Rodolfo's all right," Bernardo mused.

"Who is he?" I asked.

"My eldest brother," Bernardo said.

I thought about whether I would ever talk about Gina this way, so casually that you wouldn't guess we were sisters.

"Do you think we got enough done tonight to satisfy your grandfather?" Bernardo asked, changing the subject.

"Probably. He's in a hurry, but he'll understand." Emilio made a Nonno face. "*Roma non fu fatta in un giorno.* Rome wasn't made in a day."

"Thank God we're not making Rome," Bernardo said, and helped himself to some more pickled asparagus.

"Need to go soon; kickoff is at eight forty-five," said Emilio when he came back to the table.

I decided that I hated soccer.

Bernardo didn't rush the asparagus, however; it seemed to me he preferred to rush the driving. He dropped us off quickly, giving a final opinion on AC Milan's chances in the game instead of saying good-bye. Emilio and I got back to the apartment in just enough time for Emilio to race back to his place for a shower and a loaf of bread, and for me to set the table. Dinner wasn't its usual two-hour affair; instead, we took our dessert *(torta di mele)* and coffee into the *soggiorno* to watch the game. I don't remember who won, to be honest. I mostly remember thinking about how Bernardo smiled at me when I made a joke, as my relations made noises I never thought they could make.

"What do you think of this, eh?" asked Francesco.

"I think you sound like a bunch of *elefanti*," I told him. He slapped his leg, laughing, and accidentally knocked my coffee over, spattering everyone but me.

"*Francesco!*"

"*Aiuto!*"

"*Mi dispiace!*"

"Clean it up before it stains my carpet, you *elefante*!" Nonna ordered amid the chaos. We missed a goal, I don't know whose, and Aunt Brigida chewed her son out for not automatically bringing me another cup right away.

"She will think you were raised in a cave, my child, not in our apartment! Shame on you."

I heard my mother's voice saying, "Who raised you?!"

Falling asleep that night, I felt as if I could cup the memory of the afternoon and evening in my palm—all the hard work followed by good food and talk and jokes, and the feeling that I belonged. Most of the time, anyway.

The next day was Francesco's half day, so he joined Bernardo and me. Every day after that, though, I spent more time up on the scaffolding than anyone but Bernardo. Then again, I was the only Della Torre besides Nonno without a day job. Despite everybody's busy schedules, however, we always had two or three family members with us, to my disappointment. *It's not like he's a demon, for goodness' sake,* I thought to myself.

It wasn't that bad. I was happy. Every day that week, I got to work near him, smelling his Italian-boy cologne and his sweat.

Every day, I started out shy, like I had in the van the first night, and got over it when he showed me how to prepare the wall or square off the doorframe. Once he corrected my grip on the *cacciavite* by laying his palms over my hands while he stood behind me. I found it totally impossible to remember what he'd shown me, and hoped he wouldn't notice that I stripped the next five screws and had to work them out with the claw of a hammer.

About eight screws after that, Emilio came over to show me how to place the silver nails, like the ones in my demon-catching case. Turning his back on Bernardo, he murmured a soft chant. I felt dizzy at the sound of his low voice, but I was used to feeling this way around Emilio. I did as he did, using an old-fashioned square iron nail to tap a hole in the wood, then fitting the silver nail in place, watching my steel hammer flatten the head against the board. I could begin to see the pattern they would form as we placed them around the Second Door.

Bernardo was working on the other side of the balcony and didn't seem to notice what Emilio and I were doing. I couldn't tell if he was pretending. Our families had known each other for so long that he must know something about what we did. I made a note to ask Emilio about it later. I did notice that Emilio chanted under his breath, so low I could hardly hear what he was saying. Bernardo had hung a radio off a beam, and Emilio used the sound to mask his words. I also realized that Bernardo made sure to let us know when he was moving closer to our side of the balcony or dropping down the scaffolding to go to the van.

Some days, I thought for sure I had caught Bernardo looking at me the same way I looked at him; other days, he seemed so intent on the job that I could have been Emilio, or possibly a wall, for all he cared. But then he would look over and pass me a box of screws right when I had run out, or say, "Don't forget to measure it, first," just as I was raising the drill, and I would change my mind, thinking he was watching me after all.

When Emilio and Francesco both joined us one day, they started telling whore jokes and it got worse from there. Guys are bizarre, I decided, grinding my teeth and driving one screw after another into the balcony floor. Every now and then I had to stop and ask Emilio for a silver nail. They don't work well for actual building; that's what the screws were for, but they were needed to make the Second Door functional.

"Here you go," he said, pulling one from a battered wooden box. He caught sight of my face. "What's going on?"

I shrugged and turned away. A voice in my head said firmly, *You are worth more than that. You need to speak up.* I thought about what Anna Maria would say if she had been here.

"You guys tell these jokes like I'm not even here," I said, feeling like a spoilsport. He lifted an eyebrow.

"I'm sorry to be a jerk about it," I said.

"What are you apologizing for?" Emilio asked. He turned to the others. "Hey, guys. Knock it off with the whore jokes, okay? We have Mia with us, in case you hadn't noticed."

Bernardo was hanging over the side of the scaffolding,

working on the bracing, and Francesco was kneeling on the floor. They both stopped dead, mouths dropped open, heads tilted at comical angles, looking like the two frontrunners for the Dope of the Year Award.

"They were just jokes," Francesco offered lamely.

"No, Emilio's right," Bernardo said to Francesco, but he was looking at me. I forgave him at once.

The next day, Anna Maria joined us for the first time. When I saw her striding up the street beside her brother, looking like a leggy goddess in her own canvas work shirt and worn jeans, I prayed that Bernardo wouldn't notice her. Although I had no idea how he wouldn't.

She climbed the scaffolding, pulled on a pair of stout work gloves, and looked around. "Can you explain the structure to me, please? I have only worked on a very simple Second Door, nothing like this," she said to Bernardo. He nodded and took her on a guided tour that included me, sweating over a corner.

"And this is your cousin, who's gotten very good at framing," he said.

Anna Maria pretended to look at me like a tourist, wide-eyed. "Ah!"

Bernardo had Anna Maria hold a chalk line for him.

"So I met this guy at Plastic last night," she said, pressing the end of the line tightly against the wood. Plastic was a nightclub, a place where Nonno and Nonna would almost certainly never let me go, for reasons that probably dated back to the Middle Ages.

"Yeah?" Bernardo asked, snapping the line so that it left a long mark in blue chalk all down the wood.

"He totally reminded me of Rodolfo. Only more conceited."

"*More* conceited?" asked Francesco.

Bernardo laughed and pulled out his tape measure, telling Anna Maria, "Up. Hold it. Let me measure. My poor brother," he added, moving the line into place. "He's really not so bad, you know."

"I know. Really this guy just looked like him," said Anna Maria. "And he had spent a year in Egypt, and he wanted to tell me all about it, about how crazy Cairo was. And I thought, cool, especially since a girl doesn't go to Plastic to meet guys, you know, just to dance. But he was straight and cute. Until he kept shouting over the music for what seemed like hours. I never even got to ask if he went to see the pyramids."

"People can have the most extraordinary experiences without really benefiting from them," agreed Bernardo.

"Yes. He told me all about meeting some really great Arab poet in a café and I wanted to say, 'Did you let *him* talk at all?'"

"Be fair," Bernardo said. "Hold it there," he added, snapping the line again. "He was probably nervous."

"Too nervous to have any manners?" said Anna Maria.

"You never have any manners, and you're never nervous," Francesco pointed out.

I looked up in time to see Anna Maria look startled, then frown and aim a kick at her brother.

"No horseplay on the worksite!" barked Bernardo. I had never heard him so stern. I thought Anna Maria would bark back, but she said, perfectly seriously, "Pardon. I will kick him later."

I couldn't help laughing, and neither could the guys.

"But pay attention. This is how people get hurt," Bernardo told her, stern again.

"I know," she said, meeting his eyes. "I won't do it again."

I could see she meant it. Even in the midst of my jealousy, I liked her better for making promises I knew she would keep.

"What did you end up saying to him, the guy at Plastic?" I asked when they had moved the chalk line again.

"Oh, eventually he paused for breath long enough to tell me we should go home to his place, he really felt a connection."

At this point, we all had to stop work, we were laughing so hard.

"Did he mean it?" asked Francesco.

"I think he did," Anna Maria said meditatively. "I told him that if he'd actually given me a minute to talk we might have had a connection, but I was ready for some quiet time at home, thanks all the same."

"Oh, wow. You're so mean to them," Francesco said. "My mean sister."

Bernardo smiled faintly to himself as he placed his carpenter's square along a chalk line.

"Meaner than making a girl listen to you talk about yourself for two hours? I don't think so," Anna Maria retorted.

"She has a point," I said.

Bernardo looked over at me.

"Honesty over politeness?" he asked.

"If the other person is being rude, maybe," I mumbled. "He sounds like he was kind of a jerk."

I wanted to say, *I wish I could be so tough. And I wish I was always having to turn guys down.* But I didn't really wish that last part; I just wanted one man in Milan to ask me out so I could say yes. And maybe, *But I'm busy tonight.* I stole a glance at that one man. Listening to him and Anna Maria, I thought sadly that he wouldn't be asking *me* out. I tried to pay attention to what I was doing, but I still ended up stripping screws.

"Mia, we need to make a run to the hardware store," Bernardo said suddenly, breaking in on my thoughts. "Want to come?"

Absolutely not. I didn't want to come along and watch them flirt even more.

"No, that's okay," I replied over my shoulder.

"Oh," he said, his voice oddly flat. I turned around and he smiled his wide-open smile. "I was hoping for some company, but I can go it alone."

I froze as he climbed down the ladder and started walking away. I was an idiot. I would never ever ever get this right, and I would die young and alone, swallowed by a demon, having been kissed exactly twice.

"We've got things going fine here, Mia. Why don't you go catch up with him? You look like you could use a break," said Anna Maria as she held a board steady for her brother.

I stared at her, but she didn't look up. Bernardo had already started the van. I slithered down the scaffolding, landing so hard my feet stung, and broke into a run. He was pulling away when he saw my face in the window. His eyes crinkled and he jerked his head toward the other door, the brakes squeaking. I climbed in, hearing the roar of the car heater, taking in the smell of diesel fuel and his cologne. He grinned at me, and I blushed, hating my burning face, and turned to look straight ahead.

"Figured you needed someone to supervise you," I heard myself saying in a severe tone. He laughed. I felt the way I had the time my mom and I had taken the elevator in the Chrysler Building—stomach dropping, heart rising.

As we rattled through the streets of Milan, I knew I should make conversation, but I had no idea how, alone with him like this. Signora Gianna would tell me to act mysterious, I thought, or play hard to get; I felt fairly sure that wasn't the same thing as sitting like an embarrassed stone in the passenger seat. Bernardo didn't help, his eyes fixed on the road. As we wove through the traffic, an older guy in a snappy Alfa Romeo cut him off. He slapped his hands against the wheel, then he laughed and turned to me.

"Doesn't that get you, when someone does that?" he asked.

I smiled shyly. "I don't know how to drive," I said.

"Really?"

"I was learning when I left the United States, but I didn't have a license yet." I thought about this. "I guess I'll have to do it all over again when I go home," I said. "I don't know."

"You're going home?" he asked. I thought he sounded slightly bummed.

I shrugged. There was a place on his neck, just beneath his jaw, where his five o'clock shadow was coming in. I imagined what it would feel like under my fingers.

"Maybe. I don't have any idea, to tell you the truth," I said, and smiled at him. "I'm supposed to stay here, with the family."

He nodded. "The family is best," he agreed. "Your family, especially. They're good people." He turned down a street and asked, "Do you miss your family back home? Your parents, your sister?"

I didn't remember talking about my parents and sister to him. "Yeah," I said. "Actually, this is awful, but I don't miss them as much as I should. I love it here," I added.

"Really? Milan, or Italy?"

"Milan, I guess. I haven't really traveled around at all. Italy, I guess, too."

"Ah, no, they are not the same thing. Milan, it's different. We're so industrial here; we're in love with the future, with change. The rest of Italy, it's in love with history. But all Italians are in love with food," he said. "And maybe the Milanese are the only ones who admit that the cooking might possibly be better in another city. Like Bologna." He paused. "But not much better. We have dishes here no one else has . . . the best."

After fitting the van into an impossibly small space in front of a crowded shop front, Bernardo got out and held my door open. "You don't miss your family?" he repeated.

I pretended to give this due consideration, because standing so close to him was making it hard for me to think.

"A bit," I smiled, then added quickly. "My sister's amazing, we're lucky to have our mother, and my dad, he's tough, but he takes good care of us."

"You have to be tough to do that, sometimes. To be a father, I think," he said, opening the door of the hardware store. "It must be harder with girls, too. I have only brothers, so I don't know."

I felt offended. "Why harder with girls, though? It seems like boys give their parents a pretty hard time."

He smiled at me as we walked between the shelves, which were packed full of everything, piled, stacked, crowded. The section for nails, screws, and bolts had rows of drawers with unreliable labels. Bernardo sighed and started opening them, pulling screws from his pocket to compare. As he sorted, he looked at me, his eyes twinkling.

"I've offended you, about raising girls. I have an answer for you, but it would just get me in more trouble," he said.

"Probably," I said. I was curious, though, and asked my next question before I could be too embarrassed.

"Are men and women really so different, though?"

He looked me straight in the eye, and I felt my face get hot for the millionth time.

"By God, I hope so," he said.

I examined my shoes, wondering exactly how much I'd given away. I wished I could ask Signora Gianna for advice. This game was way, way too hard for me.

I looked up. He was busy choosing bolts and screws, putting them in sacks.

"Why does it bother you," he went on, "that we might be different, or girls might be harder to raise because . . . because of the kinds of trouble they can get into . . . the things that can happen to them? Why should that bother you?"

"I don't know," I said, picking up a box of nails and turning it over in my hands. "It just bothers me. Like . . ."

I wanted to tell him how Anna Maria had to push and push to become a demon catcher, but Emilio just got to be one. I had a notion there were other things that bothered me, too, but I couldn't put words to them.

". . . like the girls in the bar, who thought I was a boy, just because I wearing these work clothes," I said, gesturing at my canvas shirt and pants, torn and stained after only a few days.

He nodded at this. "That really got to you, didn't it? I think they know you're not a boy now, though," he said. He smiled and added, "It's not that difficult to see that you're a girl, you know."

I felt my stomach jump again. There we were, standing in our dirty work clothes in a hardware store, and I felt like we were on a movie set. *Mia's Romance. Love in Milan. That Tedesco Boy.*

"Thank you," I managed. "I guess it did bother me. But that's not the point," I added, and then wished I hadn't.

"I know it isn't. I don't have any answers, though. And so many of the differences, they are pleasant."

"I guess so," I said, uncertainly, wishing again that I could talk this over with Signora Gianna, or Anna Maria at least.

He seemed about to say something else, but decided against it, and led the way to the cash register. The old man behind the counter said, "*Ciao*, Bernardo. And who is the beautiful girl?"

Bernardo turned to smile at me, as if to say, *See? Not so hard to tell you're a girl.*

"This is Mia Della Torre," he said.

"You make your girlfriends work, now? Shame on you," said the old man.

I waited for Bernardo to say I wasn't his girlfriend, or that I was a feminist, or something clever and funny. He laughed at the old man and said, "We can't bear to be apart. What can you do?"

I didn't expect the old man to get misty-eyed, either, or to cry, "Wonderful! I remember what it was like."

He reached across the counter and patted my arm, "This is good, too. If you work together well now, you know you can always do so. It's good to know that before marriage. It's important."

I felt myself blushing yet again, and had absolutely no idea what to say.

Bernardo saved me.

"Don't scare her off, Alberto!"

"Nonsense! I'm not scaring you off, am I?" the old man asked me. "You don't look afraid."

"I'm pretty brave," I lied.

"You look it." He turned to Bernardo.

"Keep her," he advised him. "And you won't get tired of looking at her, either." He grinned. "That never hurts."

I had thought I couldn't blush any more deeply, but I found out I was wrong.

As we headed out to the van, Bernardo looked at me and said, "I hope you didn't mind? It was just easier than all the long explanations."

His voice seemed higher than usual. I made a last attempt to seem cool.

"No problem," I said lightly, smiling at him, and walked smack into the passenger door.

EIGHT

The Door Is Opened

I ended up on the ground, more bruised in spirit than in body. Bernardo didn't help me up immediately; he was laughing too hard. I wanted to sink all the way through the pavement. But then he offered me his strong hands, and pulled me up.

"Are you okay?" he asked, looking me over.

"Yeah."

He was still smiling when he opened the door of the van for me.

"I used to trip over my legs all the time," he confessed, starting the engine. He seemed to realize that hadn't helped, because he added, "You know, one day everything will stop being embarrassing every single minute."

That didn't help, either, at least not right away, but I asked, "Really?"

"Really," he said.

I wanted to cry. He thought of me as a baby sister after all.

"What do you think of Anna Maria?" I blurted out.

He shot me a quick look, eyebrows rising.

"I like her," he said mildly. "She's feisty, and funny, and smart. I think most people would find her too blunt, maybe a bit obnoxious, but I've known her a long time, and I think she simply has a strong sense of justice."

"I think so, too," I agreed. He didn't seem to be talking like he was in love with her. "Sometimes she blows me away."

"That's her mother in her," he said. "A powerful personality. I hear her grandmother was the same."

I looked over at him, and thought that I would probably never have had a conversation like this with a nineteen-year-old guy in the States. I tried to picture actually talking with Tommaso d'Antoni, our neighbor back home, about anything but cars.

"Italian guys think a *lot* about women," I said before I could stop myself.

Bernardo looked surprised. Then he laughed.

"What else is there to think about?" he asked.

"No . . . no, I mean, you were talking about Anna Maria's mother, and how she's the reason Anna Maria has such a strong personality. You were analyzing."

He looked at me oddly.

"So?" he asked. "There is something wrong with this?"

"No! I just don't remember ever hearing an American guy talk this way."

"I haven't met a lot of American guys," he said. "We had a couple of them in our school; their parents worked over here. They were okay, but they tried to be more Milanese than the Milanese. They didn't even want to be friends with each other; they both seemed embarrassed to be American."

"I feel that way sometimes," I said.

"Really?"

"Sure. We've done a lot of idiotic stuff. I didn't really know until I came over here."

Bernardo laughed.

"Oh, you are such a young nation, though! You've accomplished a lot in a short time, but you haven't had a chance to go at it for centuries, like the Romans. Give yourselves time to really screw things up," he teased.

"Every country does stupid things," he went on. "Italian politics are the laughingstock of Europe; the only people who are funnier to read about are the Greeks and the Spaniards. But that does not make me sorry to be Italian. I belong to the nation that has the best food, the best art, the highest intellectual tradition, the finest design, the most beautiful cities, the loveliest countryside, and by far the most gorgeous women," he finished cheerfully. "I'm never sorry to be Italian. That's what's strange about you Americans."

"It is strange," I agreed. He'd given me quite a lot to think about. We'd finished the conversation in the bank courtyard. My cousins were sitting in a row on the scaffolding, dangling their legs, sharing a cigarette, and looking down at us.

"What a bunch of lazybones," Bernardo said, looking up. "Or they've run into a problem. Come on, let's go."

At least I can be his friend, I thought as we got out of the van. *That's something.*

I tried to console myself with that thought over the next two weeks as we worked. I did have days to study, when nobody was free to work on the Door. But I would always look out over my books and wish I were in the Via Vincenzo Monti.

The day we finished the Second Door, though, I still felt like I would die, because now I had no excuse to see him again. Emilio took me over to the Strozzi apartment building when he got home from work, and he, Bernardo, and I finished applying a quick coat of all-weather varnish, just in case the balcony had to last longer than expected. The very last thing we did was fit the door with a tiny, ornate lock that came with an old-fashioned key. The lock was so small it looked like a lock for a dollhouse. I knelt down to examine it. Nestled in among the cast silver scrollwork and flowers there was a bird. It was the same bird that sat over the door to our shop, and was etched on the bell around my neck. I stood up.

"This is completely impractical, as well as insecure," Bernardo was saying to Emilio. "Do not, I implore you, let Signora Strozzi see the key."

Emilio laughed. "Certainly not."

"I wish I understood your family's trade better," said Bernardo.

"No, you don't," Emilio replied shortly. "Now you two go away. I can drive four screws on my own just fine, thank you."

We didn't move for a minute, not just because Emilio seemed unusually crabby, but because this was the end of the job. Didn't we have a right to stay and see it through? But then I noticed that Emilio, using his body as a screen, was tracing a pattern around the outside of the lock. Finally getting it, I turned to Bernardo.

"If he strips them, we can always use new ones," I said helpfully, smiling.

"True," said Bernardo. "Let's go clear some space in the van for the scaffolding."

"Okay," I said. I felt torn between wanting to see what Emilio was going to do, and spending a last few minutes with Bernardo. Even if Emilio hadn't been acting surly, I'm pretty sure Bernardo would have won.

We climbed down and went to work on the van. After a moment and a few whirs of the *cacciavite*, Emilio came down and said, "It's done."

"Wow," I said.

"This has been a good job," said Bernardo.

"It has," Emilio agreed. He looked up at the balcony.

"The scaffolding can wait," he said. "Nonno will want to check everything. But I think he will say we've done fine."

"He will," said Bernardo. He gazed upward at the balcony, the tiny lock winking in the dusk. I heard the utter confidence in his voice, saw the calm in his face.

"You know him that well?" I asked.

Bernardo laughed. "No. I know my work that well."

One day, I thought, *I will look like that and sound like that, about my work. I will.*

Emilio broke the silence. "Let's go get an *aperitivo* to celebrate," he suggested.

This time, when we walked into the wine bar, the girls behind the counter said, "*Ciao,* Mia! What can we do for you?"

Bernardo took a while to decide what he wanted to drink, so Emilio and I took our prosecco and found a table, eyeing the plates full of food thoughtfully, starting to make choices, enjoying the wait.

"What happens now?" I whispered to Emilio.

"Now?" He blinked, looking from me to Bernardo.

"I mean with the Second Door," I explained, and he looked at me and chuckled.

"That's not what I thought you meant."

"I see," I said, wondering when Bernardo's promise would come true and I would stop being embarrassed every other second.

Emilio looked over at Bernardo again, but when he spoke, he said, "What happens next is that Nonno will tell us what incantation he's chosen to open the Second Door. And then we go in and see what we find. If we're lucky, we only have to go in once."

We both watched Bernardo, picking his way among the dishes by the bar.

"You could just ask him out," Emilio said. "Will you die if he says no?"

I almost told him that a dead relation of ours kept insisting that I let his friend make the first move. I don't think it would have surprised him. The thought faded even as I opened my mouth.

"No, I wouldn't die," I said. "But I'll never know if he would have asked me out, then."

Emilio's eyes widened, and he laughed out loud.

"Wise," he said. In response, I kicked him under the table as Bernardo joined us.

"Who's wise about what?" asked Bernardo, setting down a plate full of the salami he so loved, along with the first fresh asparagus of the spring. When we'd started nearly a month before, there'd only been pickled asparagus up at the bar.

"Mia," said Emilio. I kicked him again and he laughed. I wanted to shake him for acting like a little boy just when I needed the serious, mature Emilio.

Bernardo lifted an eyebrow and smiled for the first time since we'd come down the scaffolding that day.

"Your cousin *is* very wise," he said to Emilio. "I noticed that from the beginning." He smiled at me. "What are you being wise about?" he asked.

I opened my mouth like a fish. I thought I had nearly gotten used to Bernardo's pale blue eyes and his smile, but I hadn't.

"Nothing, at the moment," I said with perfect truth.

Bernardo shrugged. When Emilio and I brought our full plates back to the table, we all ate quietly for a while. Then Bernardo said, "We did a good job on that balcony. Even with all the odd things you have to do," he added, shooting a look at Emilio.

"Yes, we did," Emilio replied, his eyes distant. I said nothing.

"Fair enough," said Bernardo. He smiled at me. "So, now, you go back to your books?"

"I do," I said. "This was more fun."

"I can imagine."

"And you . . . ?" I asked.

"I go back to the project we're doing for the university," he said. "This was more fun for me, too. I like working for your family."

Bernardo dropped us off at the candle shop.

"*Ciao*, Mia," he said to me. "It was a pleasure. I'll see you around."

"*Ciao*," I said. I tried to find something casual to say, something with just enough mystery to it that he would stay a moment longer, and maybe even ask me out. Emilio had already gone inside the shop.

We stood for a moment.

I could have said, "See you around, too."

Or, "Thank you for teaching me which way to hold a *cacciavite*."

Instead, I said *ciao* again and went inside feeling like someone had filled me with sawdust and metal filings. At least Emilio didn't raise his eyebrows when I came in; instead, he asked me if I wanted any wine, and Nonno poured a glass for me before I answered. I sat and listened to the van starting up and driving away.

"So! I hear you have finished. I will go look, but I'm not worried. Now we can begin," Nonno said, sounding pleased. He didn't seem to notice my mood at all. "It looks like everyone can make it tomorrow evening, which would be best. We should wait until the Strozzi family is asleep if we can."

I remembered the story Anna Maria and I had dug up, about our ancestor G. Della Torre entering the palace through the Second Door he'd built. How he'd walked in on Prince Georg and his noble lover. I hoped we wouldn't interrupt anything. The thought grossed me out.

Emilio set his glass down and asked to be excused so he could phone Alba. Nonno turned to me.

"I will explain more fully to everyone tomorrow, before we go, but I want to go over the ritual with you, since you won't be familiar with any of it."

He pulled an old, leather-bound book out of a pile on the shop table. It wasn't a notebook, but a printed tome with thick pages and detailed engravings. I was still thinking about

Bernardo, but as he paged through it, I found myself trying to make out the illustrations.

"Everywhere you walk around the city, you can see signs in shops that look like ours," he said, pointing to the shopwindow, where the gilded letters read CANDELERIA DELLA TORRE, DAL 1733.

"Now, in our case, we have been on this spot, in this shop, since 1733. Sometimes we've closed our doors for a while, because of a plague or an invasion or some other nuisance, but we've always had a shop here. On the other hand, some restaurants, they claim to be far older than they are. Even universities do that! But the point is, all those centuries seem to matter to people. They want to feel connected to the past, and older things just seem holier, stronger. Maybe that's why we learn to respect our elders.

"A man came to me a while back wanting to study with me," Giuliano continued. "He called himself a witch and claimed he came from a long line of Italian witches.

"Now, there are some who really do come from such a family. You have met one."

He waited, and after a moment, I heard a voice saying in my head, "I untie knots, and I tie them." I thought of a woman's stern face, and of stepping outside the candle shop, over and over, with some object in my hand, as she and I struggled to find a way to protect me from my demon.

I said, "Signora Negroponte."

"Yes."

"And you, yourself, come from such a family, with a long tradition in a dangerous, occult profession. But this young man, he didn't come from any such tradition, and he wanted the ancient ways to be his own.

"I am rambling like this for a reason, *carina*. The funny part about that young man, who said he came from a long line of witches? *He had power.* He had a real gift. He didn't need fifty ancestors who'd done the same thing over and over to be good at what he was doing.

"You have plenty of ancestors who have been doing the same thing over and over, and that's good; we've had a chance to get rid of some of the things that don't work. We need the notes we take, we need the centuries behind us. It's a good thing. What I am trying to say is that it is not the only thing, do you understand?"

I nodded, and he went on. "The ritual we use to open the Second Door is a newer ritual. Do you remember what G. Della Torre called it?"

I'd written it down; I could see it in my handwriting, on the page.

"The song of something," I hazarded. "The song of the gate of . . ."

"Yes. *Il canto della porta d'Orchoë*—the song of the gate of Uruk. It uses words from a much more ancient text. I do not know where G. found it, because it has only recently been found on some clay tablets and translated. He died long before those books were published."

I knew when he said "recently" he could mean anytime in the last couple hundred years; I'd even started to think that way myself.

"The text he uses is a song sung by a goddess, a great goddess, while she stands at the gates of the Land of the Dead.

"Signora Negroponte spoke to you of the gods of place, the laws of the house, and the laws of the road," he said. I couldn't tell if it was a question.

"Yes," I said. "Everyone can use the roads, no matter if they are good or evil, demon or saint or angel. . . ."

I didn't mean to wax poetic, but Giuliano smiled with approval.

"Yes," he prompted.

"But to enter a house," I went on, "you must be invited in. And you are under the protection of the roof, even if it is a roof where you are giving silver for food, or a bed, or for anything, really. You are under the wings of your host."

"Yes."

He waited. I'd gotten used to this over the last few months. Neither he nor his grandson ever liked to do my thinking for me. I suppose I should have been grateful, but it always made a place behind my eyebrows ache.

"So . . . we have to be invited into the Strozzi house."

He nodded.

"But haven't they already given their permission, because Signora Strozzi said it was okay to build the balcony?"

He nodded again.

"So . . . we have to ask someone else?"

Another nod.

"A spirit," I said, more to myself now, thinking hard, no longer looking at him to see if he agreed. "A spirit. Not the demon we are after, I am guessing. Someone else who lives there. A member of the family? Probably."

I looked up at him. He was smiling.

"Do we know who we have to ask for permission?"

He shook his head.

"Oh," I said, meeting his eyes. "That makes it complicated," I said.

He nodded, grinning like a boy up to no good.

You love *this job!* I thought, suddenly enlightened. *You love it with all your heart. The study, the danger, helping others, all of it.*

I grinned back.

I guess that was a signal. He slapped a hand down on the open book and gestured for me to pull my chair in closer. I looked down at the page, ready to read the song of a goddess, to see holy words, and saw—gibberish.

"It is a transliteration of the words found on a clay tablet, in the Akkadian language, once spoken all over Mesopotamia," he explained.

Oh, all right, then. He drew out a notebook and showed me a translation.

Goddess of the fearsome divine powers, clad in terror, riding on the great divine powers, Inanna, made perfect by the holy a-an-kar weapon, drenched in blood, rushing around in great battles, with shield resting on the ground (?), covered in storm and flood, great lady Inanna, knowing well how to plan conflicts, you destroy mighty nations with arrow and strength and overpower lands.

In heaven and on earth you roar like a lion and devastate the people. Like a huge wild bull you triumph over lands which are hostile. Like a fearsome lion you pacify the insubordinate and unsubmissive with your gall.

"This isn't the part we use for the Second Door; this is the beginning of a hymn to the goddess, though she is known by another name in the song that we use."

I had never heard of anybody talking to a goddess that way.

"So," Nonno went on. "We are using very ancient words, which people once believed were spoken to, and by, a powerful goddess. We know it has worked once before, because G. succeeded in subduing the demon of the palace. But the song of the gate is just the first part: it is a song of descent into the underworld. We are going outside of our ordinary time and place. It is the only way to reach this demon of place."

"We go to another place to reach the demon of place? No offense, but this is getting weird," I told him.

Giuliano laughed.

"It always does," he said. "That's the way it is."

I thought of the smell of stagnant water in my mind the night Tommaso Strozzi had dropped by, the night I had seen the candle go out. I shivered suddenly, thinking about Lisetta Maria Umberti's face, so still in death. Was the underworld where she had gone?

I watched Emilio outside, pacing the cobblestones while he talked on his phone. I saw his face break into a wide grin at something Alba said. The streetlamps picked out the bright glint of his hair against the gray walls of the Pinacoteca di Brera.

I thought of the Second Door we had built, and of the goddess covered in blood, and again, of Lisetta Maria Umberti's face, after we'd done our best to save her. We dealt with such vast powers and we had so much responsibility to the people we tried to help. And we were going to knock on a door using the words of someone who had been trying to get into the Land of the Dead. I shivered. As much as I wanted to learn this job, I felt afraid down to my bones.

"Nonno," I said.

"Yes?" he asked.

"I'm glad I got to help with the Second Door. But I'm too young for this. I'm not ready to go with you."

Nonno laughed.

"Don't be ridiculous," he said brusquely. "In any other age, you would already be a wife and mother—or you would have taken the veil—or you would have already stood your vigil for a witch."

He looked hard at me.

"Of course, you cannot conduct the ritual. Of course, it's a risk to bring you. You might make a mistake. But too young . . . ? No, that is no excuse."

I said nothing more for a long time. Nobody would ever say that to me back home in Center Plains, would they? Sometimes I felt so at home here, and sometimes the strangeness of this new world hit me hard.

"Nonno never allows excuses," Emilio said as he came back in, smiling to take the sting out of his words. "I have no idea what you were talking about. Just thought I should point it out."

His grandfather waggled his brows at him and told him to drink his wine.

I was still thinking about Nonno's words when I climbed into bed that night. A wife and mother? At sixteen? A witch, a nun? It was so hard to imagine.

"He's quite right," Signora Gianna agreed, speaking over my head in the dark.

"You are certainly old enough," said Gravel. (I still had no idea what his real name was.)

"Not that you know anything about it," Signora Gianna told him.

"Oh, don't I?" Gravel riposted. I started laughing.

"You guys know I have a big day tomorrow, right?" I asked.

"You do, don't you?" said Gravel, speaking to me directly for the first time.

"Yes," I answered, fascinated, sitting up in bed.

"Opening a Second Door, I hear," he continued, in his deep, rough voice.

"Yes," I said again.

"They're going about it the right way," said Signora Gianna with what sounded like professional interest. "Research, precedents."

"Thank you," I said. "We're not missing anything, are we?"

Signora Gianna and Gravel both laughed.

"There's always something missing," said Signora Gianna. "You do the best you can with what you know."

"But you would tell us, if you knew something, right?" I asked, suddenly full of hope. "You would mention it to me?"

"I would, if I remembered to," she said kindly.

"Which wouldn't be very likely," Gravel put in, less kindly.

"Hush," snapped Signora Gianna. "You are ridiculous. My memory is not what it once was, true," she went on. "And I cannot see all I would want to see, with the case you are working on. There's a great deal that I have no way of finding out."

"I hoped . . ." I began.

"I know," she said. "But you will have to do it without my help," she finished wryly. "Go to sleep, young one." I did, which would have surprised me if I'd been awake to notice.

The next night, we gathered for a rather solemn dinner, with what I was starting to think of as the usual crew for a big job: Nonno Giuliano, of course; Uncle Matteo, Emilio, Francesco, and Anna Maria.

Nonna Laura made *trofie al pesto*, a dish from the Ligurian coast that reminded me somewhat of gnocchi. She roasted chicken and pigeons, and served fresh fava beans in olive oil for a *contorno,* followed by a salad of baby greens, then cheese and fruit.

"A simple meal, before a big job," she explained. "It will sustain you, but it shouldn't be too hard on your stomachs."

"Yes, none of this should taste too bad coming back up," Francesco told me cheerfully.

I looked down at my plate, then back up at him.

"Really?" I asked faintly.

"Behave yourself," Nonna told him sharply. But she did not look at him when she said it, and both she and Francesca seemed unusually quiet. Égide squeezed Francesca's hand where it rested on the table.

At the end of the meal, Égide said, "Why don't I make the coffee, Nonna? Go sit."

She accepted his offer gratefully. Francesca stayed behind to do the dishes; her brother stood beside her at the sink, drying and teasing her, snapping his towel at her. I wiped down the table and watched them, thinking what they must have been like as kids together. It seemed like Emilio was trying to comfort her.

I ferried the coffee to the *soggiorno*, handing the first cups to Nonna and Nonno, sitting beside each other on the couch, holding hands, fingers tightly interlaced. Nonno kept her hand in his even when he opened a notebook. Emilio came in and sat down on the arm of the couch, cupping his coffee in both hands; I heard Francesca and Égide finishing up in the kitchen.

"We will be using an invocation called the *canto della porta d'Orchoë*," Giuliano said, nodding at me. "This is the same entry spell that G. Della Torre used in the account Anna Maria and Mia found. I will also bring Nonno Francesco's spell in case the *canto* does not work, but I believe it will. It's a straightforward enough recital, and then we fit the key in the lock. We may not be welcomed in, precisely, but we should be allowed to enter. Emilio will wait with his candle ready in case anyone comes out at us right away."

He paused and met his grandson's eye, then looked around at the rest of us.

"Once inside, we do not know what we will find. Keep together. Keep to the patterns of exorcism you know. Keep your senses wide open. We may have to wait to do an exorcism; we must see what we find. Is it understood?"

My cousins nodded, and so did I. Uncle Matteo got up with a grunt and went out on the balcony to light a cigarillo. Emilio moved to a chair and leaned back, running a hand through his curls. Anna Maria asked, "Can I see what's on?" and got a nod from Nonna.

She settled on a Roberto Benigni film that was halfway through. I wasn't the only one who kept glancing at the clock. The second hand ticked round and round, but the minute and hour hands seemed to stay in the same place. Then, somehow, they moved, and it was midnight.

The doorbell rang and Anna Maria jumped up. Nobody else seemed surprised that we might be having visitors. Then Anna Maria opened the door, smiled, and said, *"Buona sera,"* letting in an older man who seemed familiar, and a younger man who looked very much like him: Bernardo.

He glanced down at me once, smiling slightly. At least this time, he got to see me dressed entirely in black. I looked good, I thought, though not as stunning as Emilio and Anna Maria.

The older man kissed Nonno and Uncle Matteo on both cheeks, and I understood that he was Rinaldo Tedesco, Bernardo's father.

Bernardo and his father were dressed in ordinary clothes. Bernardo wore a dark shirt and a smooth chocolate-brown leather jacket. Standing calmly beside his father, listening to the small talk of the older men, he looked even more beautiful than I remembered.

Then we were all rising, and I was touching my shaking fingers to my breast pocket to make sure I had my case, and following Anna Maria down into the courtyard, where we crowded into her father's Fiat. Everyone else was riding a *motorino* tonight: even Giuliano had one. He took Emilio on his; Bernardo took Francesco; Signore Tedesco rode alone, talking on a cell phone, his tight scarf unfurling over his shoulder as we followed him out under the archway and into the Via Fiori Oscuri. The drive to the Via Vincenzo Monti didn't take long. I watched the streetlights flash over Signore Tedesco's back as he leaned and dodged from street to street.

"Why is everyone but us on *motorini*?" I asked Uncle Matteo and Anna Maria.

Uncle Matteo grunted, eyes on the road.

Anna Maria said, "So we can scatter faster if we have to. Papa is bringing us like this because we get to stay behind and do a bit of—information management—if anything happens."

"Oh," I said, worried I would be expected to help out with that. I was afraid all I could do was stand there if the police showed up. It hadn't even occurred to me that they might. Or was that what she meant by "if anything happens"?

We parked in the courtyard belonging to the Intesa Sanpaolo. All the BMWs had gone home to wherever BMWs live; there was only a lone Mercedes, grand and forlorn, close to the door of the bank. The Strozzi apartment building rose up before us in the dark. The balcony and the door were faintly lit by the streetlights. No lamp shone in the windows of the Strozzi apartment.

Nonno had decided earlier we would leave the scaffolding up for an easier climb tonight. Francesco started up first. Emilio stood apart, speaking in a low voice with Uncle Matteo while Bernardo and his father waited. Then I saw Bernardo head out to the street. Uncle Matteo faded into the shadow of the courtyard with Signore Tedesco.

"Mia," whispered Francesco, and I saw him gesturing to me. I started climbing, looking over my shoulder one more time. I saw Bernardo standing near the bank, looking back at me.

I felt my body freeze with embarrassment. It didn't matter that he'd seen me climb this a hundred times. My foot slipped and I felt a firm hand on my calf.

"Take it slowly," said Giuliano. "But go."

I remembered myself and pulled myself off the scaffolding and onto the balcony, feeling it creak under my weight.

Nonno took his time, and Anna Maria came last. Emilio remained on the ground, looking up.

"I believe this is the lock our ancestor used for the door to the palace," Giuliano whispered solemnly.

"Er, no—it isn't," I whispered back, before I could stop myself. Three pairs of eyes widened toward me in the dark. "I went ahead in the notes. It got blown to bits by another demon, a couple of years later."

Giuliano blinked. I heard a smothered snort, probably from Anna Maria.

"Oh! Oh, well. It's got strong wards, anyway," he said, and chuckled.

He took the key from his pocket. It was so small it would have slipped through the floorboards if he had dropped it. Thankfully, he didn't.

I hadn't thought about it when Emilio had fitted the lock, but I found that now I wanted a big, ponderous lock, with a large, clanking piece of iron for a key. I wanted a lock that would keep in the dead.

I wanted it even more when Nonno began to recite the transliterated Akkadian poem, the words soft, then crunchy, then sonorous by turns: the chant of a goddess as she stood before the portals of the Land of the Dead. Earlier, I'd seen the translation.

> *Gatekeeper, ho, open thy gate!*
> *Open thy gate that I may enter!*
> *If thou openest not the gate to let me enter,*
> *I will break the door, I will wrench the lock,*
> *I will smash the doorposts, I will force the doors.*
> *I will bring up the dead to eat the living.*
> *And the dead will outnumber the living.*

I shivered, staring at the plain wooden door with its iron fittings and silver nails, the tiny silver lock beneath a battered brass knob, and just for a moment I felt farther from home than

I ever had in my life. Then Giuliano reached forward, fitting the key in the lock while he went on reciting the commands of the ancient Queen of Heaven.

He turned the key, put his hand to the doorknob, and opened the Second Door.

The first thing that happened was that a cold wind blew past us, almost throwing me into Francesco. Giuliano lost his balance ever so briefly, then whipped his head around and called softly into the courtyard, "Emilio!"

Emilio spoke from below. "Here, Nonno. I've got it."

I turned and peered down over the edge of the balcony, just in time to see Emilio apply a match to a large candle. The wind that had blown past us was whipping around him. I watched Emilio's black collar flap against his neck. He held up the candle, its slip of a flame wavering frantically, and as I watched, a knot of wind tied itself around the flame, narrower and narrower, until with a final sucking sound the last breath of air disappeared into the flame. It swelled, slightly, then ceased to flicker and burned straight upward, calmly, as if nothing at all had happened. Emilio slid a silver candle snuffer over it.

He placed the candle in Giuliano's black bag, then passed the bag to Uncle Matteo as he emerged from the shadows at the foot of the scaffolding.

"Safely stowed for now," Emilio said. Uncle Matteo nodded and walked off with the bag. I saw a movement up by the street, Bernardo turning to watch us again. I saw his father leaning against the wall of the bank, nearly invisible in the darkness.

Then Emilio climbed up to us. His grandfather had turned back to the door and stood facing it, waiting. The balcony creaked once more with Emilio's weight. For a moment, I thought we were waiting for the others—Bernardo and his father, Uncle Matteo—but then I realized Giuliano was waiting for something else. I looked around at Anna Maria, Emilio, and Francesco. They, too, were intent on the Second Door.

"Nothing more," Nonno said at last. He lifted his notebook and read the final, guttural request of the goddess: *Let me in.*

The air in the doorway condensed into a heavy, broad-shouldered form.

"Enter, then," a voice said, and blurred back into the dark.

Giuliano looked at us.

"I think that is all the invitation we can expect," he said.

He stepped through the doorway, Anna Maria following him, then Francesco. As Francesco's shoulders disappeared into the dark, I realized I was frozen to the spot. Now, at last, face-to-face with this moment, I was terrified to enter the Second House, because I'd been there before.

NINE

The Second House

Behind me, Emilio said, "Mia? Your turn."

I turned my face to his in the pale streetlight.

"I can't," I said.

He frowned, raising one eyebrow.

"Why on earth not?" he asked.

"It's . . . the Second Door. It takes us into Left-Hand Land, doesn't it? It's the other world. I've been there before, when I was possessed. I can't go back," I said. "I know it's awful timing, but . . ."

We both looked at the doorway. I could see him thinking fast. He took my hand.

"This time, you are not alone, however," he said. "This time, you go by choice."

I gripped his hand tightly. Then I faced the door, took a deep breath—and let his hand go.

"You are sure?" he asked.

"Yes," I said, and stepped forward into the dark.

It was like stepping inside a closet, only stuffier. What amazed me most was what I didn't feel: neither the nauseating disorientation of possession, nor the excitement of being able to hear inside people's heads and see through walls. I couldn't see much of anything, here, but I didn't feel as sick as I had during my possssion. My fear bled from me, replaced by relief—and then, suddenly, I could feel my demon: a distant flutter, far outside these walls. *You are here,* I thought I heard him say. But perhaps I was the one saying it.

"Mia," Emilio whispered behind me. I didn't move. I felt my demon more strongly, as if he'd moved closer, testing the protections around me—the bell around my neck, the family I walked with. I found myself wanting to feel his mind a little longer, to learn him. He must have sensed this, because I felt him pull farther and farther away, until I could not sense him at all.

"Sorry," I whispered in response, and moved forward again.

"Pools of stagnation everywhere," Francesco whispered from up ahead, and Giuliano grunted in agreement. The sounds pushed against my ear as if there were no room for them.

My sight felt weak, the walls faint outlines, the hall table looming up suddenly and only just avoided. I could smell every inch of the upholstery fabric, could taste the wood polish, could hear *everything*—mice as loud as elephants in the walls, the thunder of our footsteps, the scratching of our shirts. I wondered if everyone else was experiencing the Second House the same way I was.

I wasn't exactly sure what they meant by pools of stagnation, until I walked through an air pocket that felt constricted, rotten, as if my skin could smell something my nose couldn't.

"Can't the Strozzis hear us? Shouldn't we whisper?" I asked.

Giuliano answered in what I knew would have been a soft voice, barely above a whisper, if it hadn't been roaring in my ears.

"We are inside the Second House," he said. "They can't hear us at all. They could probably feel us, if they knew how."

He added after a moment, "The demon will feel us soon."

We kept walking. I heard Nonno choke and gag suddenly, then Anna Maria.

Then I could smell it and feel Francesco convulsing in front of me, as we both tried not to vomit. There's no reason I should have known what a dead body left three days in a river would smell like, but I was pretty sure it smelled like that. The stench overwhelmed us, forced us backward, until we heard Giuliano growl, "Step through it."

We forced ourselves forward, and I felt very glad my cousins were ahead of me, struggling just as I was. Ten steps seemed like a hundred, but they got me through to the other side of our pocket, and I caught Francesco's arm for support. He leaned against me.

Suddenly, I thought I heard my demon whisper beside me. Sweating with fear and anger, I waited for the bell around my neck to ring, until I realized the sound came from near the portraits on the walls—not from my demon, after all.

The spirits weren't talking to us, at least, not yet. They were arguing, but it sounded like an argument that had taken place over and over, so that everyone just repeated themselves in dull, exhausted hisses.

"*È una fonte necessario, una fonte necessario,*" growled the spirit of a stern old woman, shadowed and blurred, seated under a portrait of herself. "It is a necessary source, a necessary source."

"*Sì, è una fonte di pericolo, di pericolo,*" replied the spirit of a bishop opposite her. "Yes, it is a source of danger, of danger."

The spirit of a monsignor whispered at both of them, "*Chi lo sa? Chi lo sa?* Who knows? Who knows?"

We kept moving, and the portrait I remembered from my visit with Nonno came into view, the man who looked exactly like Tommaso Strozzi, his powerful hands full of rings. His spirit faded in and out of his portrait and spoke in the softest whisper of all.

"*Non . . . vale . . . la . . . pena,*" he struggled to say. It's something Italians say all the time—"it's not worth the trouble"—an ordinary, flippant everyday phrase that translated easily inside my head. But the way his voice dragged out every syllable made it sound like a terrible warning.

Listening to him, I remembered the candle, the one that had burned down when Tommaso Strozzi had come to the shop. I remembered thinking then that the key to the problem was a sensation, a smell like a stagnant pond: the same sensation I'd felt as I walked through the strange, tight air pockets.

Avidità, I thought. Greed. And then realized I'd spoken out loud. Francesco turned in front of me. Ahead of him, Giuliano and Anna Maria stopped.

"Yes," Nonno said. "But be quiet about it."

The ancestors went on arguing in low voices that walked across our skins. Maybe all families kept on arguing until they were nothing but air and sound and spirit.

Now Giuliano walked ahead, leaving the voices behind, and leading us to Signore Strozzi's study. Even though we were inside the Second House, we still had to open the ordinary door. Giuliano's hand slipped on the handle a couple of times, but he seemed to expect that and finally got a grip. We stepped inside.

The room wasn't empty. Signore Strozzi stood in his nightclothes and gown, his back to us, looking down into the courtyard, his shoulders tight and square.

He wasn't what I saw first. The demon enveloped him in a huge, dark, human form, blurring and flickering, fading in and out so that Signore Strozzi's broad back was visible through the spirit. When I could see the demon more clearly, I saw that he glowed dimly, as if underneath he were filled with magma. His skin writhed, as if creatures of some kind were crawling all over it. We could smell him, too. I felt as if I had my face pressed against a corpse or I was drowning in a rotting pond. My head spun. I felt fear in the pit of my stomach.

The bell around my neck began to shiver as if it were about to ring. I came back to myself, still trembling, and felt the same calm come over me that I'd tasted on Christmas Eve, when I'd discovered that I *could* face my demon—that while I might still be scared, I wasn't the terrified, shell-shocked girl who had arrived in Milan three months earlier. I straightened up.

As calm as I felt, I nearly screamed when the demon turned around. Crawling over his skin were hundreds of tiny human hands. They inched and walked and turned over, wriggling like bugs to right themselves. They grasped at the air; they plucked and pulled at the demon's skin. "Your symbolism is pathetic and obvious," Emilio said coolly.

The demon roared so loudly he burst through the muffled, thick air of the Second House like the siren on an ambulance. Hundreds of hands suddenly shot out toward us. Emilio and Francesco each grabbed one of my shoulders and pushed me behind them, at the same time that Giuliano thrust his mirror in front of the demon.

"Behold yourself!" roared Nonno, almost as loud as his adversary.

I guess the demon had eyes, though I couldn't see them. Above the wriggling torso was a hump, shadowed and blurred, and it was this that leaned toward the mirror, even as the hands fell limp, withdrawing. The demon tipped the hump back and forth as he gazed at himself.

"Is that me?" asked an elegant voice. I thought I saw a blur move within the hump, something that might be a mouth. "Good gracious, I *am* handsome."

I couldn't help laughing out loud. I couldn't imagine a more hideous being, stink and all, and I certainly hadn't expected him to talk like some upper-class Italian.

"I suppose so, if you like that sort of thing," Giuliano said severely. "But now you must go."

"The rite of Ticinum, Emilio," he added after a moment.

"Yes, Nonno," said Emilio, pulling out his case.

"Francesco, candle," Nonno ordered.

"Yes, Nonno," said Francesco.

I saw Francesco place a stubby candle in a thumb holder, then pull a box of matches from his case. Emilio began to chant. I didn't recognize the passage he read from his notebook, nor could I understand it easily, since he seemed to be speaking in the old Milanese dialect, but I did recognize the sweet, solemn sound of Anna Maria's Tibetan bell.

The demon screamed and roared, his elegant voice abandoned for the moment. I was reminded of Signore Strozzi, and of the contrast between his calm voice and his thick-fingered, dangerous hands. Standing a few feet from Francesco, I could smell the beeswax candle in its holder—here inside the Second House, the honeyed scent was overpowering, a blessing, since it helped block out the demon's stench. I could hardly see the flame, however, a blurred, shuddering light that bowed with every roar.

The demon stopped.

"Wait," he said to Giuliano in his cultured accent. "I can see I started out on the wrong note. Forgive me. Maybe we can work out a deal. There's something that troubles you, something terrible you're going to have to do."

The hump of his head blurred and tipped toward me. I blinked, but Nonno did not move.

"Perhaps I might have information . . . answers?" the demon said to Giuliano.

I knew what he meant when he said *something terrible.* Sooner or later when my demon attacked again, my family would almost certainly have to let me die rather than allow it another chance at this earthly plane. A huge hope leaped up in me.

Through all of this, Signore Strozzi had not done more than shift his weight inside the monstrous shadow that enveloped him.

"No," said Giuliano firmly to the demon. "You must go."

"Wait! Shouldn't she have a say?" the demon asked slyly, his crawling torso bowing toward me. "After all, she's the one who is going to suffer."

"Don't listen to him, Mia," said Emilio. "Demons play games like this. Think, *cara*! If you're going to possess a banker, you've got to be cunning."

"Yes," agreed Giuliano, still facing the writhing hulk in front of us. "It's time to go," he told the demon.

The demon shuddered. "You shouldn't just let them talk you out of it," he said to me. "I only want to help. What you face, it's horrific, and what your family will have to do is even worse, I fear."

As far as I could tell, the demon had no eyes, yet I felt I was staring into them. That's how strange it was inside the Second House, halfway into the Left-Hand Land. I wanted to say, *more horrific than you?* But I knew the answer to that, having lived it. I took a deep breath, still wanting to believe in the demon.

"No," I said. "It's time for you to go." He shuddered again. I wondered if I had made the right choice.

Emilio began chanting once more. The demon's body jerked with every word now, convulsed with every stroke of Anna Maria's bell. Inside the creature's boiling, blurring body, Signore Strozzi twisted and shuddered at the same time. The banker whipped about, and I thought his spine would snap.

Inside the Second House, the demon's roars rose and fell as if someone were fiddling with the volume on a stereo. One minute the sound would fill my whole head, and the next it would fall away, leaving me shaking. Inside the demon, Signore Strozzi threw his head back and screamed, but I could not hear him. I wondered what he sounded like inside the ordinary apartment, and whether his family was awake.

Emilio and Anna Maria settled into a rhythm: he would chant a verse, and when he paused for breath, she would ring the bell three times. I couldn't tell what power the words or the bell had over the demon, if any. I thought I recognized single Milanese words, as Emilio's voice flowed in and out of range just like the demon's roars. "*Radice*—Root." "*Terra*—Earth." I didn't understand them all, but I could guess at most of them. "*Disagio*—Unease." "*Legge*—Law."

Until now, I had not understood why Giuliano had decided that this creature was a demon of place. I still wasn't sure what place he was referring to, but I could *feel* what he meant. Each time the demon and Signore Strozzi shuddered, the room seemed to shake as well. I saw Anna Maria shift her footing, saw Emilio rock on the balls of his feet, and Francesco throw out a hand. Only Nonno held still. As I struggled to keep my balance, I tried to figure out how he did it.

Another shudder, and I realized that I could hear another faint sound. I waited for the next convulsion and heard it again, a voice—no, more than one voice—from the portraits. The old woman was growling. The monsignor was screaming in terror and surprise. The look-alike Tommaso portrait was shouting for joy. There were other voices I did not recognize.

"Anna Maria," I whispered under Emilio's chant.

"What?" she snapped, holding her silver stick beside her bell.

"Can you hear them?"

As the verse came to an end, she didn't answer. She struck her bell three times, pausing in between for the sound to carry as far as it could in the Second House. The demon quivered.

"The people from the portraits. They are shouting when the demon shakes. When the room moves."

"Can't hear them over the bell," she said after a while. "Can't focus. Try Francesco."

Francesco heard his name and edged over to us, carefully holding his candle.

"Need to swap stubs," he whispered.

"Don't talk, just do it!" snarled Anna Maria. "There are two in my case."

"Got my own," he said.

"Shut up. Mia, tell him."

He rolled his eyes. "Crabby."

"Working," I retorted.

"So am I," he shrugged, not sounding particularly hurt. "What's up?"

"Voices. From the portraits," I managed as the demon's roars filled our heads again. "Listen."

Francesco didn't ask what I meant. Instead, he occupied himself with replacing the failing stub in his thumb holder with a longer beeswax candle, and sheltered it with his palm against the next trembling outcry.

"Ah!" he said, turning his eyes toward me, frowning.

"Yes," I said.

We stood silent, listening. I took a few deep breaths, trying to call the Madonna to mind, trying to pull back from the roaring, the stifling air.

I watched the demon writhe. Whenever he screamed, the tiny hands would stretch out their fingers as though reaching far beyond him, pulling the air toward him. They never stopped crawling and plucking at his skin. I watched him bellow, hands reaching outward, listening to the cries of joy and fear.

Then I noticed that the look-alike Tommaso portrait had gone silent, and one by one, the other voices faded. The hands, reaching and grasping outward, seemed to weaken, too. Even Signore Strozzi's body seemed to hang, wrung out, within the body of the demon. I had not noticed, or felt, how tightly the tiny hands had held on to everything around them—the air, the walls, the spirits, all of us—until Emilio's words and Giuliano's will forced them to let go. I had a momentary, bizarre fear that the apartment would collapse around us once they lost their grip. I felt as if we were pulling the demon out of this place, bit by bit, and it might not stand up without him. *That,* I thought, *is what Nonno meant by a demon of place.*

I wanted to know if time was passing as slowly in the ordinary world as inside the Second House. It seemed like we had been here for hours, days, years. The creature's roars faded to whispers, and we could see Francesco's candle tugging at him, now. The hands lifted a final time; Anna Maria suspended her hand beside her bell; Emilio fell silent; Nonno, watching carefully, lowered his mirror—and the demon lost his grip upon Signore Strozzi in one last convulsion, pouring toward the flickering light in Francesco's hand.

He vanished inside the candle with a hiss.

Francesco placed a snuffer over the flame. When he drew it away, I could smell a faint scent of pond muck in the smoke. Giuliano, Francesco, and I stood quietly, while Anna Maria and Emilio went forward to help Signore Strozzi collapse into his chair, though helping him was as awkward and slippery as it had been for Nonno to grasp the handle of the door to this room. They guided him down as best they could, but he still struck his desk hard as he settled. We heard a muffled thump that must have sounded much louder in the ordinary world. Over the banker's shoulder, I could see that it was still dark outside.

"We must leave the Second House and help him," Giuliano said. "I will go last, to close the Second Door."

Signore Strozzi began to raise his head and snarl at the air. We had to struggle to make out his voice.

"How could you take him?" shouted Signore Strozzi. "Come out, wherever you are, come out where I can see you, and explain yourselves! How could you take him? My family will murder me, they'll smother me in my sleep, they'll drive me mad with their whispers. . . . He was the luck of our house. How could you take him?"

We watched him search the air for us.

"Gone," Signore Strozzi said to himself. "Gone like the cowards they are." He began searching his desk. "Got to get out, get out, get out . . ."

He found what he was looking for, a clattering bunch of keys. The sound grated distantly in my ears.

"Back to the Second Door! We've got to go. Quickly!" cried Nonno, and Signore Strozzi lifted his head as if he almost could hear us.

We ran back through the hall, bumping into furniture that our confused senses couldn't warn us about, hearing Signore Strozzi's agonized roars above it all. I heard his wife awaken with a scream, his son call a terrified question.

I didn't expect to hear any voices from the portraits as we passed through. The look-alike Tommaso portrait was silent, and so were the ones of the monsignor and the old woman, but I could hear a handful of others, more distant, shouting at one another. As we came through, they shouted at us, too.

"Della Torres! You've always wanted everyone else's power! Want that consulship back, don't you? Never got to be dukes! Shameful traitors! Revenge!"

Part of me wanted to scream that all we had been trying to do was help. I slowed down, but Emilio caught my shoulder and said, "We have to reason with the living! Come on!"

I felt the air thicken as we forced our way through the Second Door and tumbled out onto the balcony, gasping for fresh air. I wasn't prepared for my senses to return to normal.

Suddenly, I could see so clearly in the dim streetlights. My lungs could expand; my nose didn't smell every single atom of scent; my skin didn't react to the sound of voices. I stood blinking until Anna Maria swore at me to get out of the way.

Down in the courtyard, Uncle Matteo was rocking impatiently on the balls of his feet. "He's starting his car!" he called. Signore Tedesco and Bernardo were running toward their *motorini*. I realized I could see the *motorini* clearly in the shadows of the courtyard; the sky was just getting to get light.

Nonno swung down the scaffolding faster than I would have thought possible for an eighty-year-old man. I landed on the street beside him, feet smacking hard onto the pavement. Bernardo pulled up on his *motorino*. Giuliano walked swiftly to his own, jumping on and stamping the gas pedal with a grunt. Before I knew it, Bernardo held out a hand to me, shouting to Nonno and Emilio, "I'll take Mia!" Emilio scrambled on behind his grandfather, looking as if he was commending his soul to heaven.

"What about me!?" moaned Francesco.

"You must call the Greek," Giuliano commanded. I made no sense of that. "Follow us as fast as you can. Matteo! Anna Maria! Stay behind, for the wife and son!"

We heard the roar of an engine from the courtyard on the other side of the apartment building, then Signore Strozzi raced past in a black Mercedes, head bent over the wheel. Nonno took off after him, *motorino* wobbling wildly, Emilio fighting to hang on while Giuliano repeated over his shoulder, "Call . . . the . . . *Greek*!"

"Hang on," Bernardo ordered.

He didn't wait for me to tighten my grip, jerking his *motorino* forward so that my fingers slid across the leather of his jacket. As we bounced over the uneven curb into the Via Vincenzo Monti, Bernardo felt me slide, and braked hard, so I slammed into him.

"Hang on," he repeated, but it sounded like he was laughing. "Put your arms around my waist and lock your hands!"

I still hesitated. Put my arms around his waist? I could smell the scent of his cologne.

"Mia! Don't be scared," he said, turning his head, his voice thrumming inside his chest. "But do hang on."

I took a deep breath and wrapped my arms around him, pressing my face to the back of his jacket. It took me a minute to remember we were supposed to be chasing Signore Strozzi; nothing much mattered at that moment, beyond the smell of leather.

As we leaped down the road, I worked out how to keep my seat. I pushed down on the footrests with my feet and threw my head and chest forward, bumping into Bernardo's back but not falling off. Then we were careening onto the Via Mario Pagano, weaving across lanes as we followed the Mercedes.

I matched my rhythm to Bernardo's, following the bend of his spine as he leaned this way and that, turning sharply around a delivery van with an enormous fish painted on the side, crossing in front of a Smart car, veering past a BMW as he expertly gunned the motor. Someone shouted from a car, "Hey, Bernardo! Come to Plastic!"

"Later!" he shouted back. I felt a stab of envy.

They yelled something else, but we were gone, whipping past, caught up in the river of lights and car exhaust and early morning drivers. Bernardo muttered under his breath, "He's cutting right, he's cutting right." And sure enough Signore Strozzi's engine roared again, and he shot across three lanes of traffic. Bernardo whipped the *motorino* around and followed.

Watched over by the angels and saints who protect almost all Italian drivers, Bernardo chased after Giuliano and Emilio, and the Mercedes wove erratically ahead of us all. Then up ahead, Signore Strozzi jerked the Mercedes hard left, alongside the enormous forested darkness of the Parco Sempione. By the time we reached the other side of the Largo Cairoli, Bernardo swore and changed his mind.

"Shortcut!" he exclaimed, before swerving between two buildings and bumping down a set of steps into a narrow alley. The *motorino's* voice compressed into a whining rumble.

All we need now is to run into someone's clothesline, I thought madly. *And have a dog chase us.*

Instead, we had to weave between traffic bollards. I leaned against Bernardo, feeling like an expert, even—like a girlfriend.

We rounded a corner and nearly ran into a couple. Steering around them, Bernardo called *"mi dispiace"* over his shoulder before we shot forward again, bouncing up another set of steps, just in time to see the Mercedes gunning across the Via Mercato and into the Via Brera. We saw Giuliano and Emilio ripping past, Emilio whooping with delight or adrenaline or both, his hair blowing back, one arm waving wildly. For a split second, I saw Francesco in him, gangly and happy.

Bernardo whooped back, his rib cage expanding against my arms in a most satisfying way. I wanted to shout, too, but I didn't want to deafen my driver. We curved out in a mad joyful arc, turning into the Via Madonnina.

"He must be going toward your shop," announced Bernardo.

He was right. We had to slow down in the Via Fiori Chiari, but we were still in time to see the Mercedes slam to a stop in front of the candle shop, its owner leaping out to pound on our door, screaming, "Bring him back, bring him back, you cowards, you bastards!"

Giuliano and Emilio pulled to a stop ahead of us.

I had never seen anyone like this. Signore Strozzi had begun battering his hands against the doorframe, not seeming to care about the pain.

"Tranquillo," counseled Giuliano, approaching him.

Bernardo brought his *motorino* to a stop, but caught my sleeve when I started to climb off.

"Wait," he whispered. "That man is dangerous."

I was happy to wait on the back of the *motorino*, touched by his concern. How did other demon catchers focus on their work when they were in love?

Signore Strozzi was spitting and foaming at the mouth. My eye was drawn to the doorframe, where his hands were leaving smears of blood. I felt my stomach turn.

Giuliano came to stand beside him, facing the door to our shop. Francesco had pulled up beside us, on the back of a *motorino* driven by Dottore Komnenos, of all people.

The Greek, I said to myself, comprehending.

"Don't open the door, don't open the door," chanted Francesco under his breath as he alighted. I frowned, wondering where Anna Maria and Uncle Matteo were, before I remembered they would have stayed behind at the Strozzi apartment.

Signore Strozzi had stopped screaming and was looking straight at Nonno.

"You have destroyed me," he told Giuliano, in a voice wholly his own, a voice of such utter despair that it brought tears to my eyes.

Nonno held out a hand to Signore Strozzi.

"There is hope yet," he said. "Come inside."

With that, he unlocked the door.

Signore Strozzi stared at him, then walked into the shop. The rest of us unfroze from where we were standing and followed the two of them. As I started forward, Bernardo beside me, I saw his father reach out and take his arm. They did not enter the shop.

"I tell you, you have destroyed me," Signore Strozzi was repeating as we entered.

Once inside, I could feel clearly that the exorcism really had worked; there was no sign of the hump-headed demon with the crawling hands, no feel of him, no smell of stagnant water or corpse-stink. The few candles that were still lit shuddered with our movements and nothing else. Emilio, Francesco, and Dottore Komnenos came in behind me.

Giuliano turned on the lamp.

I don't think even he guessed what would happen next.

"I cannot bear you to look at me," Signore Strozzi said calmly. And, reaching under the lampshade, he crushed the burning bulb in his bare hand.

TEN

A Man's Business

I screamed. I know I wasn't the only one. Signore Strozzi didn't even seem to notice the smell of singed flesh, or the pain, or the blood that dripped from his fist.

I heard Emilio gasp. We stood in the dark, and I half expected to hear and feel as I had inside the Second House.

"You have destroyed me. You have destroyed my family," Signore Strozzi said, his voice even. Then, softly, "Don't you understand? He was the root. Without him, I'm nothing. Our money will flow away like water, and no more will come in. I will lose my wife, my son, my home, my car, my clothes. Everything. Don't you understand? Everything! He was the root, the source, and you pulled him up, like a weed! You damned Della Torre fools!" he finished, his voice breaking at last.

The sky was brightening, but the only real light came from the handful of candles. All I could see were Signore Strozzi's shuddering shoulders, against the darkness of the shop, and the faint light shining on Giuliano's face. I could see his eyes calculating rapidly, watching Signore Strozzi heave and rock, but he made no answer. He simply stood and listened and watched.

A light bloomed out of the corner of my eye. Francesco was lighting more candles. I saw Emilio's bright head tilt toward him in thanks.

I realized someone was moving his hands beside me, blurred in the dim light. He was weaving his hands back and forth, pinching his fingers together as if tying knots, then parting his hands, running his fingers along invisible lines. I turned my head to see Dottore Komnenos. His eyes were fixed on Signore Strozzi, but he must have noticed me out of the corner of his eye, because he whispered impatiently, "Don't look at what I'm doing. It makes it fall apart."

I turned my head away quickly, embarrassed, realizing that no one else was looking either. I tried to focus on Signore Strozzi, who was now staring Nonno full in the face. I could see his eyes, fixed and calm, looking straight back into those of the banker, could feel the tension rising in the room. My own nerves were tingling wildly.

Yet I also felt my mind opening outward, taking in the

room and everyone in it, even, out of the corner of my eye, the continuing movement of Dottore Komnenos's hands. I couldn't tell what was sparkling between his fingers. Was it really a net, with a pearl at every knot? I could feel, now, that my consciousness of what he was doing was indeed interfering, so I turned my head again, and glanced toward the shelves on the wall beside the door. The candle that had gone out the night Tommaso Strozzi had visited us sat dark and dormant. Francesco hadn't started on that shelf yet.

I found myself expecting to see the candle burst into flame. Something was straining, struggling in the air; I smelled the faintest whiff of stagnant water. Yet I knew no demon could enter here without being invited by a member of my family.

Signore Strozzi leaped at Giuliano.

Everyone cried out at once, then Emilio and Francesco caught the banker in their arms; by the dim candlelight, I could see his bloody hands waving.

Dottore Komnenos hadn't moved. He kept weaving his hands, back and forth. Now I really could see the pearls, floating in the darkness.

Giuliano hadn't moved, either. He stood firm, but his shoulders were tight.

"Nearly done, Augusto?" he asked.

"Nearly," the Greek replied evenly. "Now," he added. "Hold him!" he said to Emilio and Francesco as they restrained Signore Strozzi.

Dottore Komnenos opened his hands outward and flung the net of pearl knots over Signore Strozzi. I thought I saw pearls passing through the arms and hands of Francesco and Emilio. Dottore Komnenos yanked back on a set of strings only he could see, pulling tight.

Signore Strozzi sank to his knees. I saw the pearls emerge again, this time with something invisible struggling inside them, that fought and shook as the net trembled and shivered. Dottore Komnenos pulled it tight, the pearls closing together until they were no more than an inch apart, still jerking and shuddering to the movements of their captive. I expected to smell rot and stagnation again, but I didn't. What was this, if it wasn't the demon? The Greek turned and headed for the door.

"O Dio, O Dio," sobbed Signore Strozzi. "É partito, partito. It's gone, gone."

This was the way I got to see a man go completely mad for the first time. In the movies, people shudder and laugh maniacally when they lose it. But Signore Strozzi just stopped being there. He began to repeat that one word, *partito*, over and over to himself. *"Par-ti-to. Par-ti-to."* He reminded me of one of the homeless people that wandered around downtown in Center Plains. He even looked like they did, like he was staring into a world that had nothing to do with this one or the next.

I felt my eyes fill with tears. Signore Strozzi bowed his head, clasping his hands, and I could see the bruises and blood on them. Outside, daylight had begun to creep into the Via Fiori Oscuri.

Dottore Komnenos returned, and Giuliano asked him a question with his eyes.

"It worked," Dottore Komnenos said. "Whether it did any good, I do not know."

Signore Strozzi didn't seem to hear him. He knelt on the floor, chanting his word.

"Should I call the Ospedale San Giuseppe?" suggested Emilio.

"I suppose you had better," Giuliano said, looking down at the man in front of him.

That's when I saw how Nonno's shoulders hunched, how he held his fists tight at his sides. He was furious, but why?

Francesco and Emilio stayed by Signore Strozzi. I watched in a daze as Emilio dialed the mental hospital. Dottore Komnenos took my arm and said, "You know you are shaking? Perhaps we should step outside."

I followed him obediently. Signore Tedesco was sitting on his *motorino*, lighting a cigarette. It dawned on me that we hadn't been inside for very long. Bernardo looked at us as we approached.

"Can Mia sit with you a moment, gentlemen?" asked Dottore Komnenos.

Bernardo started toward me, asking, "Are you all right?"

"I'm fine," I said, shuddering. "I just need to sit."

He patted the seat of the *motorino*, and I accepted the invitation, sinking down. I felt it rock on its kickstand and adjusted my weight.

"I need to go back in," Dottore Komnenos told us. "Can you look after her?"

Both men nodded. Signore Tedesco smiled at me, showing crooked teeth.

"Cigarette?" he offered.

"She doesn't smoke," said his son.

"I could use one, though," I said. "If I did."

Rinaldo Tedesco chuckled. "Well, take a puff of mine, then."

I did. I'm not a fan of the smoky taste, and I'm just barely old enough to remember the last restaurants in our town that had smoking sections, but somehow it made me feel better. I took a second puff and wheezed. Handing it back to Signore Tedesco, I decided I wouldn't be making a habit of it.

Time passed like the rising sun, pouring slowly down the sides of the buildings. Sebastiano, one of the guys from the Bar Brera, came down from the Via Pontaccio, and stopped in front of the café door, feeling for his keys. Presently, we heard the rhythmic wail of a siren and saw the flashing lights reflected in the windows along the Via Borgonuovo.

The ambulance pulled up in front of our shop, and Emilio stepped out to meet it. They all disappeared inside. Eventually, Giuliano and Emilio emerged with the head EMT, heads bowed together.

"What's going on, I wonder?" asked Signore Tedesco. He looked at me. "Do you know?"

"I don't," I said. "Shouldn't they be taking him away?"

"Yes," he said. "I think so. But perhaps there is no one here who can sign papers for his admission to the mental ward."

Both Bernardo and I looked at him, enlightened.

We waited in the cold, Bernardo offering me his seat on his *motorino* again. I had to make myself stop thinking about how much nicer and warmer it would be if I had Bernardo's arms wrapped around me.

"Can't you go in?" Signore Tedesco asked.

"Oh," I said. "Are you waiting so you can go?"

"No," he said. "I want to see this to the end."

"Me, too," I said.

He nodded. "But when the café opens I think I'm going to send Bernardo for something hot to drink," he added with a grin.

Emilio was standing off to the side now, on his cell phone. We heard a shout from inside the shop, and then the EMTs were wrestling Signore Strozzi through the door and into the street. He struggled, then seemed to lose heart again, and fell back onto his knees on the cobblestones. I could see his bloody hands trailing the bandages they had tried to put on him, and the smears where he had pressed his hands to his face. He began to mumble to himself again, and the head EMT gestured to him and said something to Giuliano, as if this clinched the argument. Dottore

Komnenos and Francesco emerged from the shop, and I saw them go over to Emilio and Giuliano. Then they came to us.

"Francesco is taking me home," Dottore Komnenos said to us. "I can't do anything more here."

"It was amazing to watch you," I said. "I mean, not watch you."

His solemn face was transformed by a broad smile.

"Thank you," he said. "I love what I do." He touched his brow in a salute to the Tedeschi. "Good evening, gentlemen, and thank you, as always."

Signore Tedesco touched the butt of his cigarette to his forehead in the same gesture and smiled. "You're welcome. Going all the way back to Venice tonight?"

"No, I have a place here," said Dottore Komnenos. "That would be a long way for Francesco on a *motorino,*" he added, grinning. Then he looked from me to the banker kneeling on the ground.

"That's the part of the job I don't like," he said. "Well, nice to see you again, Cousin Mia, regardless of the circumstances. *Buona notte o buon giorno, non lo so.* Good-night or good morning, I don't know."

"Nice to see you again, too," I said. *"Arrivederci."*

He chuckled, then kissed my cheek and went away with Francesco. We waited some more, while the EMTs finished binding Signore Strozzi's hands. The head EMT was getting frustrated with Nonno.

"You look cold," Bernardo said to me.

"I am," I said. "Aren't you?"

He smiled. "A little. But not cold enough not to be a gentleman," he said, and shrugged off his jacket. He put it around my shoulders, enveloping me in the smell of warm leather and cologne. My face felt incredibly hot all of a sudden. I wanted to joke that his coat had warmed me up quickly, but I felt too shy to say anything except, *"Gr-grazie."*

"Niente," Bernardo replied. His father smiled slightly and took another drag of his cigarette.

A BMW rumbled over the paving toward us and pulled up, blocking an entrance to the Pinacoteca di Brera. Tommaso Strozzi got out and opened the door for his mother.

I had never seen her look so tired. She didn't seem to notice any of us, her gaze fastened on her kneeling husband. Emilio came forward to meet her, opening his mouth, but she held up a hand.

"Do not speak to me," she told him. The diamonds in her ears flashed.

She walked over to Signore Strozzi, her son trailing after her. She looked down, and her husband raised his head. He seemed to have trouble focusing on her.

"Tell me what you have done," she said. "Tell me!"

He began to laugh. Tommaso clutched her arm and said, "Mamma, no, not in front of all of these people."

She flung her arm up, freeing herself from him.

"Don't touch me, Tommaso!" she snarled. "Did you know? *Did you?* What has been going on?"

"Mamma, this is a man's business," he said, his thick neck swelling, his shoulders tightening.

I didn't need to see the men around me shudder to know Tommaso had gone too far. Signora Strozzi shot him a freezing look.

"Then I am not surprised that it has been completely screwed up," she said.

I heard someone gasp and someone else chuckle.

Tommaso dropped his head. Signora Strozzi turned from him abruptly and knelt beside her husband. She put a hand out to his shoulder. Signore Strozzi stared at the cobblestones, muttering to himself. She leaned in, whispering in his ear. He lifted his head, listening, and then whispered back. As she listened to him, I saw that there were tears streaming down her face, catching the light from the pale sky. I shifted my feet and shivered. Tommaso Strozzi had gone back to lean on the hood of his BMW. I actually saw him check his jacket before he did, in case he was going to crease it, I guess.

Signora Strozzi took her husband's head in her hands, and kissed him fiercely, like she would have bitten him instead if she could. Then she stood up and faced the head EMT.

"We will speak apart from these people," she said. He nodded and followed her off to one side.

I watched her sign some papers. At a signal from the head

EMT, a man went into the ambulance and returned with a straitjacket. Signore Strozzi shouted once, then let himself be wrapped in it. They guided him into the ambulance. He did not look back toward his wife or his son. Tommaso put his face in his hands. The ambulance put on one warning light, but kept the siren silent, and pulled up the street. In the flickering blue light, I saw Signora Strozzi walk over to her son and begin slapping his face, over and over, screaming words I didn't know yet. He let her, half lifting his hands to protect his face, then dropping them again.

Giuliano gripped Emilio's shoulder like a signal. His grandson nodded and hurried to Signora Strozzi, taking her arm, speaking in his voice that could persuade a woman to do anything. She began to sob, shuddering. Tommaso put his hands on the car and stared at the wall, his face wet.

Emilio's words carried, now: "Come inside. You need a drink, something to restore you. Then I will drive you both home."

Signora Strozzi drew herself up, taking a shaking breath. She shuddered once more, then stopped, touching her eyes with the corner of a handkerchief. I saw the corner of the fabric flutter, bright against the dark street.

"Thank you, but we will go now," said Signora Strozzi. "I am well enough to drive."

Tommaso raised his head as if he was going to speak, but thought better of it. Emilio, too, seemed to know that he shouldn't argue.

"We will call you in the afternoon. Try to get some rest," Emilio said.

As they drove away, Giuliano came up to Emilio, scanning his grandson's face. He said to Emilio, "We can talk it over after we *all* get some rest."

Emilio said, *"Sì,"* without taking his eyes from the BMW turning into the Via Brera. Suddenly, he said, "Nonno, I don't like this. I think we should follow them."

Giuliano didn't question him. He said only, "Okay. You drive. Mia, stay here. Go to bed. *Buona notte,* Signore Tedesco, Bernardo. You know how grateful I am to you. Would you see Mia safely inside?"

It was only about twenty steps to our shop door, but for once I didn't mind Nonno acting medieval. As Emilio and Giuliano hurried to Emilio's *motorino,* Rinaldo Tedesco said, "Your mother will be worrying. I'll go home to her. Don't be too long behind me." He clouted his son's shoulder. *"Buona notte,* Mia. You are a brave young woman."

"Thank you," I said. *"Buona notte,* Signore Tedesco, and thank you, too."

Then they were all gone, except for Bernardo. He walked me into the shop, and I stood still, waiting to calm down the way I did after an exorcism, but my heart kept racing. I didn't feel wiped out, even though it had been a very long night. I could hear my breathing, and the snap of an impurity in the wick of one of the candles.

It was warmer inside. I reluctantly drew off his jacket and handed it to him.

"Thanks," I said.

"No problem," he said, looking at me as he reached out for it. The antique shop clock chimed seven times.

"*Santa Maria,* is it that late . . . that early?" I said.

I remembered the stab of envy I'd felt when his friends called out to him in the street. "Still time for you to go to Plastic," I found myself saying.

He smiled, shrugging on his jacket. "It's closed by now. You have any energy for a club, yourself?"

I lowered my eyes, afraid they'd give me away. "No . . ." I began, but he'd crossed the room to stand very close to me. I could smell him again, like I had on the *motorino*: the leather of his jacket, the warm scent of his skin, and just a tad too much cologne, though he didn't smell like he'd showered in it, like so many guys I'd passed in the Piazza del Duomo.

"Tired," he said, touching my shoulder.

"No . . ." I tried again. My heart kept pounding. "Thank you for the ride," I managed, and smiled at him.

"It was a pleasure," he said simply, and leaned down and kissed me.

I think if he'd taken his time I'd have found a way to freak out and avoid it, so thank goodness he didn't. He just put his lips to mine and held my jaw, stroking it with one finger, so that my whole body shivered. His mouth was so warm and smooth, and he kept his lips together, touching mine lightly, like a question I had no idea how to answer. I didn't move, but I shut my eyes. He drew back.

"You liked that," he said, making it half a question, half a truth.

I didn't know what to do, yet I couldn't stand to have him step away, so I just pushed my face into his shoulder and mumbled randomly. Not smooth, I'm afraid. At least from there I could hear the laugh in his chest, feel the muscles pull and ripple as he put both arms around me.

"Come back here," he whispered. "It's okay."

He let go of me with one arm, slipping his fingers gently into the hollow behind my jaw, coaxing my face slowly out of his shirtfront, tipping my head upward. He held me carefully, but I could feel him shaking. I didn't know the language he was trying to speak to me, badly as I wanted to learn it.

I finally found myself able to look up at him. Despite the dark circles under his eyes, he still looked more beautiful to me than any man living, his pale blue eyes gazing down at me, his broad mouth curving. Even his breath seemed sweet, never mind the faint whiff of sage from his dinner.

He smiled down at me.

"Why," I said, and started to hide my face again.

"Why what?" he asked, keeping his hand under my jaw.

"Why are you . . . why are you shaking?" I finished in a burst of embarrassment.

He threw his head back and I though he was going to shout

with laughter, which could have been heard upstairs; instead, he shook silently, and then smiled down at me again.

"Why are you so scared, *cara*?" He paused, then answered his own question. "This is all new to you, maybe?"

I fastened my eyes on the hollow of his throat. I think I said, *Yes, but not all of it.*

"What?" he whispered, bringing his face down to mine. "Not all of it."

He lowered his hand from my face, standing back, and asked quite seriously, "Mia, do you like me?"

I couldn't look him in the eye anymore. My face felt hot. All I could do was nod yes.

"Good," he said. "I like you. I liked you from the beginning. But there is no hurry, I think? If you don't like—"

I surprised both of us by reaching for him, putting my arms around his neck, and bringing my face close to his. Still, somehow, I couldn't kiss him back. He turned his head and took care of that, his arms back around me, his lips parting; nothing was enough. I pressed myself against him even though it felt like I was giving myself electric shocks.

We both heard the returning *motorino* at the same time. I felt him tighten his arms just as I tightened mine, before we jumped apart, staring at each other.

"I can call you?" he whispered.

"Yes, please," I said. He nodded and smiled. I could see the glint of his eyes in the dark.

Nonno came into the shop. I'd never been less glad to see

him, which made me feel horribly ungrateful, especially when he looked so tired.

"Still here?" he asked. "Ah, looking after Mia. Thank you, Bernardo."

"Now you're here I'll go. She'll be okay, sir," Bernardo said. "She should go to bed, though," he added, giving me a mischievous flick of his light eyes.

"We all should," said Giuliano. "What a night! They made it safely home, but what went on after, I don't know," he added. "Go carefully, Bernardo. And thank you."

"*Niente, signore,*" said Bernardo. "It was nothing, sir."

"Thank you for the ride, Bernardo," I said, then remembered I'd already told him that.

"It was a pleasure," he repeated, grinning, and slipped out the door, the candle flames bending and fluttering in his wake.

Suddenly, I'd never been so afraid of dying, of losing to the demon. There had never been so much to leave behind.

ELEVEN

The Price

Later that morning, I woke up with absolutely no memory of the fact that I'd been kissed, more than once, the night before. Then I sat up, and the whole night came back to me. I could hear Nonna Laura and Nonno Giuliano talking in the kitchen, and I wondered if they would guess, if I would look different or something. I hugged the memory to myself. Finally, the smell of Nonna's coffee drew me out.

When I came into the kitchen, she and Giuliano were sitting at the table, nursing their *caffè latte*. They both smiled at me and we all said *buon giorno* before she stood up, already knocking the used espresso out of the coffeemaker as she asked me, "Coffee?"

"Yes, please," I said, sitting down.

"You slept well?" asked Nonno.

"Yes, but not long enough," I said.

Giuliano nodded. "Never enough after an exorcism, and you went to bed after seven. Take a nap after lunch," he recommended. "And remember to take your walk. And do your meditations."

"Yes, Nonno," I said automatically, my eyes on the espresso maker. But then I woke up some and looked at him closely.

"Nonno, have you slept yourself yet?"

"Me? No. I was at the hospital."

"How did it go?"

"Not well. They are transferring him to a locked ward."

"And Signora Strozzi? Signore Tommaso?"

Over his head, I saw Nonna nod to herself as she made more espresso.

"We will check on them this afternoon, but they arrived at the hospital when I was there; they could not sleep, of course. You caught that exchange between them in the street? I think Signore Strozzi must have told Tommaso, though not his wife, that the family is beholden to the Left-Hand Land. I wonder how much detail he went into."

"I couldn't have told that from the way Tommaso behaved when he first came to us," I said. "Did you guess?" I asked.

"No," said Nonno. He seemed put out. "I truly thought it was a recent problem, not something so deep-rooted. I only began to figure that out when we heard the portraits, but by then, it was too late. What is troubling me is that I saw nothing about the *famiglia* Strozzi in the notes, nothing in the history books to suggest that they were dependent on a demon for their wealth. Nothing that seemed out of place in the history of a banking family."

"And we know how banking families always come by their fortunes through honest hard work," Nonna said sarcastically. "*'A man's business!'*" Behind her, the coffee shower began to hiss and gurgle. Nonno grinned at me. "Laura was not any more impressed by Tommaso's words than his mother was," he said.

I smiled back, thinking about what it would mean if all the banks involved in the recession a few years ago had been run by possessed people. Maybe this kind of demon was a lot more common than we knew.

Giuliano lifted a hand and turned to look up at her.

"But human beings don't need to be ridden by a demon in order to cheat, lie, and steal," he pointed out. "We do it all on our own."

"So you don't think this is all that common?" I asked.

Nonno shook his head. "I doubt it. After a while, a family can get tired of the price. There is always a price."

Nonna turned to look at him over her shoulder while she mixed my coffee and milk in a bowl. "And the price for Signore Strozzi?" she asked.

"He was slowly losing his mind," said Nonno. "I spoke to Tommaso when they arrived at the Ospedale San Giuseppe. He said that his father had mentioned how the men of the family were often short-lived. I could see Tommaso trying to decide how much to tell me."

"And he decided . . . ?" asked Nonna.

"Not to say much. He has a lot to think about. At least he and his mother did not have to be told what was going on; they sent for us, after all.

"Signora Strozzi said to me, 'I will thank you for saving my husband when you have saved him.' And Tommaso looked at her and said, 'Mama, can't you see that he is free of it? It isn't there anymore.' She told him, 'Free of it, yes. But you can see that he is not free.'

"She looked furious and heartbroken, just as she did this morning. I think there is a great deal her husband didn't tell her, and that was fine, while it worked. I think she didn't mind until now.

"Before I left, I caught Tommaso alone and asked him, 'If I could bring it back, would you want that?' "

Nonna sat down again. I looked at my coffee and made it ripple back and forth across the bowl.

"And what did he say?" asked Nonna.

"Nothing," said Nonno.

"Ah," she said. After a moment, she added, "As long as I have stood at that stove," nodding toward the big gas range behind Giuliano, "hearing about these cases, I have never stopped feeling total amazement at the stupidity of human beings."

She met her husband's eye, and I saw an entire conversation

pass between them in a look. I tried to picture the moment when, a year and a day after his wedding, the young Giuliano Della Torre had told his wife what his true profession was. Had she understood what he was telling her, what it meant?

Because my grandfather had tried to make sure his descendants would never be involved in the family profession, my father had never had to have this conversation with my mother. I decided that someday I would ask Nonna about what it had felt like when she found out she had married into a world of such danger and sorrow.

Or maybe I wouldn't. She had, after all, lost a son to the family profession. Maybe she hadn't known, not really, how sad our job could be, until that happened. *A family can get tired of the price.*

I thought of Signora Strozzi, never quite understanding the price of what her husband did, until now.

I looked up at them.

"How did it go, after all?" Nonna asked her husband. "The exorcism itself."

Again, as on the day after the *San Valentino* exorcism, I thought I could hear another question behind her words, and I couldn't tell what it was.

"It went well as can be," Nonno said. "With something like that, you have even less of an idea going into it than you usually do."

He wasn't looking at her as he said this. He took another sip of coffee.

"Emilio and Anna Maria worked well together, Francesco caught the demon in the candle and didn't drop it"—she smiled—"and Mia was a good observer, noticing things we would not have seen otherwise. And she didn't get attacked, either."

"I don't think I was in a lot of danger. More than usual, I mean," I put in.

"I thought you did well when he offered us a deal. The Strozzi demon offered us help with Mia's demon," Giuliano explained to Nonna. "I am proud of her for not taking the bait."

I sat up. "Was that really all it was, bait?" I asked.

His eyes crinkled at the corners, and his mouth lifted in the one-cornered smile I'd seen so often on Emilio's face.

"I do not know. Sometimes it is just bait, sometimes it isn't," he admitted. "But as we saw last night, it is wise not to make deals with demons. You never know what price they will exact." He met my eyes. "And you can be sure that you will not escape without paying, one way or another. I think you did well," Nonno added more lightly. "Do you feel you learned a lot?"

"I am still trying to make sense of it," I said. "But yes, it was like a big puzzle. Scary, but intriguing." I went on, "The clues we had weren't that much help, because we just had to pull the demon out, like we were uprooting a big tree."

"Yes," said Giuliano. "And we had no idea that we were

uprooting the source of the family's wealth."

"If that's true," Nonna said. "Do you think maybe it's just something they believed in?"

"Good question," said Nonno.

"Perhaps they just believed it, and it gave them a reason to do all the bad things you can do in that profession. A justification. What if *they* really are the source of their own wealth and don't owe it to some monster from the other world?" Nonna Laura asked.

I blinked. I hadn't ever heard her put out her opinions like this. Giuliano frowned, but I couldn't tell if he was offended.

"I can't say," he said. "We will have to wait and see. But I had not thought of that. My brilliant wife," he added with a grin.

Nonna shrugged.

"If you're married to this, you pick up a few things over the years," she said.

Finishing my coffee, I thought more about the offer the demon had made. Then I realized that I had forgotten another detail about last night. Nonno looked so tired, I wasn't sure I should tell him. I felt too worried to wait, however.

"There was something else that happened," I said. "While we were in the Second House."

Nonno and Nonna sat, expectant.

"I could feel my demon. We touched . . . we touched minds, just for a moment. He kept far away, because of my bell, and the family. But we seemed to be examining each other."

"Ah," Giuliano said, raising his eyebrows. Nonna looked at me intently.

"I don't know exactly what I learned. It just felt like, *there you are*. I thought he said that, or I did. But I was afraid, too, to enter," I added, feeling ashamed.

Nonno nodded. "Emilio told me. Yet you went in."

"With his help."

"Yet you went in," repeated Giuliano.

I accepted this. "Yes. And I don't know what it was like for everyone else, but it didn't feel like it did when I was possessed. It felt stuffy and strange, but not nauseating, and I didn't have the same . . . powers. And I was there by choice this time."

I had not understood, until the moment I told them, how entering the Second House had changed the fear inside me, the terrifying memories of possession, into something else.

I couldn't read the expression in Nonno's eyes. He seemed to be appraising this new knowledge, trying to put it together with what he knew. I thought of how it had felt, that moment of contact with the demon, over distance. I thought I had felt him wanting answers, too—what are you doing here? How can you come into my world?

"Can you feel him now?" asked Giuliano.

I shook my head.

"Did he remain throughout the exorcism?"

"No, it was very brief, and then he was gone; he . . . he

doesn't like not being able to get close to me," I said, unsettled by my knowledge.

Nonno took a deep breath and leaned back in his chair.

"We must think about this. Another piece of the puzzle . . . keep looking for that poem, Mia. I will bother Fernando and the crabby poet again," he finished. Nonna gave me another grave look and then stood up, starting to clear the dishes. Nonno and I rose together. Nonna looked at her husband and said, "Go to bed," with a slight smile on her lips. "Overworking idiot."

He smiled back, and said, "Not too dumb to take your advice."

I picked up a dishtowel and began to dry, still thinking. Nonna seemed wrapped up in her own thoughts, too.

I wondered what the Strozzi demon would have demanded in exchange for helping us with my demon. The price probably would have been too high—though if I was going to die anyway, maybe it would have been worth it. What sacrifices would I make to stop my demon? What sacrifices would I make for my family?

I felt my gut turn over when I thought about dying. I wanted to live so badly, now that dying would mean never kissing Bernardo again.

Of course, he might not call. But he had to, didn't he? I had followed Signora Gianna's advice, and he had chased me. Not the other way round. He had asked if he could call. He would call, right?

He didn't call. After finishing the dishes I went down into the shop and tried to focus on finding the poem. Later, after lunch, I succumbed to a long nap. When I woke, I found Nonno downstairs in the shop, reading the paper. When he saw me, he remembered the crabby poet. Then he phoned Fernando at the Biblioteca Ambrosiana. I heard the librarian's cheerful voice on the other end of the line.

"*Buon giorno,* Fernando. I'm doing fine, thanks. Listen, this poet, he's not talking to us. . . . I know." He laughed suddenly at something Fernando said. I raised my eyebrows and he said to me, "He says that the artistic temperament can happen to anyone. Yes, Mia's here," he said, turning back to the phone. "That's all very well, but most artists I've known are very professional; they have to eat. I've lived my life in the Brera district. Well, let's just call it a dead end. I'm wondering if you have other ideas?"

He listened, nodded, made a few notes, and said at last, "Thank you so much. I will let you know how our quest goes. We will stop in on you sometime soon. *Ciao.*"

I looked at him over my barricade of books.

"He's given me a few more names," Giuliano said. "But I think we are scraping the bottom of the barrel, at least when it comes to poets translated into Italian."

"Nonno," I said, struck by a sudden thought, "I understood someone—oh, I can't remember who—why can't I remember?" I pressed my lips together, thinking. "Anyway, I understood someone in the spirit world who spoke Italian, at least I think it was Italian, before I spoke Italian myself. Right when I arrived here. And I'm pretty sure the demon was speaking in Italian when he recited the poem to me at Peck; I remember the feel of the words. But what if he wasn't? What if he was speaking, say, ancient Greek, and I just understood him like I did the other spirit?"

Giuliano gazed at me intently. "You understood a spirit that spoke to you in Italian?" He asked. "You've mentioned something about another spirit before, haven't you. Why can't *I* remember . . . ?" He rubbed his forehead, then shook his head as if to clear it. "So you are saying you might have understood the demon no matter what language he was speaking, and you might have remembered it as Italian?"

"Maybe." I looked at him in despair. "It just makes it harder."

His eyes warmed. "Oh, *cara.* It's always hard. We must just keep going. And it's past time for us to enlist the rest of the family, don't you think?"

"Yes," I said.

"Very well then." Nonno indicated my wall of books with a flick of his finger. "Though it may yet be in one of those," he added.

"Not likely," I said. "I'm still reading about the Visconti and the Sforzas."

Giuliano smiled. "Our successors," he said. Neither he nor

any other Della Torre had ever mentioned to me that our family had once ruled Milan. I had found that out from the history books. "I can't say that they did a better job than we did, but then we didn't do much of a job. I think we were better off out of it," he said.

My phone buzzed with a text, and I jumped.

But it wasn't Bernardo. It was Emilio, asking, "How are you doing?"

I put my phone down, disappointed, then picked it up again to type back, "Okay. How are you?" After all, it wasn't Emilio's fault that he wasn't Bernardo.

Only then did it occur to me that as far as I knew Bernardo didn't even have my number. Would he ask someone for it? What if he didn't want to be bugged—which relative of mine could he ask who wouldn't tease him mercilessly?

I couldn't keep my mind on my books. I went up to see if Nonna needed help with anything, which she didn't, and ended up meditating in front of my Madonna. Even with months of practice, I still found it hard to calm down and stop listening for my phone.

I envied her. Whoever had carved her had done a great job capturing the mixture of sorrow and joy in her diminutive features. Her face was framed by the fall of her blue robe, with golden stars hidden in its wooden folds. *A holy face framed by the sky,* I thought, and for some reason, the words gave me a feeling of peace.

Here I am again, talking to you about a boy, I told the Madonna in my thoughts. I didn't want to take a chance on anyone hearing me, especially since Francesca would probably be home soon for a nap before dinner, as she seemed to do a lot these days. *But not a Satanist like last time,* I added. *At least I'm pretty sure not. His family has known ours for a long time. Signora Gianna says they are good people.*

I wanted to ask her a hundred questions. I wanted to Skype with my own mom, too, and pour out the story of how I got to know him and ask, "Do you think he will call?"—and get annoyed with her if she didn't say, "Yes." I wanted to tell Gina about him, his translucent skin and elegant bones and red-brown hair, his kind voice and clear eyes.

As I sat there, though, I realized I wasn't going to try to get in touch with Mom or Gina. I wasn't going to ask the Madonna any of the hundred questions I had. I shut my eyes and saw the golden light all around the Madonna, and felt my heart beating slowly and steadily. I thought of Bernardo again and knew that nobody, not a statue or a parent, would be able to give me the answers I was looking for; there was only one way to get them. The idea didn't cheer me, yet I felt calmer as I came down the stairs to the shop. Nonno was standing, his hands clasped behind him, examining the candles. He turned as I came in.

"Sometimes I just stare at them in order to think," Giuliano said, smiling. I smiled back, and sat down at the desk, pulling a book at random out of the pile and tugging my notebook toward me. He stood gazing into the candle flames for a while longer, then sat down at the table, making his own notes.

"Thank goodness for work," I said.

Nonno nodded. "It helps, doesn't it?" he said. "Studying, sweeping the floor, all of it. That wasn't a hint," he said, as I stood up and got the broom. "We had to go over it pretty well last night. Because of the glass."

I'd almost forgotten. I began to sweep anyway. When I got near the door, I opened it, making myself look at the door-frame. I felt a rush of gratitude to whoever had cleaned up the blood. I came back in and shut the door.

"Has anyone checked? How is he?" I asked, letting the regular movements and the sound of the broom soothe me.

"Emilio. Bad," Nonno said, and frowned, looking out the window.

"One thing gets me," I said.

"And that is?"

"How were we supposed to know? I mean, were we supposed to just leave the demon hanging around, driving him crazy?"

"Do you know, I think I know the answer to that, and then I think of him in a locked ward, and wonder if I know after all."

"So he, and his family, chose madness and wealth over sanity and, perhaps, poverty? That's just dumb," I said. "My mom and dad have never had much money, and maybe they aren't happy all the time, but Dad doesn't go around thinking his hands are rotting off."

"Our family hasn't been rich for centuries. If we were, we would lose more than the brass plate by the door, Mia. We would lose much of our identity . . . if not all of it."

"Everybody's got to figure out who they are on their own," I said, feeling wise. "You can't depend on an identity like that!"

"You and I may know that, yes. Yet do we know the real cost, to one who has always had everything?"

I couldn't be sure that I did. "Have you had a chance to work out where the demon came from?" I asked. "Has he always been in the Strozzi family?"

"I have not. I have just been making my notes, in as much detail as I can, and adding a card for the Strozzi family to the catalog, because now we must track the family. I do not know if they have some way of calling the demon back."

I blinked.

"We have a catalog?"

"Yes. I have been meaning to show you. One thing at a time, though," Nonno said.

We went into the back office, where he unlocked a cupboard that seemed to blend into the wall. Only a small brass keyhole gave it away. Inside was a nine-drawer card file, made of light wood with black metal fittings, and faded cards in the label slots in front, in alphabetical order. He drew open R-S-T, and reached into the back for a fresh index card.

"A new invention, really. My father had it made. We are still compiling it. Now, of course, Emilio wants to go onto the computer and have a searchable database. I say, 'What if one day you can't turn it on?' We can't afford to do anything that won't work for centuries. I notice that Nonna and I keep having to buy a new computer, more than once in a decade even!"

I tried not to smile. Even my parents know that you need to replace your computer about every three years, and they took a geologic age to get cell phones.

He showed me how to fill out a card for the Strozzi family, with brief details of the case and who participated in the ritual. He showed me the family tree that he had begun that morning, not having found one for the Strozzi among our family's notes, and demonstrated how to figure out the code for the generation and branch of the family tree that Signore Strozzi belonged to, so that later, we could refer back to it. He reminded me to note the address of their apartment, and to include as many details as I could about that location, since years from now our family might attend another case in the same area or even, he feared, the same apartment, since this was a demon of place as well as of family. He showed me how to make a second card for the address. Finally, he wrote in his own neat handwriting the name and number of the notebook where an account of the exorcism could be found. "Leave room for more names and numbers, because you will be writing your own, and so will the others," he said. I read what he had written: *Giuliano Della Torre, Taccuino numero 154.*

Nonno was on his 154th notebook. I was on my first.

That thought stayed with me as I read history, trimmed wicks, dusted shelves, and turned the pages of notebooks while wearing the white cotton Mickey Mouse gloves.

In the evening, Nonno came back from errands and brought out a bottle of wine. It was unlabeled, from friends outside of Genoa. He set out three glasses and poured slowly; I didn't have to look at the clock to know when the shop door would jingle and Emilio would come in, smelling of pinesap, wishing us a good evening.

"How was the rest of your day? Still recovering all right?" he asked me, taking a glass from his grandfather and settling into a chair.

"Yes, thank you. I have a lot of questions, but I don't know where to start. And seeing Signore Strozzi like that . . ."

"Yes," Emilio nodded. "*Par-ti-to.* Gone."

"Yes," Nonno agreed.

They shared a look. Giuliano pushed himself up out of his chair and went upstairs, to consult with Nonna about the plan for dinner.

"It's not often a case goes wrong for my grandfather," Emilio said.

"I was wondering about that," I said. "I mean, we succeeded in getting rid of the demon, right? So why is everyone so dissatisfied? I know why I am, but is it the same reason?"

"Because Signore Strozzi isn't better?"

"Yes."

"Yes. We don't come into people's lives to make them worse. So yes, I think we are all disappointed."

"But surely, his life is better without the demon?" I asked.

"Do you think he thinks so?" countered Emilio.

"What did you think of how his wife and son took it? Did they have anything more to say?"

Emilio compressed his lips and looked out the shopwindow, looking more like his grandfather than usual.

"They talked about suing when I saw them this afternoon. They wanted results, they said, not a locked ward. Because it may be permanent, you know. He may never recover. It's not been a full day, but he looked very, very bad, Mia. I don't hold out much hope. And, of course, they need him, not just because he is her husband, his father. They need him for the money, I think. The money the demon was bringing in."

"So he wasn't good at his job on his own?"

"It seems not."

"That is so bizarre." After a moment, I asked, "And how would they sue? What would they say?"

Emilio gave me a grim smile. "That gets tricky, doesn't it?"

I nodded, smiling grimly back.

The shop bells jingled, and we both looked up.

Bernardo stood on the threshold. He seemed taller than I remembered, and his eyes crinkled at the corners when he looked at me.

"Come in," said Emilio, since I didn't seem able to speak.

TWELVE

The Story of the
Soup Bone

For a split second, I felt nothing. Then I felt my heart jump up from the table and start dancing. But the rest of me sat perfectly still.

"*Ciao,*" he said. "How is everyone today? I came to check on you."

"I didn't have a chance to thank you last night," said Emilio. "Good job."

"*Niente.* But how are you doing?" He was looking at me when he repeated the question.

"Fine, fine," Emilio said easily.

"Me, too," I said, wishing my voice didn't creak with longing and embarrassment.

"I'll go get a glass for you," Emilio told Bernardo.

"No, I can't stay, I'm on my way to dinner," Bernardo replied, and my heart did actually sink in my chest.

"I really came to check on Mia, and to ask you, Mia, if you could ask your *nonno* and *nonna* if it is okay if I take you out to dinner some night this week? If you would like to go, that is," he added, and he actually seemed shy about it.

Emilio was grinning. "Should I be here?" he asked.

"Shut up," advised Bernardo, smiling. "If I were some kind of coward, I would have waited until you weren't around."

Emilio shrugged, accepting this.

Bernardo looked at me. "Mia?"

"Yes!" I gasped, then decided I sounded way overeager. Never mind, it was too late. He smiled warmly at me.

"Good," he said. He pulled out his phone. "Let me text you so that you have my number." He looked up, chuckling. "I said I'd call you, but I couldn't . . ." I smiled back and gave him my number. "Call and tell me their answer," he said. "And don't forget to tell me what kind of food you like, when you call back."

"Okay," I said.

"Good," he said.

Then he was gone, and I was left facing my cousin's enormous grin.

"Excellent," he said. "Now you can stop stripping screws, and he can stop asking me about you."

"We're not building anything right now," I said absently. His words settled in my brain. "Wait. What do you mean, asking about me?"

Emilio started laughing like an obnoxious boy.

"Really?" I persisted.

"Oh, yes! Asking, asking. How old are you? How long have you been here, how well do I know you? Do you have a boyfriend at home? Does he have a chance? On and on and on."

He caught himself. "I shouldn't be informing on him," he added, "but I couldn't help it. Now you know."

He was still laughing as I went up the stairs two at a time to find Nonno and Nonna.

"Giuliano is on the phone," Nonna told me.

"Oh." I thought maybe if I asked her alone, she would say no. She seemed crabby.

"He'll be off in a minute. Do you have guests downstairs? I heard Emilio laughing."

"No, it's only the two of us."

"Go get him. I need you two to help with dinner."

When I hesitated, she asked, "What?" still looking annoyed. "I have a pot boiling."

"It's just . . ."

"Come into the kitchen."

I followed her. She stirred the pot, tasted the sauce she was making, frowned, added a large pinch of salt, and stirred again. I waited, then blurted out, "Bernardo Tedesco wants to take me to dinner, and he said to ask you and Nonno if it was okay."

She blinked, then frowned again.

"Bernardo? Is that the older brother?"

"No! That's Rodolfo," I said. "This is the youngest one."

Her face lightened; she began to smile.

"That tall boy is old enough to ask girls out?" Nonna asked.

I knew she wasn't really asking me that question.

"And he told you to ask our permission?" she said. "That's good. Things have changed a lot since I was a girl, and it's nice to see a boy with some sense."

I waited.

"I like him," Nonna finished.

"Like who?" asked her husband from the doorway, sliding his phone into his pocket.

"Bernardo Tedesco."

"Yes," agreed Nonno. "He's a good boy."

He looked at me, raising his eyebrows. "We are talking about him because . . . ?"

"He wants to take Mia to dinner, and he says she must ask us," said Nonna.

Nonno lifted his chin, pressing his lips together. "I don't think any young man has come to me with a question like this in many years," he said.

I wasn't sure who these young men would have been asking about. Francesca? Probably. I tried to picture Égide asking, and found I could. I watched Nonno look at Nonna, raising his eyebrows again. She nodded.

"You may go," he said. "But take your cell phone, and don't stay out past eleven, not this first time, yes? We will be up listening for you, you know," he added kindly, and gripped my arm. "This is good. I like him."

I danced down the steps to get Emilio.

"Well?" he asked. "I don't need to ask, I see," he added as I came into the shop.

I blushed. "Emilio?" I asked.

"Yes, *carina*."

"Can we not mention this to the entire family? I mean, for a bit?"

"You told Nonno and Nonna that an actual boy asked you out on a date, and you think they won't talk about it?"

"You don't have to sound like it's such a miracle that somebody asked me out," I reproached him.

He grinned again. "It isn't," he said. "Not a miracle: a matter of time. Good first choice, too."

He was nice enough not to count Lucifero as my first choice. I didn't tell him that Bernardo felt like the *only* choice.

"Call him after dinner," he advised.

"I don't want to look too eager," I said.

"Too late. But that's all right," he added, standing up. "They want us to come up and help cook, right?"

"Yes."

I followed him up the wooden stairs again, grinning my head off. I thought of everyone I'd ever known who'd been asked out on a date—at least, one they wanted to go on. Now I understood the dorky looks on their faces.

Of course, I should have known that, after nearly seven months among my relations, it would be hopeless to keep this secret. Anna Maria showed up with a loaf of bread and a knowing smirk. "About time," she said, pinching my arm hard. "I couldn't figure out which one of you would burst first."

I grabbed at her arm and whispered, "Did *everyone* know before me?"

She laughed. "Just those of us that were working with you all the time," she said. "Though my parents are pleased. I think my mom was worried he was going to ask me out," she added wickedly. "As if I would have said yes."

I glared at her. "He's awesome."

"Yes, yes," she replied, waving a hand. "And I've known him for a hundred years. I can't get interested in some boy I can still remember from when he was covered in snot." She laughed. "Don't get all heated up. You know it doesn't matter anyway: *I* wasn't the one he wanted to ask out."

I hadn't known, but I didn't say that.

"Let me give this bread to Nonna," she said, leaving me to answer the doorbell and get pinched on the arm by her brother as he came in. "Good job, Mia," Francesco said. "Because I'm pretty sure he's not a Satanist, I've known him all my life."

I gaped at him, feeling like I had been slapped. He caught my arm and added quickly, "I can't believe I said that!"

"You are such an idiot," Anna Maria said to him, having emerged from the kitchen just in time to hear him. She looked at me and mused, "Not that somebody wasn't going to say it, you know. In this family, no stupid action ever gets forgotten. But you should still punch my brother," she advised. "It would do him good."

Francesco still looked as stricken as I felt.

"That's okay," I said. The door opened to admit Égide, who smiled broadly at me, pinched my arm, and said, "What restaurant are you going to?"

I looked around at all of them and asked, "Is everyone telepathic or something?"

"Yes, of course," Égide said. "But having a cell phone helps, too."

He clouted me on the shoulder. "Go to Alhambra, near the Corso Buenos Aires. The food is great."

"Yes, but you'll never get to talk alone with Bernardo," put in Anna Maria. "It's the neighborhood restaurant, everybody is always sitting at everyone else's tables."

"That could be helpful if things get awkward," said Francesco.

"Things are *supposed* to be awkward," Égide said. "On my first date with Francesca, I ordered the tourist special out of sheer fear."

"Oh, *Santa Maria*! Did you actually eat it?" asked Anna Maria.

"No," said Égide. "I let it get cold." He smiled at the memory.

"Really?" I said, happy to make sure we stayed on this new topic.

"Really," he replied. "I was looking at her the whole time. Listening."

"He had to. I talked the whole time," said Francesca from the doorway to their bedroom. "I was so nervous. Poor you," she said to Égide. "I don't think I've ever talked so much . . . and about so little! I went home terrified you would think I was just a chatterbox."

Égide went over and pulled her to him with one arm, kissing her cheek.

"I knew you weren't," he told her.

"Dinner is going to be hell for you," Anna Maria told me. "Everyone is going to get sappy about their first dates . . . except for my brother, of course "

"Hey!" cried her brother.

"And you will die of an overdose of family sentimentality before you ever see Bernardo again. Which is just as well," she added, throwing a glance at her sibling. "Men are a pain."

"Bad news from the professor, Cousin?" Emilio asked Anna Maria, leaning over the threshold to the kitchen. He ignored her scowl, saying, "Everyone come sit, dinner is ready."

As we sat down, Nonno looked at me with a pleased

expression and declared, "I had to leave my first date with my wife halfway through."

Anna Maria widened her eyes at me and mouthed, "I told you so." I fought to stay straight-faced.

"Well, when I say a date," Giuliano continued, "it's not like the ones you young people go on. Her aunt and her sister walked in with her, but sat at another table in the same café and pretended not to listen. Then Bertoldo Strachetti came to get me, because his brother-in-law's mother had started reciting in Latin," he went on. "My father told him to say it was a family emergency. But my Laura knew he was lying."

I looked around the table and realized I was the only one who had not heard this story a hundred times.

"I left," Nonno said. "And she thought I had arranged with him beforehand, to get me out of this. She thought I didn't want to be there because our relations had set us up."

Everyone was listening politely, even Anna Maria. I had expected her to make some smart-ass comment. Instead, she was looking at Nonna. I did, too, then, and saw one corner of Nonna's mouth lift in a smile uncannily like that of her grandson Emilio.

"She never dreamed that I'd worked on my family and hers behind the scenes for *weeks*, months," Nonno continued. "I'd tried to get everybody to think that it was their idea, because I didn't want anyone to suspect."

I tilted my head, waiting, but he only smiled at his wife.

"Suspect what?" I asked, finally, realizing as I did so that I had asked the question somebody was always supposed to ask at this point in the story. He reminded me so much of my own grandfather sometimes.

"That I had been madly in love with her for more than a year. I didn't want anyone to know, until I was sure."

I smiled.

"You must have been sure," I said.

"Well, yes, after another date I was. When I could get one. I had to chase her down myself, then. It took another month to see her again. I thought I would die. It was only a few years after the war; it was still hard to get things and nobody had any money. And there I was, going all over the city for whatever I had heard she wanted . . ."

Nonno laughed.

Nonna laughed, too, now. I could see that the grandchildren were all looking more interested. It seemed the story had gone off its usual path. I wondered what the normal punch line was, and if I would ever hear it.

"Shoes in the wrong size," Laura remembered. "A card of buttons, the ugliest buttons you'd ever seen. A book about modern art, in French."

"With good pictures," Giuliano amended solemnly.

She smiled at him. "Bertoldo Strachetti was always a bad liar," she said.

"Buttons?" Emilio asked. "I thought you just . . ." He

paused, and I guessed that he hadn't meant to lead his grand-parents back to the usual ending of the story.

Nonno waved his hands. "A lot more went on. I shorten it. I don't want to bore my relations," he explained grandly. "But Mia has never heard the story," he added.

"I can't think why not," Anna Maria retorted.

"It's a special occasion story," Emilio told her. "Respect, my cousin. Respect!"

Nonna smiled at me and said, "This went on and on. Half the time, I didn't even know who had gotten me the gift. My family wasn't very good at passing messages, everyone always at work. But then . . ."

She shot her husband a look. I guessed that the end of the story was his to tell, that it was important to him still.

"Your mother got sick," Nonno continued. "And you wanted to make a meat stew, you wanted a soup bone. And I saved up and went all over and got you the biggest piece of beef I could find, with a good big bone in it, and I brought it to your door. I didn't say anything, I just looked at you. After a while, I found my voice and said, 'For your mother.' You took it and didn't say anything, either.

"For four days, nothing. I thought of stopping by. I thought of sending a cousin. But I knew I should not. Something told me I should not. So I waited, and my heart did these flips—one . . . two . . . three . . . four!—all the time. I waited for news, but nobody mentioned your mother.

"Then on the fifth day, a note, from your mother. She told me to come to dinner.

"I had one suit, so I wore that, even though it was too tight; I'd put on a lot of muscle that year. It was winter, I couldn't find any flowers, I brought half a bar of chocolate wrapped in a newspaper, and a bottle of wine. I stood on your doorstep again. I thought I must have worn a hole in the stone, I had been there so many times with something in my hand.

"Your mother let me in. She wanted me to see how well she was, on that soup bone. She had cooked for hours, I could see that. Hours. Risotto, two kinds of meat, a *contorno* of winter greens . . . I still haven't figured out the secret ingredients. I ate everything, and you never said a word. I talked to your mother, your aunt, your grandfather, your grandmother, your big sister, your middle sister, your great-aunt, your niece . . . everyone but you!

"And finally, the Madonna smiled on me and your grandmother suggested we all go for a walk. It was freezing, but it was close to Christmas, everybody was out strolling around. They let me talk to you alone, your mother and your aunt walking ahead and everyone else behind, and everybody pretended not to hear. You kids have it so easy," Giuliano added severely, looking around the table.

"Yes, but maybe we make more bad choices," suggested Francesca.

Nonno shrugged and finished the story. "I will remember that night until the end of my days, the crispness of the air, the lights near the Duomo, and the curl of your hair, sneaking out from under your winter cap. And the way you smiled at me, with those eyes that are still the most beautiful in the world, and thanked me for the soup bone."

Nonna smiled at him then, and pinched his cheek.

I imagined that walk. Maybe it was like all the times I had had to go out surrounded by family. I hadn't missed that in his list of her relations there was only one man, her grandfather. I had begun to comprehend the toll of war. For Nonna to have made a young man chase her was gutsy.

"You'll have a good time with this young man," Nonno told me. "Just remember to come in before eleven."

Anna Maria rolled her eyes. "I never understood that," she said. "Why the curfew? You can get just as pregnant at ten o'clock as at midnight."

We were all used to her bluntness, but I noticed I wasn't the only one who looked a bit shocked.

Nonna answered her. "It's not for *that*, my self-centered niece. It's so that we can stop worrying and go to sleep."

Anna Maria stared at her and seemed to recollect herself. "Oh," she said.

During coffee, I asked to be excused and slipped away to call Bernardo. He answered on the first ring, and his calm voice made my spine quiver.

"They say I may go," I told him.

"Good! I'm glad," he said.

"Me, too," I said shyly. I heard him chuckle.

"And what kind of food do you like to eat?" He asked, solemn once again.

"Uh, I don't know. I . . . good food. Whatever's really good."

He laughed. "Have they taken you out much? I know you will be eating well, at home. *Cucina tipica.* There's no need to go out for traditional Milanese. Any kinds of cuisine you don't like?"

"No . . . I haven't really tried that many things, though. My town at home doesn't have all that many restaurants. Not like here."

"Yes, here we have everything," he agreed proudly. "Okay. I will pick someplace good, and foreign. If you don't like it we can figure it out."

"Thank you."

"Thank *you.* . . . I will see you then."

He hung up. I stood looking out the living room window into the dark. A minute later, my phone rang again—just as I realized why he'd called back.

"Pronto," I said, trying not to laugh.

"Ciao," he said, not succeeding himself. "What night would be good for you?" he asked.

I wanted to pretend I had a life, and say I was busy tomorrow; then I remembered I really was, because we were all going to Aunt Brigida and Uncle Matteo's.

"Thursday?"

"Excellent," he said. "I will come for you at seven?"

"Um, sure."

"That's great. See you then. Good-night," he added.

"Good-night," I said, smiling into the phone.

So that was that.

I didn't sleep all that well Wednesday night, and I knew it wasn't because of Aunt Brigida's excellent dinner. Thursday afternoon, I fell asleep over my books and woke long enough to go upstairs for a nap. Later, I tried on the five outfits I had planned, but nothing seemed to fit. My hair was a mess. One dress made it look like I was trying too hard; jeans and my blue shirt made me look like I didn't care.

Finally, Francesca caught me standing in front of the mirror and said, "The brown dress."

"But . . . that's the nicest thing I own," I said. "And it's really an autumn-winter dress."

"It's still early spring, and you look good in it. Bernardo's got style, but he's not going to notice the season of the dress. He's going to notice *you*," she said. "Besides, it won't be the nicest thing you own for long. We need to go shopping." She grinned and patted me on the shoulder. "Go! Get ready."

I went back into my room still in doubt. All afternoon, I'd waited to hear Signora Gianna offer her advice, but she was out or something, just when I needed her most.

I put on the brown dress, feeling exposed and frozen at the same time.

At seven o'clock, I was sitting downstairs, my hair as nice as

I could get it. Emilio, horribly, had just shown up, and he and Nonno were jabbering about the upcoming elections as if nothing were happening. I almost texted Bernardo and asked him to meet me at the corner of the Via Brera. I wanted to sneak off, not conduct my—well, it was early to call it a love life—in front of my entire family.

7:01. 7:02. 7:05 . . . I heard a *motorino* outside. It came into view, and passed our shop, ridden by a girl, her giant portfolio strapped onto the back.

At 7:07, I heard the sound of the engine I already knew was his, the *motorino* I had ridden on the night of Signore Strozzi's exorcism. He pulled up and parked. He was wearing his chocolate brown leather jacket, a pale blue scarf knotted under his chin, beautifully cut, dark navy jeans, and a pair of well-made brown Oxfords. He pulled off his helmet and set it carefully on the luggage rack, running a hand through his hair. I saw the flash of his shirt collar and wished my whole high school back home could see him—he was so ridiculously handsome and well dressed. For a fleeting moment, I felt almost grateful for the circumstances that had brought me to Italy. If it weren't for my demon, this first date would be happening at home with some guy who thought putting on a clean T-shirt was the most anyone could do for a girl.

I stayed at the table, watching him come to the door, my knees like jelly. Emilio and Nonno looked up as he entered, the bells ringing their bright greeting as if he were just anyone. He smiled in his calm way.

"*Buona sera,* Mia. *Buona sera,* Signore Giuliano, Emilio."

Nonno waved a hand at him. "*Buona sera,* Bernardo. Wine?"

"Thank you, no," Bernardo said. "Our reservation is at seven thirty. Thank you, sir, for letting Mia come out with me."

Nonno made a gesture that looked like he was shooing him out. "*Va bene.*"

My knees did not cave in under me. I turned to my cousins and said, "See you later."

Emilio laughed. "*Ciao,*" he said.

"Eleven," Nonno admonished, raising his eyebrows at me. "Have a good time."

I smiled at him, and Bernardo opened the shop door for me.

"That didn't go too badly," said Bernardo, smiling at me as he held the *motorino* steady for me to get on. I rolled my eyes and forgot my nervousness for a moment, remembering the last two days. He caught my expression and said, "Oh, I missed the worst of it, did I?"

I nodded.

He grinned. "Families are a pain. Was it awful?"

"I know the details of the first dates of every *single* couple in my family," I said, forgetting to blush. We might have been back on the scaffolding, or in the bar after work.

He threw his head back and laughed. "Perfect!" he said.

"Tonight, you wear a helmet," he added, settling it on my head. "Then I don't have to worry so much." I hadn't realized he was worrying at all, the night we had chased Signore Strozzi through the streets. He climbed on in front of me, then turned to look me in the eye.

"Your story will always be different," he said. "Let's get out of here."

"Yes," was all I had the breath to say.

For a moment, as he stood on the starter, I felt sad that he hadn't said "*our* story." But then I felt relieved. I could almost hear someone's voice—Mom's? Signora Gianna's?—saying, "Time enough for that."

We didn't ride very far, unfortunately. I had just gotten used to the feeling of my arms around his waist again when he pulled up in front of a restaurant in the Via Solferino. It was an Indian place, with low lights and strings of marigolds hanging like streamers. We sat in a corner, looking out into the street.

"I hope you like Indian food," he said. "I'm addicted."

Now that we were sitting down in a restaurant, on an actual date, I felt as if all that time we'd spent working together on the balcony or joking over *aperitivi* had evaporated. I found myself staring at the candle between us, wondering if I should check the restaurant for the presence of annoying Satanists. If I didn't say a word with more than one syllable in it soon, Bernardo was going to think I'd been possessed by a very shy demon. At that thought, I wondered how much he knew about what had gone on the other night.

"You look like you're over the other night," Bernardo said.

"Has anyone heard anything about Signore Strozzi? I meant to ask Emilio, but I forgot," he added, flicking a smile at me.

I smiled back, remembering, but then gave him the bad news.

"Signore Strozzi is still in the locked ward at the Ospedale San Giuseppe. We don't know if he'll ever recover his senses," I told him.

"Wow." He shook his head. I waited for some way of telling how much he knew.

"Yeah, it's kind of crazy, isn't it?" I said.

He nodded. "Hard on his family, I imagine."

"They're very upset, Nonno and Emilio say."

He shook his head. "They shouldn't be. Your family are good people; they only try to help."

I stared at the menu. I'd had Indian food once and hadn't really liked it, because most of the dishes had practically burned my head off. But I would try anything that he suggested.

"Can you recommend anything?" I asked, finally, remembering Signora Negroponte asking the same question of the waiter at the Caffè Vecchia Brera, the day we first figured out how to protect me in the street. Bernardo smiled with his eyes this time.

"Menu overwhelming?" he asked gently.

"A bit."

"Will you allow me to order for both of us, then?" he suggested.

I had a sudden flash, of a very different guy telling a waiter what I wanted before I'd ever agreed to it. Lucifero hadn't waited to hear my opinion. *Maybe not all dates have to end in demonic possession,* I told myself.

"Why are you smiling?" he asked.

"Long story. Yes, I would appreciate it very much if you would order for both of us, please," I added. "And . . ."

"Yes?"

"Well . . ."

"Come on," he coaxed.

"Well, the last time I had Indian food, everything burned my mouth."

"So, mild, mild," he said.

"Yes, please," I agreed, relieved.

He laughed. "Of course! How am I supposed to talk with you if you have to spend the whole time like this?" he asked, fanning his mouth as if it were on fire.

The words were out before I could stop them. "How come you're so kind? I thought guys were supposed to be, I don't know, tough," I said.

He laughed. "Oh, I can be tough. You've seen me dealing with a bad wood order, right? Me, I'm macho."

We were both laughing by now. All that time on the scaffolding hadn't gone away after all, and yet I still had butterflies in my stomach. He waved the waiter over in what he clearly considered a very macho fashion.

"Ciao, ragazzo," said the waiter. "Haven't seen any of you for weeks. How's your father? And who is this beautiful girl?"

"My father is fine. And this beautiful girl is named Mia Della Torre," said Bernardo. "She's hungry, and she needs mildness, gentleness in the food. No heat."

"No heat, eh?" The waiter raised his eyebrows at me. What would my sister do in an embarrassing situation like this? I decided to try acting innocent, even though I was pretty sure Bernardo would see through it.

"No," I said demurely.

"Yes, she is to be protected," Bernardo said firmly.

"I will bring extra raita, just in case," the waiter told him.

"Thank you."

"And I will warn the kitchen."

"Thank you."

"So, what will you have?"

"The set menu . . . unless . . . Mia, are you a vegetarian?" asked Bernardo, suddenly worried, as if this might be a serious problem.

"Bernardo," I replied in a severe tone, dropping the innocence, "you've seen me eat a metric ton of that amazing salami at the wine bar in the Via Vincenzo Monti after work, haven't you?"

"Not vegetarian," noted the waiter, eyes on his pad.

After he left, we laughed some more.

What my sister and the girls I knew back home had failed

to mention was how friendly a date could feel, even if you spent a lot of it thinking about kissing the man across from you. Sometimes I would remember the kiss in the darkness of the shop, and several minutes would go by before I could speak again. Bernardo noticed, but he didn't seem to mind. He just seemed happy to be there, looking at me, tasting course after course of the wonderful food that was set in front of us, nearly all of it very mild. The waiter made a point of bringing Bernardo a selection of hot chutneys, "In case you miss the heat," he informed him.

"Not in this company, I don't," Bernardo rebuked him.

I smiled at my date.

Worthy enough for you, Signora Gianna? I asked in my head. Though I wasn't sure that was what she had meant.

After dinner, I looked at my phone.

"We only have an hour," I said. He must have seen how sad I looked, because he put his arm around me and said, "That's okay. I know just the thing."

He walked me across the street and settled me on the *motorino* before he climbed on.

"You're a better passenger tonight," he told me.

"I'm sorry I wasn't before! I hadn't ever ridden on a *motorino*, you see?"

"Really? Wow."

"Yeah, I know."

"Well, this time, put your arms around my waist, like

258

before, but then put your hands in my pockets. So."

I was glad he couldn't see my face. I was also glad my family couldn't see him.

I loved the feel of his back.

"Lean where I lean, and keep your feet on the footrests. Don't bring them down when we stop someplace. And lean forward, into me, not back. You don't want to fall off if I have to jet forward. You can learn to push off with me, but that will come. Ready?"

"Yes," I said.

It turned out I had forgotten to tuck my dress under, so I almost didn't make it out of Via Solferino without dying of embarrassment. I hoped nobody I knew had seen my underwear. I worked the skirt around my legs while we waited to turn into the Bastioni di Porta Nuova.

We drove through the warm air, the smell of leather and diesel fuel in my nostrils, flowing with the river of traffic, just another couple like all the others. Sometimes I'd look over and see some guys scoping me out from a car, or some girl checking out Bernardo and looking enviously at me—at me! I clung like the luckiest girl in the world to the back of the most beautiful boy, riding between the lofty buildings, passing the models and the businesswomen in their perfect evening clothes, jouncing together over cobblestones or rough pavement.

He got me home at 10:46. I didn't come inside right away, though.

In fact, I would have stayed outside a lot longer, because he had turned around on the seat of the *motorino*, removed my helmet, and taken me in his arms. But he had taken Nonno's words seriously, as well. In his voice that made the shivers run up and down my spine, he said, "I, too, would like one more kiss, Mia. We can have one soon?"

"Yes, please," I said as we drew apart . . . and then knocked heads.

"Ow!"

"Ow!"

"Your necklace is caught on a button," he said, chuckling into my hair.

We had a bit of work to do disentangling it. He held the bell between his fingers for a moment, turning it.

"You always wear this," he observed. "It's beautiful work-manship, so fine."

"Thank you."

He let it fall, and it rang once. He raised his eyes to me, a mischievous look in them.

"Do you wear it so the boys will hear you coming?" he asked.

I stared at him.

"Like a leper?" I asked.

"What?" he barked, astonished.

He put his long fingers under my chin and lifted it with great care, as if I might break.

"Is that what you really thought I meant?" he asked. He held my eyes for a moment. I could see the light at the end of the street reflected in his pale irises.

"I don't like kissing lepers," he declared. "I meant, like a *cat* . . . so that all of us poor bird-boys will have some warning before we are caught by your beauty . . ." He grinned but gave me a sad look as he added, "Someday maybe you will tell me what ever happened to you, that you would think that I would say such a mean thing."

"Someday," I said. I thought of my neighbor Tommaso d'Antoni's afterthought of a kiss, of walking boyfriend-less through the halls of my high school, and of Lucifero, turning his handsome face upward and smiling as the demon descended from the roof of the Galleria.

Bernardo eased his weight off the *motorino* and held out a hand for me.

"Let's make sure you're on time. I don't want to get you into trouble."

I wanted to retort that I was already in plenty of trouble, but I wasn't feeling as sure of myself as I had before. He walked me to the shop door and waited until I had let myself inside.

Then we did kiss once more, there on the threshold.

"*Not* a leper," he whispered into my ear, holding me tight. Then he let me go and waited a moment while I locked the shop door from the inside, before he smiled at me and walked back to his *motorino,* waving once more as he climbed on. I watched him turn on to the Via Brera. The shop was dark, not one solitary flame left burning. As I slipped up the stairs and passed down the hall, I noticed Nonna and Nonno's door stood slightly open. When I opened the door to my own room, I heard it close with a soft click.

Nobody scolded me, not even Signora Gianna. She said nothing when I came in and sat down on the bed, but I knew she was smiling.

When Anna Maria cornered me in the shop around lunchtime the next day, I thought she wanted to know about my date. Instead, she called me to follow her into the back office, where she started emptying her satchel of all the notebooks she had borrowed for the Strozzi case, gently setting each one on the table.

"Two things," she said abruptly. "One, I've seen Lucifero again, on a shoot. He looks bad, like he's been doing heroin, but I know that's not it. . . . Well, he could be doing that, too, but I can see that something's eating him.

"You need to look out," she went on. "I don't know what Emilio's thinking, I heard about the so-called 'trap' he set the night of Nonna's birthday dinner. I don't think much of a grandson who would risk ruining that for her."

"I honestly don't think he thought it would," I said. "I don't think failure crossed his mind."

At that, she drew her lips in a thin smile, her eyes hard.

"You're right. And he is good, very good. We know that. Some humility wouldn't hurt him, though."

I didn't think that Emilio lacked humility. It just seemed like it wasn't a consistent quality in him.

"The second thing is . . . I want to help you," she said.

THIRTEEN

The Dream of the Bear

I stared at Anna Maria.

"Help me? How? What do you mean?"

She paused again, putting the notebook she was holding down on the table, stroking its leather cover with her archival gloves. She looked toward the door that led upstairs.

"Let's talk somewhere else. Have you eaten lunch? Is Nonna expecting you?"

"No . . . she's out at some meeting," I said.

"Let's go, then. It's a beautiful day. Want to bike?"

We grabbed bikes at the BikeMi Brera *stazione* and took off. We stopped at the *panetteria* in the Via Solferino and took sandwiches and fruit to the Parco Sempione.

We dropped our bikes at a stand on the near side of the

park. Anna Maria chose a bench facing the stream that runs by the ampitheater. She looked around, as if one of our relations might be behind a chestnut tree or something.

The sun sparkled on the water, and a man and a woman, hair streaked with gray, passed down the gravel path opposite us, hand in hand, heads bent together, laughing. I pictured myself walking with Bernardo, streaks of gray in his red-brown hair. It seemed so easy.

"There are things you should know," said Anna Maria, watching me. "Things you're not learning."

I turned away from my daydream.

"I study every day," I said. "Every weekday, anyway. And we are still searching for the poem," I added with a sigh.

"The poem? Oh, yeah, the one the demon recited to you when you were out at Peck that day? Yes, that may be one of the keys." She waved her hand. "But they aren't teaching you everything," she said, knitting her brows. "I believe there are things you have a right to know."

I frowned, too.

"But you know they can't, right? Because if I lose, if the demon succeeds, he'll know everything I know. We can't risk it," I finished.

She snorted.

"I don't believe that. The demon took my cousin Luciano, and he was good, better than his son may ever be. What of his knowledge?"

I drew myself up.

"Emilio says that we learn ways of sequestering parts of our minds, just in case." She narrowed her eyes, looking fierce. "And are they teaching you how?" she asked.

I blinked at her, then I opened my mouth and shut it. She could tell the answer was no.

"Of all the people in the family who should be learning those techniques, you are the one," she said. "Don't you think?"

I just sat there, still gaping. After a long moment, I hazarded, "Maybe we haven't gotten to that yet. I'm just starting with the basics. I've only been here since September, after all."

She gave me a look that was hard to read, and I remembered that she'd had to sneak her way into an exorcism before they'd agreed to teach her. With that kind of persistence, I thought they were lucky to have her in the family business.

We both sat quietly for a moment. I am embarrassed to admit it, but my mind was roaming the streets of Milan, on the back of a *motorino*. *Focus. You want to survive this, don't you?* I said to myself.

Anna Maria seemed content, for now, to let her words sink in, and we paid attention to our lunch. The panini were delicious. I don't know how one thin slice of cured meat and a slightly thicker slice of cheese can taste so much better than the pile of meat and cheese you get in American sandwiches—and fill you up the same, too, especially if you are eating slowly. I looked across the stream, wondering what Gina would be doing right now. She'd still be deep in sleep, I thought. Right there, facing the moat of the Castello Sforzesco, I remembered the smell of our school's hallways: metal lockers, old sandwiches, cement, institutional paint, stinky sneakers, orange peel. I didn't miss that at all, I realized, thinking of the smell of Bernardo's leather jacket.

Anna Maria asked, "What are you thinking about?"

I couldn't help myself. I smiled.

"You went out with Bernardo Tedesco last night, didn't you?" she said.

"Yes."

"No wonder your mind isn't on the job." She laughed reluctantly. "You had a good time."

"Yes."

"I'm glad. I remember when he was a pain in the butt, always dirty. Francesca hit his brother on the head with a huge squash once. Did you know that? Whatever he did, he must have deserved it, though."

I smiled again. I knew a story Anna Maria didn't, about her own family; I knew Rodolfo had tried to kiss Francesca. I couldn't help feeling smug.

She shook her head. "Maybe now isn't the time for us to discuss this."

I dragged my mind back and looked her in the eye.

"There are things to tell you, to show you," she repeated. "You are right, we have to go carefully. But I think you have a right to know."

"Okay," I said uncertainly.

She blew out an exasperated breath between her perfectly made-up lips.

"You do want to survive, don't you? You want to defeat this bastard?"

For a moment, I resented the question. She hadn't been inhabited by this being. She hadn't been there, inside my head, when he had made me throw my own sister at the wall.

She saw the hard glint in my eye. "Then let me help you," she said.

"Okay," I said finally.

She breathed out a long sigh of relief. "Okay," she echoed. "I will think about what's best to start with. We'll have to be careful about when and how we meet. I may talk to my brother, if that's all right with you . . ."

"Let me think about it," I said. "This is still a lot to take in."

She looked impatient, and I turned to her. "Anna Maria," I said. "Thank you. Thank you for this."

"*Niente,*" she said, shrugging. "So. Tell me about this date. Where did he take you for dinner?"

That's all it took. I ended up telling her exactly where we went, and what he wore, and what I wore, and what we ate, and how the waiter teased me for not wanting the food too hot. I wished for all of my life to be this ordinary—sitting in the sunshine on a spring day, telling a girlfriend about my first date with a guy. We sat for an hour or two, I don't know how long. Then we went back to the bike stand, and she took me to a bookstore in the Via Ulrico Hoepli and bought me a novel.

"You have a lot to learn, but you might as well enjoy the language you are learning," she said. "Italo Calvino, he's one of our greats, and this is a very good one—*Il barone rampante.* See what you think."

I tucked it in the purse she had given to me for Christmas. "Thank you," I said. She punched my shoulder as if I was her brother. Her cell phone rang.

"It's the professor," she said, surprised. She pursed her lips at her phone. "Let him leave a message," she said.

On the way home, she entertained me with gossip about all the people in the advertisements we passed on our way back toward the Brera. I went to sleep turning her questions over in my mind.

The next day, Bernardo turned the book over in his hands, picking it up from the desk in the shop.

"I liked *Le città invisibili* better," he said. "This one is kind of intellectual. Well, all of them are. But this, it's all about the Age of Enlightenment. I prefer Marco Polo and Kublai Khan chatting, and the images."

"I haven't started it yet," I said, deciding to go back to the Libreria Hoepli and buy *Le città invisibili* first chance I got. "I've never been much of a reader," I added.

"But you're surrounded by books all day! Are you studying for exams in America or something? I meant to ask."

"No, just keeping up with school, and studying Italian culture and history," I said, hoping he couldn't see I wasn't telling the whole truth. "I don't know anybody in my hometown who even speaks another language."

I thought about how I had successfully dodged foreign languages for the first part of high school. I would have been in Señora Driscoll's Spanish class this year, if my ordinary life had gone on. Instead, I'd learned a language by being sent to a place where many people did not speak English as their second or even third language.

"Do you need to stay and study now?" Bernardo asked. "Or can I take you out for an *aperitivo*? Promise I'll have you back by dinner."

Nonna waved her hand at me from the stove when I ran upstairs, breathless, to ask. On the way back, I tripped over the threshold into the shop and flew into Bernardo's arms, stiff with embarrassment.

"Pian piano," he laughed. "They'll still have something for us to eat when we get there, you know."

So we climbed on the back of his *motorino,* and, once more, we flew down the streets of the city.

"I have a boyfriend," I announced to Gina the next night when we Skyped.

"Excellent!" said my sister.

"You're not surprised?" I asked.

She laughed. "Why would I be surprised? You're different. I

can't wait to see you in person. You've really gotten more confident since you went to Italy. And you look great."

"Thanks." Then, worried, I confessed, "At least, I think I have a boyfriend."

"What do you mean?" she asked, laughing at me.

"We've only been on two dates. But he really likes me. He kept asking my cousins about me. It's probably too soon. How did you know with Luke?"

Gina thought about this.

"It seems like forever ago. I think I knew when he called me his girlfriend to his mom," she said. "Maybe a month after our first date. Seriously, what's his name? What does he look like?"

"His name is Bernardo Tedesco, and he is the best-looking guy in Milan. He's tall, and has kind of red-brown hair, and blue eyes. He's sweet. He had me check with Nonno Giuliano and Nonna Laura if it was okay for him to take me out."

"He didn't ask them himself?"

I rolled my eyes.

"We don't live in the Middle Ages," I said. "Did Luke ask Mom and Dad, or did he ask you?"

Gina giggled. "He asked me. But when he came to get me, I had to snag my purse, and Dad gave him a Dad Talk."

"Jeez. What did Dad say?"

"I asked Luke, but he just shrugged and told me Dad had said he'd kill him if anything happened to me. I think I was way more freaked out than Luke was. He said he wished his own dad would talk that way about his sister Jenny."

I remembered her telling me that Luke had spent Thanksgiving at our house because there would actually be a turkey, as well as stuffing, Aunt Maggie's sweet potato casserole, and so on—as opposed to a twelve-pack of Miller Genuine Draft and a fight, which I guess was a typical Thanksgiving at his house.

"It's weird, the stuff you take for granted, isn't it?" I said. "Like how Dad will always be like Zeus the Thunderer when it comes to us. You know?"

Gina laughed. "It's a pain. But kind of nice to know that if you chose a total jerk Dad would just *destroy* him if something happened, right?"

"Yeah," I said. I wondered what Dad would have done about Lucifero. I had a sudden picture of Nonno putting his hand on Dad's arm and saying, "He'll have his own punishment."

That would never happen; Nonno and Dad were separated by thousands of miles and, more importantly, by my grandfather's anger. And maybe, now, my father's, too.

"What are you thinking about?"

"I wish Dad were here," I said suddenly. "And all of you."

"You'd want Dad giving Bernardo a Dad Talk?"

"Sure," I said. "Not that Bernardo would need it."

"He sounds nice. Have you kissed?"

I blushed, wondering if she could see my face turning red.

"Yeah," I said.

"Was he any good?"

"I don't really have much to compare it to," I pointed out.

She laughed. "How experienced do you think I am? I mean, to you, was he any good."

I smiled. "Way better than Tommaso d'Antoni," I said.

She laughed again, louder.

"OMG, you kissed Tommaso?"

"He kissed me," I corrected her.

"I always kind of wondered what that would be like," she mused.

"It was okay," I said. "Bernardo is . . ."

I smiled, trying to find the right word.

"That's the thing I like about Luke," said Gina.

"His kissing?"

"Yes, but the way he's all the way there when he kisses me. One hundred percent."

"I know what you mean," I said.

And I did.

About a week later, when I'd run into the kitchen doorframe for the fifth time because I wasn't looking, Nonna said, "It's a good thing you don't see that boy every night! He's gone to your head. Any more of him and you wouldn't notice the stairs, either."

I decided not to tell her I had already tripped on them more than once, thinking of Bernardo. I steadied myself and caught her eye. Her lips were pressed firm, but her eyes were crinkling at the corners.

"Never mind," she said. "Every day of your youth dawns only once. Come set the table."

She was right, though. I still studied and searched for the demon's poem, did chores around the shop, ran errands, helped cook, and paid attention to the follow-ups Nonno did with various clients—Signora Galeazzo was healing steadily, the *San Valentino* couple were doing slightly better, Signore Strozzi was about the same, sadly. Anna Maria and I had met once, but all she'd done was ask me to describe what I'd experienced in the Second House in as much detail as I could. Still—really even the important stuff was just a way of passing time until I saw Bernardo again.

One afternoon he suggested we visit the roof of the Duomo, so we went to buy tickets at the office across the street from the back of the cathedral. The line in front of us was like a mini United Nations, something I hadn't quite gotten used to, even after living here since September. Now, in the Brera, the tourists were flying fast and thick; they seemed to spontaneously generate in the warm spring air.

Instead of the sprinkling we'd had during the cold months, we got flocks, crowds even, following guides holding up sticks with some noticeable object attached at the top, as if they were the priestesses of some odd new religion involving plastic flags and giant flowers. I was a tad overdressed that day, in a scarf, linen blazer, and a cotton shift dress of Francesca-approved cut that even Anna Maria had swooned over. My new heeled sandals pinched a little, only because I was breaking them in.

Bernardo placed his long, broad hand in the small of my back. I leaned back, to be close to him.

Ahead of us, an older Asian couple in extremely well-cut clothes were struggling, in a combination of Italian and English, to explain that they wanted two tickets to the roof of the Duomo.

"Tourists," he whispered to me with a grin.

"Yes," I said. "Did I tell you I saw an American completely lose it in the Bar Brera the other day? He kept saying, 'You call this pasta? You call this *pasta*?!'"

"Oh, no! The poor waiter."

"Yeah. It was Sebastiano. He said, 'No: I call that calamari.' There was a special," I added with a poker face. Bernardo burst out laughing, startling the French family right in front of us.

"In English, he said it? Sebastiano?"

"Yes. I love how he never lets on that he can speak it until someone gets uppity. Sometimes he makes me pretend to be his translator. I use my best Brooklyn accent."

"Brooklyn?"

"A part of New York City."

"Oh."

He gently walked me forward as the line moved, his hand still resting on my back. I thought, *I have butterflies in my stomach, all the time.*

"I want to go there with you someday," he announced.

The Asians left, tickets in hand. I watched an Indian couple who spoke English with Australian accents get their tickets. The French family selected a representative, who spoke in precise, heavily accented Italian.

Home, home, home, my heart said, and I couldn't be sure which home it spoke of, though I knew I was happy. I would survive my demon and live, and bring my handsome, pale Italian boyfriend home to meet my parents, to walk down the streets of Center Plains. He would fall in love with Gina like everyone else—that couldn't be avoided, I thought, swallowing hard—but he would realize, just in time not to lose me, that he really loved me and not my sister, and they would end up good friends, sparing me and Luke a soap opera. Bernardo and I would come back to Milan quickly, because Bernardo wouldn't like the bad American food. We would marry young, like Mom and Dad, or Luciano and Giulietta. We would trip through the Giardini Pubblici and get our wedding pictures taken by the big circular fountain, like any other couple.

We wouldn't be quite like Luciano and Giulietta, though, because we would grow old together like Nonno and Nonna. All our children would be good at demon catching. We would live in an apartment in the Via dei Giardini, across the street from the Giardino Perego, and we would sit on a green bench, reading the *Corriere* while the kids played on the large wooden snails and the huge spiderweb. I would put my feet in Bernardo's lap. Old women would smile at us.

I would have an ordinary Milanese life. Of course, there'd be differences, involving getting up in the middle of the night to get into an Audi—my own, of course—to go rescue people from demons. I tried not to think too much about how Bernardo would feel about this, reminding myself that obviously all of my cousins managed to date or marry ordinary people.

Then I touched the bell at my throat and thought about the demon. I remembered his eyes looking into my own from the eyes of that child in the Piazza del Carmine. If Luciano Della Torre hadn't stood a chance, what about his distant cousin, a young girl with only a fraction of his training?

No apartment, no bench, no *Corriere*, and no children. No holding hands in Center Plains and not much of a chance for Gina and my parents to meet Bernardo. I felt sad about all these plans that wouldn't come to anything.

Bernardo bought us two tickets, the guy at the counter looking slightly relieved at the sound of a Milanese accent. My thoughts were far away, thinking about all the dreams that people never got to live. Lisetta Maria Umberti, the girl from Christmas Eve, she'd been an art student. How many paintings had she dreamed of making, how many brushstrokes had she left undone? Luciano Della Torre must have planned to grow old with Giulietta. He'd never seen his son, Emilio, as a grown man, straight-backed, luminous, standing in the candle shop, still dressed for work at the bank, pulling out his demon-catching case. He'd never seen his daughter, Francesca, packing her briefcase, her sleek head bowed over her papers, or seen her come home and wait halfway through dinner to say, with quiet pride, "We won the case."

Bernardo touched my hair lightly, so lightly I hardly felt it, yet his fingers brought me back to the present. We stepped out into the street.

"What are you thinking about?" he asked. "You look sad."

I wanted to tell him my daydream . . . and so many other things.

"I was thinking of home," I said.

He smiled.

"I do want to go there with you, you know," he repeated as we got into line for the stairs to the Duomo roof. Bernardo presented our tickets to the grumpy attendant, and then we began to climb the narrow steps, 201 of them. Every now and then, we saw the buildings across the street at another angle through a window in the dank stone. The air smelled warm and musty. Bernardo let me go ahead, and I felt his eyes on me. What was he looking at?

We stepped out on the roof. The cathedral, from the piazza, looks like a huge marble confection, like a sand castle you'd make at the beach, only whiter, with sharper edges. The folks who had built it over the last six hundred years (the last bronze door was added three years before my dad had been born) clearly felt that a church wasn't a church unless every spare inch was covered with gargoyles and gloomy saints. Yet somehow the whole crazed mass of marble creatures looked incredibly elegant, a very Milanese cathedral, indeed. The shingles on the roof were gigantic, plain slabs of marble. Above us, the gilded statue of the Virgin Mary, called the Madonnina, inclined her gilded head over her city. We walked along the edge of the roof, gazing across at the rooftop garden of La Rinascente, the big department store, and then looking between gargoyles to the people milling below.

So easy to swoop down on one of them, take over their body . . . *Where did that thought come from?* I shook my head to get rid of it.

"Don't lean out too far," Bernardo advised. "It's a long drop."

I smiled, glad he worried about me. He took my hand and led me to the far side, saying, "Look," as we came over the peak of the roof. The gray city spread out beneath us, past the roofs of the Palazzo Reale, roof after tiled roof stretching away. In the far distance, I could see the Alps, still carrying a big burden of snow.

"Wow," I said in English.

"Uoaou," he imitated me. I squeezed his hand and laughed.

"I haven't been up here in years," Bernardo confessed. "Living here, one doesn't act like a tourist all that often. Especially with the crowds. But I couldn't believe you hadn't seen this view."

The Alps seemed close enough that I could reach out and prick my finger on their frozen peaks. "It's like you can touch the mountains from here," I said.

Bernardo looked proud of himself.

"That's why I told you we had to wait. The rain has washed away the smog. No point in coming here when the air isn't clear."

What would it be like to step out into the nothingness over the piazza, if you didn't need to be afraid to fall? If you could float over the roofs, lighter than that single cloud drifting in the sky to the south? Your heart would tug you upward, inside your rib cage, and under its deft, inexorable power you could fly as far as the mountains, and feel the cold breath of the snowfields on your face.

I had been lifted into the air in my own room, at home in Center Plains, by the demon that had taken over my body. I'd been pushed down the stairs, my feet banging against the steps, leaving destruction behind me. Was that the only way to fly? I felt as if Bernardo's hand was the only thing keeping my feet flat on the marble roof. I smiled at him, and his face filled with light. I almost felt our shoes start to rise off the ground, as he shut his eyes and leaned down to kiss me.

That night, I had a vivid dream, full of shifting images. First, I saw a round lake, as still as a mirror, reflecting the steep hills around it. The hills were covered in ancient trees, all oaks.

Then I was on the sea, watching a bird building a nest among the waves. The bird seemed confident and unhurried, as if it had done this many times before; it hovered on glittering blue wings, weaving bits of straw and slender sticks together above the deep. The water shone and rocked beneath the nest, and I could see great fish swimming far, far down, at impossible depths. The bird did not drop a single stick from its beak, and presently, a nest floated in the water.

Then I was hovering above a town in a narrow gorge, watching two men walk down the street, talking intently. I couldn't see their faces, but I thought I might have known them, once.

Next I was back in Milan, near the Biblioteca Ambrosiana. The air was warm. As I passed over the city, I saw a great black bear moving with massive and deliberate steps out into the Via Armorari. Its pelt was as smooth and sleek as one of the mink coats in the shops on the Via Montenapoleone, and it walked with a serious, heavy gait, putting down each paw as if it could plan an earthquake. I doubt that Milan has seen a bear in its streets in a long time.

The bear passed under a streetlight and I felt a fresh wave of muggy heat slide over me. No one was in the street, and yet I knew that everyone who was awake at this hour was watching, standing in the shadows so that the streetlight would not catch their faces, so that the bear would not turn to look at them. It continued down the Via Spadari, then turned toward the Piazza del Duomo.

Presently, it came and stood before the cathedral. It looked up at the Madonnina, high on her pedestal above the roof. I didn't see her move, but she looked down at the bear, as if she had been waiting for it. The bear opened its mouth and spoke.

I woke to find myself sitting straight up in bed, one foot on the floor, as if I meant to go look for the bear. All the next day, I found myself forgetting it was just a dream and turning toward the Piazza del Duomo to see if I could find—what? The stones of the piazza would not yield a single pawprint. Still, by six o'clock, when the books in front of me made my eyes swim, I slipped away from the shop, full of the smells of Nonna's cooking and the sound of Emilio on his cell phone. He was talking to Alba, and I don't think he even noticed when I left. I took a bike from the BikeMi *stazione* and headed down the Via Brera, pausing on the corner to stare at the stone street sign set in the opposite building: Via dell'Orso, the Street of the Bear. Then I thought of the black bear holding up the Madonna in Santa Maria del Carmine, the sculpture my ancestors had given the church.

Someone honked behind me and I realized I had to get out of the narrow street or move forward. I biked down past La Scala, turning into the side streets by the Galleria, and parked my bike at the *stazione* by the Duomo. I turned, and walked slowly toward the cathedral, trying to see exactly where the bear could have stood.

All around me the crowds swirled, their conversations rising in the air. "It's much cheaper in the States—" *"Fünfunddreißig euro?!"* *"Mi dispiace,* I was supposed to call earlier . . ." Most people hardly noticed me as I wandered toward the center of the great stone grid, though some guys called out, "Hey, gorgeous!" and "Let me take you home to meet my mother," and so on. They didn't bother me, not now. I had a boyfriend, for one thing. And I was a demon catcher. I'd seen things that would make these tough guys shrivel up.

"Well, *buona sera*! It's Mia Della Torre, of all people," said a voice.

My whole body went cold as Lucifero came up beside me. I didn't have to look to know that his friend had come up on my other side.

"Buona sera," I heard myself say.

"Yes."

We kept walking. Neither of them had touched me, but I still felt like they had gotten inside my skin. I noticed they were steering me slowly toward the rear of the cathedral, away from the main doors—and farther from home.

A quick glance at Lucifero showed he didn't look at all well, just as Anna Maria had said. I wished ferociously that she were there beside me.

Part of me started to cry inside with rage. I hated being so afraid . . . hated it.

Then, right there, I could feel myself opening up a way into myself, like a road, a place for the power to flow in, the only power I'd ever really known, the power of the demon . . .

"So you will help us, you see? You will help us," Lucifero was saying, his voice soft and cold, but I knew that in a moment I would have the power to turn his face whiter than it already was, and smash every one of his sharp teeth. I felt the demon's gloating joy, just as I had felt it during my possession. I felt sick.

I stopped dead and stamped my foot. Lucifero and his friend stopped, too, staring at me.

"Damn you *all*," I growled, my voice shaking. "None of you can have me. Do you hear me? *None of you!*"

I was snarling at him and his stupid follower and the demon I had almost opened the way for. For one split second, I felt another power, like a shadow stooping over me, rising up from my feet at the same time. I thought I could smell the musk of some animal, and for one split second, I thought I had black fur and earthquake paws. Then my eyes cleared and the feeling was gone.

So were Lucifero and his friend. I caught a flash of them as they disappeared between two shops.

I stood there, staring, shaking, making sure they were gone. Then I turned and started to run in the other direction, toward home.

FOURTEEN

Alcione

I told Nonno what had happened when I got back to the shop. He frowned, pouring out the wine. Emilio frowned, too.

"Do we need to go back to the old days, when I couldn't go out without an escort?"

Emilio smiled. "We might be able to enlist some help with that, now," he said.

I blushed. "No, he has to work all day," I replied. "And anyway he's not family." But I couldn't help liking the idea.

I wanted to tell Bernardo everything, but I knew I couldn't. He met me the next evening, shaking hands with Nonno, as always, and telling him what restaurant we were going to and promising I would be home by eleven. When we stepped out into the spring air, Bernardo said, "Are you hungry just yet? Because it's such a lovely evening." We drove to the Parco Sempione instead. The sun was just starting to angle over the trees as we found ourselves a bench on a path mostly free of Milanese out enjoying the sweet, if muggy, air.

It felt so good to sit beside him. I sat still, trying to decide how much I actually could tell him, and while I was thinking he pulled me into his lap as easily as if I'd been a cat. That's one great thing about dating a building contractor's apprentice, I can tell you. I wrapped my arms around him in the dark.

I didn't have a lot of experience, yet I knew I was with someone really patient. I thought of the way he ate, of watching him during our first *aperitivo* at the wine bar in the Via Vincenzo Monti, the night we started the Second Door. So maybe it wasn't patience; maybe he was just enjoying himself right where he was, and he didn't need to try anything new, get to any bases or whatever. He just tipped his head so that he could smile down at me.

"*Cara,*" he said. "It's so good to hold you."

I could hear only our breathing. Then my senses widened, and I could hear the leaves, back and forth in the trees above us. Farther out, the cars and *motorini* on the Foro Buonaparte zipped through the dusk.

Bernardo's arms tightened around me. I leaned into him, still trying to decide how, or what, to tell him about the day before, what to call Lucifero. My ex? Hardly. I had already made up my mind that the dream would sound too weird to him. Somehow it seemed too important to tell in passing.

"So good to hold you, at last," he said.

"You hold me all the time," I teased.

"I know," he said, and wrapped his arms around me even more tightly. I pressed my face into his neck, loving his sweet smell—always a bit too much cologne, and the day's sweat. His heart was pounding like mine. That made me feel better. I'd learned by now that he was really good at holding back, so it was nice to know that at least part of him didn't want to.

I sat there in the evening light, my head against his chest. *We could sit like this for hours,* I thought. *You don't just want to sit,* I said to myself. *But the waiting is fun, too.*

An old man crunched past us on the gravel, smiling at us as he went. "What are you thinking?" Bernardo murmured against my head.

"I don't know," I said, not wanting to explain.

He chuckled, then fell silent again, and we listened together to the trees, the passersby, the traffic, the sighing air.

That's when I felt the double pulse.

Bernardo's heart has a certain sound. It's firm, even when it's pounding with hope, or desire, or whatever he felt that night. It's steady even when it is too fast. Now there was another rhythm, darting in and out between his heartbeats, irregular, fearsome, hurried. It swam upstream through his heartbeat, the way I remembered from before.

My sweat turned icy.

Bernardo's arms tightened around me, too tight.

I lifted my head just in time to see my boyfriend's spirit vanish. He widened his eyes in surprise and terror. I had never seen him afraid. Then he began to recede—whatever made him Bernardo pulled back into the dark, beyond the irises of his eyes. And someone else came. I knew who it was.

"Not going anywhere, now," he whispered. I could hear the straining of Bernardo's vocal cords as they were forced to speak. "Not going anywhere. At last, at last."

For a moment, I couldn't move. He had struck home. There was no better way he could break me than by trapping me like this, in Bernardo's arms. I felt rage surge up inside me, thawing my frozen muscles. I tried to pull away, even though I knew it would be useless. I had to do something before my breath was squeezed out of me. I got our chests apart long enough to hear the bell around my neck trembling and ringing. My demon grimaced.

"Such a little thing," he hissed, "such a little thing to keep us apart for so long."

He reached for the bell, and in that split second, I felt a brief, paralyzing stab of elation. It shocked me. *He's coming back and I will have all the power again,* said a voice in my mind. *And I will save Bernardo,* said another. *What on earth are you thinking?* I cried out to them in my mind.

It didn't matter. My demon reached for the bell again, but then drew back, baring Bernardo's teeth like a vampire in some film. He tried again and again to touch it, his other arm still holding me in a bruising grip. My bell kept ringing bravely. I would have been proud of it if I hadn't been so terrified—and so angry.

Then he grinned at the bell and told it, "You don't matter. Because I have her at last. I took the road into her heart, yes."

He looked down at me, Bernardo's face distorted, his jaw elongated, his brow rippling as my demon continued to make himself at home in his flesh. *Oh, Santa Maria. Oh, God.*

"Listen to me, *alcione*, listen to me," he rasped, his voice gravelly and cold. I could hear him again as if he were inside my skull. "I have waited so long. I looked for you, and you were not there, your mouth was stopped with dust. But you've come back, so there's hope for me now. You've come back. You must listen. You must!"

His harsh voice had a pleading note in it. I thought of the poem he'd recited to me. I thought, too, of Lisetta Maria Umberti's exorcism. He sounded different: his voice was the same, but his words, his way of addressing me, were different.

The scent of cinnamon started to rise from Bernardo's body.

What had my demon called me? *Alcione?* What did that mean? It sounded Italian, but I couldn't remember hearing it, or reading it, before.

Only a few months ago, I would have gone to pieces, or died of fright. I still couldn't think clearly; I had no idea what to do, but I knew I had some time. He needed me to listen to him.

My whole body shook with terror and anger. He could feel it.

"I can't breathe," I managed. "You're holding me so tight. I can't breathe."

"That is because I cannot let you go," he whispered. "I did before, and you did not come away with me. You went down into the dark, and the world ended."

My vision was fading, and I knew I was about to faint.

"If I can't breathe, I can't listen," I gasped.

It was a good point. If I hadn't been so terrified and furious I would have laughed, to hear him pause, thinking. He made Bernardo's arms slacken just slightly. I struggled again, and he tightened them once more, the smell of cinnamon growing stronger. He began to whisper in my ear again, the hideous double pulse beating beneath his words.

"Oh, no, you don't," he hissed. I couldn't see his face now, but I could see Bernardo's shoulder, tight, muscles leaping with effort.

Oh, Bernardo, caro, *I never meant to do this to you! This wasn't your danger; it was* mine!

When my demon tightened his grip yet again, I knew I would hear that sound of grinding muscle and bone in my dreams. Or one day, I would hear it in my own bones, my own muscles, and then I would know I was going to die.

One of Bernardo's hands found the lump in my jacket pocket. Even on a date, I never went without it; Bernardo never asked, or even seemed to notice.

"What is this?" my demon whispered. "Ah . . ."

With quick, shuddering fingers, he pulled out my case. I could just see the gilded letters on the side, shining faintly between his fingers.

"How I hate these," he reflected, so softly I could hardly hear him.

Smoke began to curl from under his fingers. I smelled the old leather, beginning to burn.

"How dare you!" I whispered back. "Haven't you taken enough?"

"These humble things cannot abate my anger," he told me simply.

I struggled to get my hands free and reach my case.

He held it away from me, keeping me in his crushing grip and laughing—Bernardo's laugh turned upside down. I don't know if I'd ever hated my demon more. *You are* mine, I fumed. *I will settle you, I will take care of this matter on my own.* I felt a shadow rising behind me, the shadow of the bear. I made one more flailing grab at my case.

Incredibly, I caught it in my hand. It burned me where he had set it smoldering. We tussled for it while he went on laughing.

My demon seized my arm in his ferocious grip, forcing Bernardo's beautiful, gentle fingers into my flesh.

"So easily lured," he hissed. "You're even easier to trick than I imagined!"

"Go on," I heard myself whisper fiercely. "Break it. Take

control of me. Trash my case. What good will it do you? What does it give you, to ruin someone's life? To take a father from his son, or a daughter from her father? What difference does it make to you?"

"A huge difference, you widow slut!" His voice rumbled, so low that I heard the words through my rib cage. "What do you know about it? Have you ever *really* lost anything?"

Even in the midst of my own fury I heard his words, remembering that he had called me this once before, on Christmas Eve, when he possessed Lisetta Maria. *So,* I thought, while my body reeled in pain from his wrenching grip and the hot case in my hand, *you keep talking to me like I'm someone else. Who?* When he wrapped Bernardo's other arm around me again, even tighter, I wasn't sure I would stay conscious long enough to find out.

"I have to know," he whispered at last.

I pulled my face as far away from him as I could. I gazed at him, lost in the darkness of his eye sockets, so different from getting lost in Bernardo's pale eyes.

Oh, God, Bernardo! My demon kills his hosts, nearly all of them! Don't go!

But something besides anger looked back at me out of the empty eyes.

"I have to know," he repeated. "Please tell me. Did they tell you what they meant to do? Did you know when they set out? Did you see them leave?"

I blinked at him.

"I don't know what you're talking about," I said.

"Don't lie to me! I have to know, *alcione*!" He hissed wildly, crushing me.

I heard someone screaming, and it took the longest time to realize it was me. I could feel the bell still trembling and ringing in the hollow between my collarbones. I could feel the bear, now, rising up through my spine, and still I screamed. Yet somehow the sound seemed faint, like it was being swallowed by the dark emptiness in the eyes of my demon.

"Did you know?" my demon asked. "Did you?"

"I don't know what you mean!" I gasped.

"You really don't," he rasped.

"No," I said. "No."

"You did love me, I think," he whispered. "You did! They never told you."

"Who are you talking about?" I cried. "Who am I to you? Why do you call me *alcione*? I don't even know what that word means! Who are you?" I screamed.

"You don't know?" he asked, his voice soft now.

"I don't," I whispered.

"No, it is not possible," he groaned. "You have to know. You have to . . ."

Staring into his eyes now, I could see that they were tunnels. *If the eyes are the windows of the soul,* I thought, *my demon's eyes open a view on past centuries.*

We were so still that I could hear the faintest rustle of the leaves. We held as still as lovers on a spring night, staring into each other's eyes.

Now I could feel the bear's heat spreading from my feet all the way to the top of my head. I felt its strength in me. I didn't understand it, and I wanted to, in case there was a price for me to pay. But I felt sure I could trust it. For now.

As the bear's power filled me, I tried to lower my feet to the gravel beneath the bench. *If I can just touch the earth,* I thought, wondering what instinct was speaking. I remembered what Signora Negroponte had told me months earlier about the magic of the road. We were sitting beside a path. Did that count? What had she said? *Mercury is the god of roads, the lord of thieves and messengers. Messengers . . .* I remembered the suicides who helped us from time to time.

I couldn't take my eyes away from his. *I will get lost in their darkness, and never come back,* I thought. Then, *No! I've got to find an answer.*

The law of the road had worked in my demon's favor, in the past, because I had needed the protection of my family to go outside. The wards they set on their home would not work in the street. I couldn't see a way to turn it to my advantage. I felt the strength in me, the strength of the bear, buying me time, but I could not tell how much.

Somebody was standing near us. I recognized his stained stockings, his drab waistcoat.

Help me, I thought.

Respicio opened his hand. It held a cup of hot chocolate from Zucca. Then he vanished.

Damn all messengers! I thought. Here I was, stuck on this

lonely path, trapped in the arms of my demon, unable even to reach my cell phone in my pocket . . . and all I get is . . .

You didn't think of your cell phone at first, I told myself. *You know this fight's your own.*

Someone else, however, was emerging from the trees into the evening light, his face nearly as white as that of Respicio. He was smiling, the way he'd smiled on our disastrous first date in the Galleria.

"You will help us, after all," he said.

I found my voice.

"No, Lucifero," I said.

A movement out of the corner of my eye made me turn my head; I saw Lucifero's friend and two other people I did not recognize, a man and a woman.

I suppose I should have been even more terrified. I was exasperated instead. First the useless messenger; now a pack of idiot Satanists who never knew when to give up.

My demon was eyeing them with what looked like professional interest.

"I know you," he grated out, looking at Lucifero.

"You do, my lord."

"My lord?" I said. "Are you *totally* insane?"

"Don't speak to him that way," snarled Lucifero's friend in a high voice.

"Go to hell," I said. "Oh, wait, that's kind of your plan," I added, feeling slightly hysterical.

My demon stood up, still gripping me with Bernardo's

arms. He made Bernardo's head turn slowly, taking in all four of the people closing in on us.

My feet touched the gravel of the path. I heard my next thought as clearly as if I had spoken aloud.

God of roads, lend me your wings.

I don't understand what happened then. I don't know if anyone else heard the thunder or felt the earth heave. I only knew I was out of my demon's arms and turning to face him. I stretched out one hand, fingers curled like claws, and something burst away from me like a sound wave. Then I was running as fast as I could down the path. Behind me, I heard my demon scream; I heard Lucifero shout. My fingers fumbled in my jacket for my cell phone. I came to a crossroads and turned.

I slowed down, then stabbed the toe of my shoe into the gravel as I came to a halt. I listened to my breathing, ignoring a staring couple. Half of me wanted to keep pelting away until I got to the candle shop, but the other half wanted to turn and fight. I had felt such power. *I want to finish this.* And I knew I couldn't leave Bernardo to my demon and to the fools who worshipped him.

Think, I told myself. *This isn't just about you and your fight now: don't do anything—anything more—that would put him, or his body, at risk. What would be the best thing to do? What would you tell yourself to do, if you were Nonno?*

Stand and use everything I have—wits—the strength of the bear—my own strength—to fight for myself and for Bernardo, I answered myself. *But also call for backup.*

I pulled my cell phone free of my jacket, trying to see the buttons well enough to speed dial Emilio. As I hit CALL, my cell phone slipped from my fingers. I bent down to grab it.

"Mia?"

"Parco Sempione, kind of near the amphitheater," I gasped.

"Coming," he said.

I knew the tone of my voice told him what he needed to know. I closed my phone and made myself meet the eyes of the couple. "I'm fine," I said. Then I headed back where I'd come from and stood still, panting, trying to calm my mind.

Something was drifting up the path. My beautiful Bernardo, moving through the dappled shadows beneath the trees, his feet a few inches off the ground. And behind him, like a lost army, four people, their feet dragging in the air. I understood then more clearly than ever why we could not allow this demon to take hold on this plane.

The frightened part of me thought of running again. They were not moving all that fast. But I had to figure out how to save Bernardo, though I couldn't see a way to do that. And now, I had some help coming, even if it did not arrive soon enough. I stood and planted my feet firmly in the road.

The raging part of me didn't want Emilio or anyone else to arrive soon enough. *This is my fight,* I thought.

I waited, letting my demon and his followers float closer. I tried not to think about what would happen if some passersby turned down this path. I took a deep breath, and pictured my Madonna. All my frantic thoughts fluttered and settled like an audience quieting for the second act.

I lifted my chin and looked my demon in the face, feeling a shudder of fear and sorrow. *Oh,* caro, *Bernardo.* I took another breath. I could feel my demon gathering his strength as he came steadily closer. I could see his smile on Bernardo's stolen face.

Words came to me. The simplest magic of all, perhaps.

"Tell me your name," I said to my demon.

He stopped midair.

"My *alcione,* you always surprise me," he whispered. I could hear him, even over the drone of traffic circling the park.

"Tell me your name," I repeated. I tried to sound like Nonno, perfectly calm.

"Why?"

"Why?" I said. "Because I am your *alcione.*" *Whatever that means,* I thought, but I didn't want to remind him and lose whatever power that word held over him. "Because I want to know the name of the poet who wrote the only sonnet I've ever memorized." *And because if you kill Bernardo, I will not rest until I have had my revenge on you.*

He raised both of Bernardo's hands upward, weighing my words.

"You loved the poem?"

I almost laughed at the hope in his hideous voice. This was

not the first time I had been struck by the bizarre vanity of demons.

I opened my mouth to lie, since the truth was complex. Then, suddenly, all those days of looking through books of poems and reading collections of letters came back to me and I had an idea. *Just give me one lead,* I thought. *Now that I know that you wrote it, tell me how to find you.*

"I did love it," I said. "But I hear your critics weren't that impressed."

He snarled, remembering. Again, it would have been funny, if it hadn't been my boyfriend's distorted voice.

"Monks and frauds—everyone writing of heaven and hell, as if we did not have enough of both here on Earth. They couldn't see beyond the walls of palace and cloister," he sneered.

I stared at him. *You have changed a lot since the night you first attacked me,* I thought. *What is happening to you? Just give me one name . . .* I wished we'd been able to decide which era the poem had come from, now that I was reluctantly familiar with so many poets.

"It is true," I said. "We can make heaven or hell here on Earth. That one monk, for example, the one who hated your work . . ."

"Which one? The idiot from Verona, or the one from Lodi?" he asked, laughing harshly.

"The one from Verona," I hazarded. *Just one name . . .* It felt surreal to be using my wits to find a way past his defenses, to be standing here talking about poetry in the moonlight. But it was working. I felt a surge of elation, surprisingly like the one I'd felt when filled with the strength of the bear. I felt as if that power were still nearby, as if I could call it up again. I saw his face change. Had he guessed what I was thinking?

Then I heard feet pounding along the gravel path, shouts fading in the open air. I didn't dare look away from my demon. Out of the corner of my eye, I saw my cousins come up beside me.

The demon leveled his eyes at me.

"You bitch," he said.

I heard one last set of footsteps on the path, slower, firmer: Nonno.

"Take him," my demon whispered as he brought Bernardo's fingers up to his chest. Then he made Bernardo's hand sweep outward and behind toward Lucifero and his friends, motionless in the air. "Take them all . . . more casualties of your beauty."

Bernardo's body jerked in the air; his jaws opened impossibly, a long, harsh sigh flying out of them. I screamed. Then his body, and the bodies of Lucifero and his friends, dropped to the ground as if pulled from below. They lay still, so terribly still.

I ran forward and fell to my knees beside Bernardo. His face was his own again, his own sweet proportions. But there were shadows under his eyes, and he did not move. I wanted to touch him, yet the memory of what his arms had been made to do, his lips had been made to say, made me pause, searching his features, just to be sure.

Please just open your eyes, I begged him in my mind. *And let them be* your *eyes. Please don't be dead.*

Someone knelt beside me.

"Mia," said Emilio. The kindness in his voice made the tears start in my eyes.

"He isn't dead," I told him. "He isn't."

Emilio reached out a hand to touch Bernardo's neck. I slapped his hand away.

"Don't touch him," I cried. "He isn't dead!"

"Mia, I only—"

"Don't!"

I leaned forward then and put my hand on Bernardo's chest. *Don't be dead. Don't be dead.*

I wanted to feel his heart pounding under my fingers. Was it? I couldn't tell.

"My hands are shaking," I said in amazement. "Oh, no, no. He can't be dead. He can't be dead . . ."

I didn't stop Emilio when he reached out again, sliding his hand under his friend's head and nodding. "No injury," he said. Then he placed two fingers against Bernardo's neck.

"He isn't," he said at last. I lowered my head to Bernardo's chest, sobbing too hard to hear the blessed sound of his heart. I heard voices around me, gravel underfoot. I smelled Emilio's pinesap scent and knew he remained beside me. He didn't move or speak; he just waited while I cried some more and then began to breathe more evenly again.

"I'm getting his shirt wet," I told Emilio.

"It's probably okay."

I didn't move. I could hear Bernardo's heart now, beating steadily against my ear. Other truths were sinking in. What would I say to him when he woke up?

"Who came?" I asked softly.

"Everyone," Emilio said. And after a moment, "Mia, I am sad, too. Will you let us help him? Will you?"

"I've already called," said a voice above us—Anna Maria. I jumped. I raised my head slowly, and saw Uncle Matteo and Francesco stooping over the other bodies in the moonlight. Nonno stood off to one side, surveying the pale road, the dark bodies.

"The police will be here soon," Nonno said. "We should prepare."

I shut my eyes for a moment; any energy I had left seemed to drain into the ground. In the distance, I could hear a siren, wailing closer.

"I think the danger is past, for the moment. What do you think?" Emilio asked me.

"My demon is gone. I don't feel anything, my bell isn't ringing . . ."

"Your bell," he said.

"My bell," I repeated, and looked down to where it rested on my collarbone.

It was dented, as if someone had pressed it with his thumb. The clapper wasn't moving. I shook it, and it made only the faintest whispering sound.

"Oh," I said, dumbfounded.

Emilio looked up, and I remembered something else.

"Oh, no! My case," I sobbed. "My case!"

I stood up quickly, stepping around Emilio's and Bernardo's prone form.

"Mia, wait. Someone should go with you," called Emilio. I was already halfway back to the bench when he caught up with me.

By now the sun was behind the trees, so we had to search in the shadows. We found it among the leaves by the bench. The two halves were torn from each other, the leather burned through to the wood in some places, the ancient hinges twisted and broken. A silver nail gleamed in the dusk, and I found my mirror, its face shattered, shining up from the ground like a miniature broken moon. Using our cells as flashlights, we found almost everything precious, except my small notebook. I wept with rage.

We got back in time to watch the medics lift Bernardo onto a stretcher. I went to his side; they didn't stop me from touching his cheek as they loaded him into the ambulance. I thought I saw him try to lift his head as they set him down, but I couldn't be sure. I stood waiting until the flashing lights came on and the sirens deafened us. As they drove away, I started to follow. Emilio caught my arm.

"I have to go with him," I said.

"I will find out where they are taking him," he replied, his grip on my arm very firm.

Off to one side, Nonno and Uncle Matteo were talking to the police. Two more ambulances were grinding up the gravel toward us; I saw Francesco directing them. Anna Maria was nowhere in sight. I heard a garbled cry and saw that one of the Satanists that I didn't recognize was waking.

"I didn't even check on the others," I said.

"To hell with them," Emilio growled. I blinked at him, startled by the hardness in his face. "Let others worry about them. They followed you, didn't they?"

"They must have."

"For their own cruel purpose." He touched me lightly between the shoulder blades. "Come on, *carina*," he said. "Let me get you home. You must sit down in a safe place and rest."

"But there are still things from my case we haven't found," I said.

"I sent Anna Maria to go over the ground; she knows to look," he said.

"I want to go to the hospital," I said.

"In time," Emilio said, taking my arm again. "Let's go."

It only takes maybe ten minutes to walk from our apartment to the park. I stood still, swaying, wondering if I could walk half the distance. Every step without Bernardo.

Because I knew then that even if he survived, I'd lost him. I couldn't quite believe it or bear it, just yet. But I am sure I knew, then.

We were passing our metro stop before I could speak again.

"Emilio," I began. I had to know. "How do you do it? How

do you—do we—spare our girlfriends and boyfriends, wives and husbands, the danger? Do we?"

He looked straight ahead and walked in silence for a while.

"We find another way to love," he said at last. "Just as we find another place to keep certain knowledge when we work. It's something like that."

My throat felt too tight for words. I forced them out anyway. *"Why didn't you tell me?"*

"We didn't see it coming," said Emilio. "I feel like the fool I am. I suppose we thought we had more time."

I heard the humility in him then, and felt my heart soften.

"I didn't see it coming, either. I did that to Bernardo," I whispered. "I did. It was all my fault."

"No." He surprised me with his vehemence. "You might have laid him open to it, yes, but your demon did it. This is important, Mia."

He sounded like Anna Maria, blunt and fierce. I knew she was busy back in the park, going over the ground, learning what she could learn, and maybe finding the last few missing items from my case, like my little notebook. But I knew that she could search all night for what I'd really lost, and she'd never find it. No one would.

FIFTEEN

The Halcyon Bird

Back at the shop, I sat down at the desk. I rested one hand on the smooth wood.

Emilio said, "Can I trust you to stay where you are?"

I looked up at him, frowning. "Where are you going?" I asked.

"Upstairs. To get you something to drink. Will you stay?"

"Where would I go?" I asked.

He waited, watching my eyes. "I'll be right back," he said.

I listened as his footsteps pounded up the wooden stairs. I noticed that my hand was trembling. I lifted it off the desk and cradled it in my other hand. I could feel stinging tears rolling down my cheeks. I heard Emilio returning through the office with a lighter, stiffer tread.

It wasn't Emilio; it was Nonna Laura. She set a tray holding a bottle and several glasses on the desk. Emilio emerged behind her.

"Sit," she told him.

With a penknife, she scraped the wax seal off the bottle, then drew the cork and poured out three glasses.

"Let it air a moment," she ordered.

We sat in silence. I could smell wine and spices—cinnamon, maybe, and aniseed. I thought absurdly, *I can't drink it, it smells of cinnamon.* I could tell from Nonna's expression that I would have to drink it no matter what.

When Nonna raised her glass, Emilio and I lifted ours. The liqueur burned, the fumes making me cough. But it had a sweet aftertaste, spiced with cardamom and nutmeg as well as cinnamon and aniseed. I felt the heat from it spread through me. Nonna felt in her pocket and passed me a handkerchief. I took it and wiped my face.

She didn't ask for any explanations; she let us sit. We finished our glasses, and when we set them down, she took me upstairs and put me to bed.

"I won't be able to sleep," I told her.

"Sit up in the chair by the window, then," she replied. "But rest. There will be time enough to think, to go to the hospital, all of that. Right now, look at the Madonna, meditate, sit, and sleep if you can. I'll bring you a glass of water."

I slumped in the chair by the balcony window. I'd left the

long French doors open to catch the spring air, and the gauze curtains lifted and fell slowly, bright with moonlight.

I woke up slumped in the chair, blinking in the sunshine, a glass of water on the table beside me. I had one blessed moment free of memories of the night before. Then I heard voices in the kitchen. My stomach turned over. I made myself get up.

When I came into the kitchen, I saw Anna Maria sitting at the table, looking less perfect than usual. I went over to kiss her cheek. Nonna said, *"Caffè latte?"* She spoke over her shoulder, already putting the coffee shower into action.

When she set my bowl in front of me, I sat over it, inhaling the smell of espresso and milk. I looked over at Anna Maria.

"Have you slept yet?" I asked.

She smiled to herself, swiftly and sadly. "Yes, thanks," she answered. "You?"

"I didn't expect to, but I did."

"Good," said Nonna, sitting down with us.

I swallowed hard, and asked, "Has anybody heard . . . ?"

Nonna fixed her eyes on mine. "Bernardo has not woken, but they think he will," she said. "Anna Maria will take you to see him, if you wish."

"Yes, please," I said. Though I could not imagine what I would say to him, if he woke while I was there. How could I apologize for exposing him to that terrible risk, even if I hadn't seen it coming, even if no one had?

It took forever to get out the door. I stood staring at my

open wardrobe for five minutes, before I came out to the kitchen again and said, "Anna Maria, can you help me with clothes? I can't think." She nodded and followed me back to my room, silently pulling out clothes and laying them on the bed. Then we had to get a list of things Nonna wanted, since we were going out. I heard Anna Maria ask her, "Surely, she shouldn't have to do errands?" Nonna replied, "The world keeps turning, and this family keeps eating up all the butter."

"I'm actually grateful for errands," I told Anna Maria when we climbed onto her *motorino*. "They're comforting."

Anna Maria snorted. "Tell me that again after we get the wrong kind of butter and have to take it back. I know this mood she's in."

When we arrived at the hospital, a nurse showed us up to the room. I realized I was shaking again. What would Bernardo look like? Could I bear it?

It was just as awful as I had imagined. I made myself walk straight up to the bed. He lay unconscious, stretched out like a corpse, his hands at his sides, a tube running from one wrist, an oxygen mask over his face. I stood looking down at him, taking in the dark circles under his eyes, the gauntness of his handsome face. His skin seemed even paler than usual.

"Signorine Della Torre," said a familiar voice. I turned. I hadn't seen Signore Tedesco sitting against the wall, with Uncle Matteo beside him. They both rose, and I felt a weight of guilt pressing on my heart. I fought the urge to run out of the room.

I hadn't realized that there would be things even more unbearable than seeing Bernardo in a hospital bed. Anna Maria didn't offer any protection, walking over to kiss her father on the cheek.

"I want to thank you for trying to save my son," said Rinaldo Tedesco, holding out his hand. I took it automatically, thinking, *My family has lied to this man. He doesn't realize I'm responsible for what has happened.*

It didn't matter that Emilio had said it wasn't my fault: I had exposed Bernardo to the danger.

"Working with your family, we know we run certain risks," Signore Tedesco said. "Thank you for trying to protect him from Signore Strozzi's demon. If that man ever regains his sanity . . ." he frowned.

Aha, I thought, realizing what role I would have to play. But part of me screamed inside, *You had no right to lie for me!*

I took a deep breath, fighting rage and nausea, and said, "I did my best, sir." I added fiercely, "I am sorry I could not do more."

"I don't doubt you did all you could," he said. He squeezed my hand again and stepped back, letting me stand over Bernardo alone.

I felt tears sting under my eyelids again. *Oh,* caro, *mi dispiace, veramente.* Oh, my dear, I am sorry, truly. *Ti voglio bene,* I told him in my mind, words we had never said.

"My wife will want to thank you, too," said Signore Tedesco.

I thanked the Madonna she hadn't been there when I arrived. "She will be back later." I hoped I would be gone. I had no idea how to face her, especially since we hadn't met. My chest ached.

Anna Maria had come up to the bed, too, and touched Bernardo's hand before sitting down. I saw her texting rapidly and wondered who she was talking to, and whether she was getting the full story on whatever Signore Tedesco had been told.

I wanted badly to stay, and just as badly, I wanted to run away. I remembered the vigil by Lisetta Maria Umberti's bed, after her exorcism. Nonno, Emilio, and I had sat for hours, watching, talking, even playing Briscola to pass the time. *You owe Bernardo that, at least,* a voice inside my head told me. I looked over at Signore Tedesco and wondered, if I stayed, whether I would be in the way of family.

"Rodolfo is getting off work early," Rinaldo Tedesco was telling Uncle Matteo.

I couldn't help smiling a little; if I hung around I would meet the famous brother.

"Would it be a problem if I stayed a while?" I asked Signore Tedesco.

He looked over. "No, my child. Not at all. Please."

Uncle Matteo rose. Turning to Signore Tedesco, he added, "It is our custom to watch over a . . . someone like this. But, of course, we do not do it if our friends do not wish it."

"I would be grateful," said Bernardo's father simply. "I will come back later, with my wife," he continued, rising and joining Uncle Matteo. His trust hit me like a punch in the chest. Anna Maria jumped up to say good-bye to her father, and kissed Signore Tedesco on the cheek, murmuring sympathetically. "We'll stay until you return," she told him. "I'll ask one of the boys to come in after us."

After they were gone, I turned to Anna Maria.

"Tell me what they told him," I said. I didn't have to explain exactly what I meant.

She frowned. "Yes, it would have helped if someone had filled us in," she said. "But it was what you heard—just that it was revenge."

"That it was," I agreed. "But not the Strozzi demon's revenge."

"We can't tell everybody everything," she said. "You already know that. Would you have preferred Signore Tedesco to rage at you and keep you from seeing his son?"

"I think it would keep me from feeling unbelievably guilty," I said.

"No, it wouldn't," she snapped. "You'd feel guilty anyway. You blew it, sure—but so did other people. We didn't prepare you. I don't think anyone had really thought he was in danger. I think my father and Nonno both thought they had time to teach you a few things, before . . ." she stopped. "Before your emotions were involved enough to make Bernardo a target." She shook her head. "I sometimes think they have *no* memory of what it is to be young."

I laughed suddenly.

"You sound like you've forgotten, yourself, at the ripe old age of nineteen," I said.

"Twenty next month," she put in, not in the least disturbed by my words. "Think, Mia. Who's really responsible here? Don't carry it all on your shoulders, as if you were some kind of martyr or something. Spare me."

"I'll try," I said. "But, Anna Maria, if he had been dating some ordinary girl . . ."

"Completely true," she agreed. "But he wasn't. You can talk about what might have been all day long, Mia, and it won't change what's happened. Besides, we have to date people, too," she added. "It's not like we're monks or something. For one thing, we need to make more of us." She flicked a smile at me and then frowned again. "I think nobody prepared you because we're too used to having to take precautions *later*, when things get really serious. . . . Nobody thought, hey, these are special circumstances. They acted, or didn't act, out of habit. That's my best guess."

I didn't answer. Her mention of monks reminded me of what I had learned from my demon. When I left this room, I would search until I found what I was looking for. I sat staring at Bernardo, his strong hands slack at his sides. Had I seen a movement out of the corner of my eye while we were talking? There it was again—his eyelids fluttered. Then suddenly, his eyes were wide open and full of panic. His hands lifted off the bed, weakly reaching for the mask on his face. The heart monitor began to beep, racing, and Anna Maria stepped smartly out into the hall, in time to be pushed out of the way by a nurse. Bernardo had finally reached the mask, and he was trying to pull it off. I was half out of my chair, reaching toward him, saying, "*Caro*, don't pull it off—" but the nurse had already taken charge.

"You're all right, *signore*, you need to keep the mask on. You have been in a coma. Breathe, breathe. You are all right. You are in the Ospedale San Giuseppe and it is ten in the morning. Can you tell me your name?"

He slurred out, "Bernardo. Tedesco."

"Yes. And can you tell me what day of the week it is?" she asked.

His eyes crinkled suddenly. "How long have I been asleep?" he countered.

She laughed. "A little more than ten hours," she said.

"Then it is a good day of the week," he joked. And then he saw me.

For one instant, I saw relief and joy in his face. One instant was all I got. I watched him remember. I saw the smile in his eyes fade. He made a low sound in his throat that echoed against the mask, and turned his head away.

I hadn't admitted to myself that I had hoped he might not realize exactly what had happened. But I remembered a great deal from my own possession; I recalled having to watch, trapped within my body, as my demon had used it for his own. *Bernardo knows a demon was after me,* I thought. *He knows it's my fault this happened to him.*

"I should go," I said, standing. The nurse stared at me, surprised. "You're his girlfriend, no?"

"I was," I said. He hadn't moved his head. The nurse looked so sympathetic that I couldn't keep the tears back. "I'll go," I said. "Anna Maria, can you stay, please?"

"Of course," she said. She already had her phone out. I wondered who she would text now.

I grabbed my purse and walked quickly down the hallway. It was too full of people. I kept going until I found an alcove by a supply closet, and then I leaned against the wall and cried and cried.

When I finally dried my eyes and made my way outside the hospital into the sunshine, I stood for a moment, trying to think what to do next. I didn't want to go home, but I felt too tired to wander the city. I thought of my demon, and my bell, and wondered whether its protection still held. I reached out in my mind, feeling for my demon, and was rewarded with a shock: I could feel him *precisely.* It felt so different from our meeting inside the Second House. If there was such a thing as a map of the Left-Hand Land, I would have been able to point to where he was. I also knew I had time. He couldn't cross back yet. He had to gather his strength.

I stood there, while people bustled past on their way to

lunch, trying to take this in. Finally, I turned toward home, skirting the Largo Cairoli and avoiding the Parco Sempione altogether.

When I turned down the Via Fiori Oscuri, I slowed my steps, thinking about Nonno, who would be sitting in his usual place, probably writing up notes for last night. I imagined, for one appalled moment, having to do the same. Then I gritted my teeth. Of course I would. This was my case, after all.

I didn't want to talk to Nonno Giuliano, though; I had many questions to ask him, and also some things to say, but I wasn't ready. I wondered if he would understand. I didn't know if I cared.

But when I got there, Nonna Laura was the one sitting at the desk. I kissed her cheek and asked my question with a look.

"Giuliano is at the park," she said. "Did you see Bernardo?"

"Yes," I said, my eyes beginning to smart.

She said nothing, gazing at me with such sad understanding that I just sat down and bawled. She handed me another handkerchief when mine got soaked, and waited. When I finished, she said, "I am taking you on a trip. Go upstairs and pack: clothes for a week, a jacket and sweaters, walking shoes, nice things and things to get dirty in. And some books, fun books, not study books."

When I didn't move right away, she added dryly, "I think that demon took part of your brain with it."

I stood up. "Where are we going?"

"To the coast," she said vaguely. She shooed me with her hands. "Francesca will drive. *Avanti!*"

Upstairs, I pulled clothes out at random, stuffing them in the rolling bag that had crossed the Atlantic with me. I remembered that first night, falling into bed, trying to speak my first words on Italian soil.

"Signora Gianna?" I called up toward the ceiling.

There was no answer. I could feel her nearby, but not in the room. I wondered why I had never thought about how there might be a Second House in our apartment. Had any of us ever tried to enter it, or did we leave it for our dead relations to hang out in? Who whispered from the photos on our walls?

I didn't realize that Nonno Giuliano had returned from the park until I heard his voice raised below, in the shop. The door to the stairwell must have been open. I heard Nonna reply in a low, even voice, and then I heard her lighter tread, moving up the stairs. The door at the top opened, and I heard her say, her voice muffled as if she was speaking down into the office below, "I will not argue about this." She went into the kitchen and I heard her putting dishes away, muttering to herself.

A few minutes later, I heard Nonno's footsteps on the stairs. He continued down the hall toward my door. I heard him tap on it.

"Mia, may I come in?" I found my fists were clenched. I took a breath and opened them. "Yes," I said.

He opened the door and came in slowly, glancing at the suitcase open on my bed and frowning.

"May I sit down?" he asked.

"Yes," I repeated, watching him.

He took the chair by the balcony door, the one I had fallen asleep in the night before. I still hadn't moved the glass of water Nonna Laura had left for me. I sat down on the bed.

"I don't know what to say to you, *carina*," he said.

I looked down at my hands. He sighed. When I looked up again he was staring out at the courtyard. He gripped the arms of the chair and pushed himself up out of it. He walked over to me, reaching into his coat pocket, and brought out my fountain pen, the old box of matches, and three more of my silver nails. He put them into my hand when I held it out.

"We didn't find your bell or your notebook," he said.

"I found my bell last night," I told him. "The notebook . . . it had a copy of the poem in it, and a few other small notes. But I think the important stuff was all in my study notebook, the one I keep in the shop. I'm not sure. I'll try to remember."

"Yes," he said. "Try."

We met each other's eyes.

"I will go," he said grimly, "and stand on the doorstep of that damned poet, until he speaks to me."

He went to the door. I put the things he'd given me down on the bedspread.

"Nonno," I said.

He turned. I stood up.

"I don't know what to say, either," I said.

He came back to me and hugged me, then kissed me on both cheeks.

"Have a safe trip," he said, and the words seemed to come hard.

I went back and sat on the bed and stared at nothing for what seemed like hours. Still, by the time Francesca got home, I had managed to pack. She came in, saying, "Has Nonna told you . . . Ah, you are packed. Good." As I hefted the suitcase out into the hall, I saw Égide was home, too. He held out his hands and said, "Let me take it, Mia." I followed him down to Francesca's little hybrid. He set my bag in the trunk, then turned and took me by the shoulders. He looked into my eyes.

"You think you can't bear it," he said. "But you can. And in time, you will find a use for what you have experienced."

I stared at him. If anyone else in the family, except maybe Nonno or Nonna, had said this, I would have thought, if not said, "I don't believe it." Because it was Égide, I didn't doubt a word he said. For the first time, I wondered why he had left his home. I saw a history in his eyes that seemed to dwarf anything I was going through.

Nonna came up to us, Francesca behind her, then Nonno, carrying two more bags.

"You should have let me carry those," Égide told him. Nonno rolled his eyes.

"Ready?" Nonna asked me, not looking at her husband.

"I think so, Nonna," I said.

Égide took Francesca in his arms.

"Be safe," he said.

"I will. I'll come home soon." She smiled at him, and they kissed in a way I didn't remember having witnessed before. They kissed like Bernardo and I had. I felt the tears prickle in my eyes. Francesca broke away for a moment to say good-bye to her grandfather, and I got more good-bye kisses on my cheeks from him and from Égide. Then, while Francesca, Égide, and I finished loading the car, I watched Nonno Giuliano and Nonna Laura out of the corner of my eye: they stood apart, saying nothing, until Nonno opened his arms, raising his eyebrows with a question. Nonna stepped into them, and the two of them clung to each other. He murmured something I couldn't hear. Then he let Nonna go, and Francesca started the engine.

My tears came again as we rattled down the streets and out onto the highway. I cried until I fell asleep, speeding west past fields and houses. We stopped in a rest area and ate sandwiches Nonna had made while the strange mountains around us sank into the darkness.

When I awoke, we were driving along a steep coastline in the mountains, with no barriers between us and the sea that was striking the cliffs below. We passed old houses made of stone and plaster and once even a castle that jutted out above the sea, with elaborate battlements like the Castello Sforzesco. Then we were rumbling down cobbled streets again, into a town built on either side of a steep, narrow ravine. The houses charged up the sides of it, the topmost ones looking down into their neighbor's yards. We parked in a square that could hardly hold five cars. Francesca opened the trunk and began pulling out our luggage. Then we started walking down the cramped main street, carrying our suitcases.

As we descended, I gasped.

"You all right?" asked Francesca without turning her head.

"Yes," I said. "I just . . . I saw this town in a dream."

"You did, did you?" said Nonna, sounding unsurprised. "Welcome to Vernazza, one of the Cinque Terre."

"The place where the *sciacchetrà* is from!" I said, remembering.

Francesca laughed. "Yes."

We turned up a side street and set down our bags just outside a stone house with a worn, wooden door that seemed polished by the centuries. I looked up at the crest above the doorframe.

There was a shield with a bird on it, like the one above our shop door. This bird, however, wasn't just perched there, like the shop one; instead it was building itself a nest. Wavy lines of stone undulated beneath the nest.

I pointed. "That's our bird, from the shop," I said in a voice still thick with sleep.

"Yes," Nonna said.

"Why is it building a nest? What are the wavy lines?"

"The wavy lines are waves," she said. "It is building its nest upon the sea."

"Why?" I asked.

"We should go inside. You need to lie down, and we need to make you some food."

"Why?" I repeated, standing my ground. "Why a nest on the sea?"

They both stared at me.

"Because," said Nonna, "this bird is the halcyon bird, the kingfisher. The ancients told of it. It builds its nest at the winter solstice, calming the seas for twelve days so that it can hatch its eggs in peace."

The phrase she used was *uccello d'alcione*—bird of the halcyon, but the word *alcione* tugged at my attention.

Francesca said, "Something troubles you about this?"

"My demon called me *alcione*," I said.

"Ah," said Nonna.

I held still, looking up at the stone bird, nearly afraid to breathe for fear of losing this new connection.

"Well, he has known our family for some time," Nonna reasoned.

I shook my head, thinking of the warmth and hurt in his voice when he had said that word. I felt certain there was more to it than that.

"Come," said Francesca. "You need to rest, Mia."

I let her take my arm and lead me inside. The house didn't feel like our apartment in the Via Fiori Oscuri, dark and full of old furniture. The walls were whitewashed. The furniture was plain, and there wasn't a lot of it. Francesca helped me up more stairs to a snug room with a single, shuttered window and a small bed. She said, "We need to air the sheets, but you can lie down for now. I'll bring your suitcase in a minute."

She walked over to the window and flung open the shutters to the night air. I sat on the bed and looked out, across a stone-paved courtyard with a lemon tree and a pot of basil in it, down through the gaps in the houses, to a yellow stone harbor and the Mediterranean Sea.

I put out my hand to touch the iron bedstead and ran my fingers over the chipped paint. I looked out at the water, where the moon struck pale sparks from the waves.

I don't remember lying down on the bed or falling asleep. I remember waking, rising slowly through transparent layers of dreams, filled with scenes now familiar to me: a mirrored lake with ancient oaks, a bird building a nest upon the face of the water. Some things were different. Now a great black bear walked down through the oaks toward the water. I heard Nonna's voice saying, *This is the halcyon bird* as it flew out to its floating home with another stick, its nest dark against the shining sea.

I woke all the way up to a patch of sun on my face. I smelled garlic, olive oil, and baking bread. My stomach growled.

I went to the window, looking out at the sun slowly lowering in the sky, the sea stretching to the horizon. I had slept the day away. I felt like I had when I first arrived in Milan, jet-lagged and disorientated. Suddenly, I wanted to talk to Gina. I decided to ask if we had Internet here, though from all I had seen of this stone town, I wouldn't have been surprised to see the neighbors wandering around dressed like figures from one of the paintings in Santa Maria del Carmine.

The bedroom held a single table; on it was a stack of bedding that smelled like the sun. I made the bed and came downstairs, rubbing my eyes.

"There you are," said Francesca, looking up from the pile of greens she was chopping. "Good. Did you sleep well?"

"Yes, thank you." A thought struck me. "Francesca, this house . . . Is it well warded? I mean . . ."

She smiled at me, a wry expression on her face.

"You've really become one of them, haven't you," she said. I felt proud, even though I couldn't tell if she thought this was a good thing. "Yes, it is well warded. We have owned it for a long time, longer than the shop and the apartment in Milan. It is our halcyon nest," she added, jerking her head toward the front door.

"Good," I said, and felt a shudder of relief go through me. Only later did I realize I might have offended her by suggesting that they would take me someplace that was less than safe. "Can I help with anything?" I asked.

She put down her knife again, and looked at me, considering.

"You are sure you don't want to rest?" she asked.

I shrugged. "I'd like to, but I feel weird watching you do all the work, and maybe it's better if I do something."

She nodded. "Come pit olives, then."

I brought the olives and a spare bowl to the kitchen table, and sat pitting them, the tips of my fingers turning purple-brown. I sat staring at the growing pile of olives in the bowl and thought slow, olive-pitting thoughts for a while. Then I thought of Bernardo, and tried to remember where I'd put my cell phone. *I should call him and tell him where I am,* I thought, before I remembered the look on his face as he turned his head away.

"Have you heard anything from Milan?" I asked.

Her smile was sad this time. "He is recovering," she said.

"Oh," I said, in a small voice. I kept pitting olives until my face was wet and as salty as my fingers. When I was finished, I brought the bowl back on the counter and washed my hands and face, rinsing the tear sting from my eyes. Francesca said nothing; she glanced over at me a couple of times, while checking the oven.

Finally, she told me, "Chop those olives finely, with garlic."

"Sure," I said.

She nodded and turned away to sauté the greens. Then she started heating olive oil, butter, lemon juice, garlic, salt, and pepper flakes in a pot. I watched her wash and dry two flat fish fillets.

I looked at her back, her perfect glossy chignon, her straight shoulders as she cooked. I understood that she was being kind. There was something different about her, too. I couldn't put my finger on exactly what. The front door shut and Nonna came in, holding two bottles of wine.

"Salvatore gave these to us," she announced, lifting them in the air.

"Wonderful!" said her granddaughter. "Mia, wait until you taste Salvatore's wine."

"You're up," grunted Nonna, sounding like a bear. "Good. How do you feel?"

"So-so," I said.

She nodded. "But you slept well," she stated.

"Yes, thank you."

"Good. Sleep, eat, walk along the coast, rest. That's what you need. Go sit and look at the sea. It's good for you. Breathe the air. It will all help."

"Climb up to the tower," suggested Francesca.

I had seen the tower on the way into town, standing watch over the headland. It wasn't very big, as towers go, but it was higher up than just about everything else around here. The Italian word for tower is *torre*; it felt strange to see part of my family name on signs for tourists.

"Take your time," Nonna added.

"Okay," I said.

Our eyes began to water from the pepper flakes. Francesca

laid the fish in a baking pan and spooned the sauce over them. She turned them once, sauced the other side, then took the whole pan in two potholders and set it in the oven, on a rack above a nearly finished tray of focaccia. Then she poured out a boiling pot I hadn't even noticed, mixing my olive paste with some pasta in the shape of small hats. We sat down to dinner— fresh focaccia, pasta with olive paste, fish that flaked off of our forks, sautéed greens with garlic, and a glass each of Salvatore's wine, which Nonna explained was made up the street, from grapes grown on the hills above.

"Like *sciacchetrà*," I murmured.

"Not *sciacchetrà*," corrected Nonna. "That is made from dried grapes, and it's amber, not red."

"She knows that, Nonna," said Francesca. She turned to me. "We can go down to the wine bar after dinner and have a glass of that, all of us."

"I need to know," I said, thinking out loud. "Can I go outside? Alone, I mean? You mentioned walking along the coast, like that's something I could do. But my bell didn't save me in the end," I said.

"How do you know that?" asked Nonna. "Were you wearing it at the time?"

"Yes," I said.

"Well, then. He still couldn't reach you? The bell kept him from possessing you?"

"He reached me all right," I said. Tears filled my eyes again.

"You know what I mean," she said. She thought a moment. "But it's more than that. What do you think your demon will do now?"

"Come after me?" I hazarded.

She looked me in the eye. "You really think that?"

I met her eye, then looked down. "No. I think I will need to go after him," I said.

We blinked at each other in surprise. Nonna recovered first, nodding at me. "You'll do," she said.

After dinner and dishes, we all walked down to the water together through the musty stone alleys, smelling of damp. We passed wider streets leading upward and caught the moist night breeze on our cheeks. I inhaled deeply, filling my lungs with salt air, as we came out onto the piazza, full of tables and umbrellas spilling out from the restaurants around the edges. Waiters passed us with full plates; I saw four shrimp arranged on a swirl of bright yellow sauce, and a mound of *trofie*, the pasta Nonna had served the night of the Strozzi exorcism, speckled with pesto. I sighed. So much had happened to me, and still the world went on, the tables were set, people went on cooking and eating. I thought of Nonna saying to Anna Maria, "And this family keeps eating up all the butter."

Francesca and I stopped at the top of the breakwater, looking out to the sea, watching the fishing boats heading out under the waxing moon. Nonna went on to the far end of the pier.

After a long silence, Francesca said, "You know, Mia, there's this ridiculous idea that we make women and men out of each other—that somehow you're a woman, or a man, once you've had sex."

I felt my face burn. What did she think I had done with Bernardo?

"We didn't," I blurted out. My chest ached.

She laughed. "I'm pretty sure I would have guessed if you had," she said. "It's okay, Mia. And what I am saying is I don't think that it's true, that to me sex is *not* the rite of passage that makes us women and men."

I frowned. What mysterious ritual did I still have to endure, to grow up? What was she talking about?

She went on. "I think that we become women and men after our first difficult, impossible experience even. . . . We become grown human beings after we recover from it. It's not the terrible thing that happens to us; it's when we reap strength from it. Do you see what I mean? That out of the soil of that difficulty comes a flower . . . ah, that metaphor is terrible!" She laughed at herself.

"I think I see," I said, still watching the boats.

"In the old days, the Church gave us rituals so we knew when we were grown. Before the Church, there were our older religions, and before that, our tribes. Now, there are not so many rituals, which is why people might think sex is the big one. But I believe that the moment of true adulthood comes in one's own heart. After we choose to overcome what has happened. *If* we choose to."

"But why does it have to be after such suffering?" I asked. "I've been possessed, I've watched someone dying from the same demon's attack, I've probably lost my true love—" I stopped, embarrassed. "Certainly, I will never forget the moment his face changed, in my arms. . . ." This time, my voice just died in my throat.

Francesca put an arm around my shoulders and I leaned into her. I felt a flash of fear—what if I was wrong about where my demon was—what if I turned and saw his eyes in her face? But then she spoke again, in her warm voice, as rich as her brother's. "I don't know, Mia, why we have to suffer to become grown. Did you appreciate the life you have half as much before your possession? Now that it has nearly been taken from you, does it not seem more of a gift?"

I thought about this.

"No, not after it was nearly taken. I was too busy recovering and being scared and angry. Now, though, yeah, I appreciate every minute. Even the bad ones seem like gifts, sometimes. Not all the bad ones, though."

She smiled sadly. "Yes." She went on, "That is why I believe it is not the suffering but the testing of our strength that matters. What do you know about yourself, now? You know you're strong enough to survive him once, to help pull another back from the brink, and to defend a third. You know you can survive the terror of waiting for his attacks, first cornered in a house and a circle of family, and then on your own, out in the city, the world."

She stopped, then added, "But I am not the one who should be telling you these things. You will know them all by yourself, or know what is good for you."

She looked conscience-stricken, and I smiled at her. "Actually," I said, "I appreciate the help." *Especially since that isn't the Della Torre way,* I thought.

We stood quietly for a moment. For the first time, I pondered what that moment had been for her. Was it when her father died? She'd only been nine.

I looked down the pier at Nonna, standing near the very end, the scarf she'd tied over her hair lifting in the night wind.

"What is she remembering?" I asked.

"I don't know," said Francesca. "A lot of times, we Della Torres bring our brides, or grooms, here on honeymoon. We come in the winter as well, when there are fewer tourists, though we didn't this year, because of you. . . . But no, don't feel bad! We used to come out in the summer, too, in August. We might do that this year." She looked back at Nonna.

"She's remembering walking on this pier with your father," I said, startled by my certainty. "When he was a boy."

Francesca raised her eyebrows, her blue eyes gleaming at me in the half-light.

"You think so?" she asked.

"Yes," I said.

She gazed at Nonna.

"I cannot bear imagining what it would be like to lose your only son," she said softly. And then, "Well, maybe we have let her walk with him long enough, for now? Let's go to her."

Francesca gave me her arm and we walked slowly down the pier together.

"Thank you," I said.

"You're welcome. . . . For what?"

"For not rushing to comfort me about—him; for letting me cry. For saying the things you said now. It helps to hear someone else thinking about it. Thank you for being here."

She laughed. "You are very welcome. I can hardly help being myself, you know."

Francesca touched her stomach thoughtfully, and I looked at her, wondering again what was different about her. I could almost name it, but not quite.

We caught up with Nonna. I expected to see tears on her face, but she was smiling, though her eyes were still far away.

"Luciano used to refuse to go to bed on nights like this," she said, and Francesca flicked a glance at me. "He would make at least one of us walk down to the harbor with him. Sometimes he tried to walk to the moon, especially when he was very young. He would reach out his arms for her. Sometimes he just threw rocks in that shining path. If you came down to the harbor with him, you could get him to go to bed afterward.

If you tried to be firm, it wouldn't work. It wasn't worth the pain, believe me. Such a sweet boy, and he could throw such a tantrum! A tantrum over the moon."

Nonna Laura looked at the two of us. "It's cooling off," she said. "Let's go home. Unless one of you wants to throw a tantrum?"

I shrugged. "Not really," Francesca said, deadpan.

"Me, either," I said.

On the way home, I convinced Nonna and Francesca to stop for gelato just before the shop closed. I got my favorite, *nocciola,* hazelnut, but Francesca made me promise I would try *melone* before we left. I found myself hoping we would stay here forever. I would make my home here by the sea, and cook food, and all those people with demons could look after themselves. I wouldn't even try to find out the name of a certain poet. . . . I wrinkled my forehead in thought as we left the shop, and Nonna patted my arm.

"You think too much," she informed me with a wave of her gelato spoon. "The young always do. Stop worrying for a minute."

"I'm not worrying," I retorted, then added, "sorry. I didn't mean to be rude."

She just laughed and shook her head. "Well," she said, "we've seen the moon, so now we can go home and go to bed."

I turned and put my arms around her, kissing her cheek.

I woke up the next morning while the house was still silent, and stood by the window, watching the light change on the sea as the sun rose with silent, unstoppable power.

Most of me still felt like I would never get over the moment when I felt the double pulse in Bernardo's neck. I couldn't allow myself to think that he might forgive me. I should have mentioned that I came with a few risks. "Every relationship has problems," I could imagine Gina joking.

I gripped the windowframe. I understood then what I hadn't before, even while the demon was forcing Bernardo's throat to speak, forcing his arms to hold me. I understood why Nonno did the work he did, why Emilio did it. They had brought me to Italy to learn to protect myself, but I had more to protect than myself, now.

Even if Bernardo never spoke to me again.

He wasn't the only one I would fight for, either.

My heart hurt. I mean the actual muscle just ached, while I stood there, watching the sea and the town emerge into daylight.

I stared out at the flickering water, imagining a nest out there, bobbing on the waves, and a small bird gliding out to it, a stick in its beak. It landed, rocking the nest, and wove the twig into the refuge, making the nest that much sturdier where it floated, suspended over the deep.

Then, under the waves, I saw my demon's face. There was a terrible yearning in his eyes, but that faded, and he grinned like a lizard.

"Go ahead," I told my demon. "We're not finished yet."

Acknowledgments

While I wrote this novel my whole life changed utterly. I know I'm going to forget to thank someone, so bear with me.

I would like to thank my daughter Tasmin for interrupting everything by her arrival, and teaching me precisely how to combine new motherhood and a career.

I would like to thank my stepdaughter, Rain Lochner, for her ideas about the big possession scene. It's good because of you, dear.

Stacy Braslau-Schneck and Dave and Monica Schneck, you saved my groats emotionally and physically during one of the hardest periods of my life. For shelter, comfort, and emergency holiday inclusion, I thank you.

Luna, Flipper, Minnie: we miss you. Thank you, our loyal pack mates.

Vicki Vickers, you took us in and grandmothered Tasmin on zero notice. Thank you. Rob Kent, you lent us the car and your support. Thank you.

Emmanuele, Nicola, Gianni, and Adamo of the Monastery Hostel in Milan, I am grateful for your enthusiasm, advice, and cheerful acceptance of the odd American couple and the youngest youth at your hostel. You helped us to find out where the Strozzi family would live, where Nonna would have her birthday, and a whole bunch of other important information.

Marco, owner of Candele Mum, you took the news that your shop inspired a novel very well.

The nation of Italy and the city of Milan: you welcomed my five-month-old daughter with open arms. We learned quickly to leave an extra half hour before going anywhere, so that the Milanese could talk to our daughter, and the first words Wolf learned in Italian were probably, "*Cinque mezze*—five months." Because of you, my daughter knows how to smile.

Titi, John, and Diana at the Alhambra restaurant—along with the rest of your family, especially Tasmin's Eritrean-Italian friend Christian, and your neighbors, especially Giorgio—you all fed us great food and kept us talking half the night, teaching me so much about the immigrant's view of Italy.

Wolfgang, you believed in me and took care of our tiny daughter through the first draft. Though we didn't work out, we both did our best, and we'll go on doing it for our daughter's sake. Thank you.

Haddayr Copley-Woods read the draft in record time, and raced to give me such sensible help. So did my doughty Smokey Wizard Bacon crew, Brendan Day, Carrie Ferguson, David Englestad, David Gallay, and Kelly Janda. Thank you all for the reassurances and the insights. David Gallay, especially, made sure that Mia kicked more butt.

Art Chocolate—Cathy Couture, Jane Washburn, Kim Long-Ewing, Rhea Ewing, Rio Mayoleth, and Stacie Arellano—saw me through. Cathy and Jane, thank you for housing Tasmin and me, and Cathy, thank you for being her Madison grandmother. Karen Meisner, Beth Hoover, and Stephen White, you helped me bear the hard stuff and celebrate the awesome stuff.

Thank you, Bonnie Cutler, managing editor at Egmont, for having the savvy to hire Joan Giurdanella, and for believing so much in my work. I also want to thank Andrea Cascardi, Egmont's publisher, for your forbearance when one thing after another was happening—and for setting the deadline when it mattered. Thank you to Margaret Coffee and Michelle Bayuk, and everyone else in marketing, for making it possible for my readers to find me.

Ruth Katcher, my editor, you were patient when I needed patience, and set deadlines when I needed to focus. Your edits made this a far better book. Joan Giurdanella, you caught some major howlers, and you and I made Ruth laugh with our online debates. Caitlin Blasdell, my agent, you joined with Ruth in lending emotional and professional support. I know you all know this, but still I'll remind you: you rock.

Thank you all. I couldn't have let Bernardo go without you.